I had to be in two places at the same time.

My current situation was that Bart was naked here in Betty's bedroom while Art was naked over there in Liz's shower. Therefore, my first order of business was to get Art out of the shower. Then I had to put Bart somewhere out of sight for a while until I could get some clothes on Art.

Getting his clothes on and off in the right bedroom becomes quite a problem for Art—Bart in this hilarious novel of double trouble.

Which twin gets the phony?

That's for us to know and you to find out.

Read.

"Donald Westlake is the Neil Simon of the crime novel."

—New York Times Book Review

two much

donald e. westlake

a fawcett crest book

fawcett publications, inc., greenwich, conn.

TWO MUCH

THIS BOOK CONTAINS THE COMPLETE TEXT OF THE
ORIGINAL HARDCOVER EDITION

A Fawcett Crest Book reprinted by arrangement with M. Evans
and Company, Inc.

Printed in the United States of America

First printing: March 1976

1   2   3   4   5   6   7   8   9   10

For
Steve Kesten,
who knows how,
and
for the mistress of Adams' Apple,
who knows why

Two heads are better than one.
John Heywood
Proverbs

IT ALL BEGAN INNOCENTLY enough; I wanted to get laid. So when Candy and Ralph said we were invited to a party over in Dunewood I said fine, wait while I change. Ralph said, "There'll be some singles there," and Candy stuck her tongue out at me behind Ralph's back.

I put on white slacks and a pink shirt and we headed barefoot down Central Walk toward Dunewood. Fire Island, two P.M., Sunday, August fourth. Sun straight up in a cloudless sky, air hot and smelling of ocean, rows of little houses lined up along the boardwalks stretching across the island from bay to beach. Children were everywhere, on bicycles and on foot, running wild because Fire Island doesn't permit any automobiles.

All the houses in Dunewood look alike, except for the colors. The one we wanted was up near the beach, and the music could be heard three blocks away. The owner had built an extralarge deck on the back of his place so he could tell it from all the others, and it was full of people dancing and drinking and shouting at each other over the music. Suntanned women in bikinis and big dark glasses dancing to rock music; how they moved it all around. "I guess I'll go get acquainted," I said.

"Do have a wonderful time," Candy said. Couldn't Ralph hear the spite in her voice, couldn't he figure out what was going on? (Or what had been going on, until he'd stopped going to the office.)

Apparently not. His face stayed as open and unsuspecting as a girls' choir in bandit territory. Giving me a grin and a friendly poke in the arm, he said, "Go get 'em, Art." He envied me my bachelor's access to women, the poor schnook; I wondered if he'd still envy me if he knew my main access the last six months had been to his wife.

What Ralph didn't know couldn't hurt me. "Bye-bye," I said, and drifted away from the happy couple, off to find a substitute for Candy. I do have a sweet tooth.

The place to meet women is by the liquor. Whoever my host might be, he was no piker; gin, vodka, rum, and enough tonic to float a loan. The table was already a sticky mass of mangled lemon parts, but who cared? Not me. "Thank God," I said to the big-titted brunette beside me. "No sangria."

Her sunglasses left just enough of her face exposed to show me she was grinning. "Picky, aren't you?" she said.

"Absolutely. And I pick you. Let's dance."

So we danced for a while. Her bikini was dark blue and her flesh was tanned the color of brandy. Perspiration trickled down from her throat, sun-glistening lines leading down into the soft cleft between her breasts, and I wanted to taste her. Salt is always welcome after too many sweets.

There were brief pauses between tunes, longer pauses between LPs. In one of those longer waits she put a warm damp hand on my forearm and said, "Listen, man, why don't we lie this one out?"

"Sure," I said. "You had enough?"

"I haven't had this much exercise," she said, "since my pony ran away."

So we walked over to the railing as the music started again, and she said, "Be a hero, will you? Get us a couple drinks."

"Sure. What's yours?"

"Vodka," she said.

"And what?"

"Ice and a glass and a big wet kiss," she said.

"Right."

I went away to the liquor and almost didn't go back, because women who talk that strong in front almost never follow through; it's the quiet ones that mean business. On the other hand, a girl drinking vodka straight was a very hopeful sign. Also, nobody really appealing was at the bar when I got there, so I made myself a rum and tonic, and filled another plastic glass with vodka and ice, and went back to the girl in the dark blue bikini. How different things would have been if some other piece had attracted my attention right then.

But none did, and my first choice was still alone at the rail. I gave her the glass and stood picking at my wet shirt. Now that I wasn't dancing, I could feel how moist I was.

She gave me a critical look and said, "You're over-dressed."

"I noticed. Walk with me, I'll go back and put on a bathing suit."

She hesitated, looking around at the deck heaving with people, and then she shrugged and said, "Why not?"

We carried our drinks. Candy gave me a savage look on the way by, but I pretended I didn't see it.

We walked a couple blocks, not saying much except stuff about the weather, and then she said, "How far we going, anyway?"

"Fair Harbor," I said. "Six or seven blocks, that's all."

She looked in her glass as though worried the supplies wouldn't hold out, and said, "You got anything to drink at your place?"

"We had an underground tank put in last fall," I said. "Smirnoff makes weekly deliveries."

"Good," she said.

We kept walking, and I thought it was time for intro-ductions, so I said, "My name's Art. Art Dodge."

"Hello," she said. She pointed at herself with her free thumb and said, "Liz Kerner."

"You staying in Dunewood?"

"No. We have a house in Point O' Woods."

I looked at her with suddenly increased interest. Point O' Woods? Most of Fire Island is middle-class money, but Point O' Woods is *money* money. They've built a fence across the island at their border to keep the riffraff out. That's the kind of money I like, snotty money; I've always meant to go get some of it. "It's nice in Point O' Woods," I said, as though I'd been there often.

"It's dull," she said.

"Who's 'we'?"

She looked at me, and I got the impression there was a frown down in behind those sunglasses. "What?"

"You said *we* have a house in Point O' Woods."

"Oh." She faced front again. "My sister," she said, as someone might have said, "Yes, that's my newspaper."

"Ah," I said. "She as good-looking as you?"

"Probably," she said. "We're identical twins."

"Twins!" I was thrown off stride by that. It was one of my basic questions, and it had never collected that answer before.

She glanced at me this time as though she might be thinking of getting annoyed. "Something wrong with that?"

"Not at all." I needed something to say, something to make the transition. "It's just a coincidence, that's all."

"What kind of coincidence?" She was still almost hostile.

"I'm twins, too," I said. It came out of nowhere, just words to fill a gap and smooth things over. I had no idea then where it would lead me, no plot in my mind at all. Not that it would have been possible anyway; nobody could have schemed out in advance everything that would follow from that one innocent remark. I have a natural glibness, that's all, and I'd merely chosen a statement intended to heal a potential rupture and give us a small something extra in common. A little white lie, nothing more.

It did its job. She gave me a surprised look and said, "You are?"

"Absolutely. I have a brother Bart, identical." The name was a logical follow-through; Art and Bart, just the tacky kind of thing done by the parents of twins.

She said, "Is he here?"

"No," I said. But then I had to explain his absence, and once again I simply fell into it. The scheme built itself, with only the most minimal help from me. "We split the week," I said.

"Split the week?"

"One of us always has to be in the office. So I'm here the first part of the week, and then we switch."

"Complicated," she said, meaning she'd lost interest.

So I dropped the subject, permanently, so far as I knew. "You live in Manhattan?"

"Sometimes," she said. She brooded at her glass, which was empty, and frowned out ahead of her at Central Walk, stretching away on a straight line in the shimmering heat all the way through Fair Harbor and as far as Saltaire. "It's hot out here," she said. "Bad as dancing. How much farther is this place?"

"Two blocks." I pointed, saying, "See the house with the American flag? We turn there."

"So that's what that is," she said.

We kept walking, elbow-deep in running children, and when we got to the house with the flag I saw the patriot himself out on his front deck, glowering at the world. He was wearing Bermuda shorts and an undershirt, and his snow-white hair made a nice contrast with his lobster-red skin. "Howdy," I called, and gestured at his flag. "I'm from the States myself," I said.

His mouth moved but he didn't actually say anything, maybe because he didn't have his teeth in.

We made our turn onto the boardwalk and I led the way to Ralph and Candy's house. The kids, happily, were away. We stepped into the cooler dimmer interior and Liz handed me her glass. "Don't mind if I do," she said.

I handed it back. "That's the refrigerator," I told her,

"and that bottle has something in it you'll like." I gave her my own empty glass and said, "And I'm drinking rum and tonic."

She shrugged and went behind the counter to make the drinks. The left side of this house was living room and dining room and kitchen combined in one open area, with a counter separating the kitchen work space. A doorway led to the two bedrooms and bath, and a ladder next to the doorway led up to the sleeping loft, which at this time of day would be as hot as a stolen nymphomaniac. In theory, that was my place up there, though of course I'd been planning to spend most of my time in the master's bedroom. With Ralph in residence, however, I'd taken to sleeping on the living room sofa, where the three children could rollick me awake every morning.

My wet shirt was sticking to me like an airmail stamp. Standing in the living room, waiting for my drink, I unbuttoned it and peeled it off and threw it away in a corner. I slid my palm down my slippery chest and dried it on my pants, and Liz brought me my drink. "You're wet," she said.

"I thought I was." I sipped at my glass and said, "The tonic gets here later?"

"Too strong?" She reached for my drink, saying, "Here, I'll fix it."

"No, it's fine," I said, and as long as her hand was extended toward me I took her by the wrist and brought her in close. She gave me a quizzical look, and when we kissed she had exactly the salt and musk and sex taste I'd been looking for. "You're overdressed, too," I told her.

2   2

C ANDY, HER EYES BLAZING and her voice an angry half-whisper, said, "Did you have to use *our* bed?"

A very ambivalent pronoun. "I was so used to it," I said. I spoke in a normal tone of voice. We were both in the kitchen, me making drinks and Candy making hamburgers. The kids were out someplace beneath the setting sun, and Ralph had taken *Newsweek* into the bathroom.

Candy was so enraged already she paid no attention to what I'd said. "What if Ralph notices something?" she demanded.

"That's not the kind of Ralph-noticing you have to worry about," I told her. "You keep making faces at me in front of him, even Ralph is going to tip wise."

"I could *smell* her on my pillow last night, I couldn't sleep."

"I slept like a top," I said. "Until seven-thirty, of course, when the kids came in and did their reenactment of the Battle of Blenheim."

She suddenly dissolved into cunning little tears. "Why are you so mean? It isn't my fault Ralph is here. Don't you see how jealous I am? I wanted that to be *me* in bed with you." She waved the spatula in distraction.

"I know, Candy," I said gently. She was after all my hostess, and I had after all sublet my apartment. I rested my hand on her shoulder; the flesh was warm from either sun or passion. "This is hard on both of us," I said.

13

She put the spatula down and folded herself in against me. Her bathing suit top and cut-down blue jean shorts left a lot of skin available to my soothing hands. I kissed the side of her neck, and found it less interesting. She kissed my mouth, hungrily, and whispered, "Maybe later tonight, when Ralph starts on his paper work, we'll say we're going to Hommel's for a drink."

"And screw in the poison ivy?"

"We'll find a place!" she whispered shrilly, and the phone rang. She gave it a look of fury, then glanced with sudden caution over toward the doorway leading to the bathroom. Backing away from me, she whispered more calmly, "We've found places before, Art, and we can do it again." Then she hurried around the end of the counter and picked up the phone on the second ring. "Hello?" Her face became angry again; she seemed about to hang up, or say something loud, but then she took a deep breath and said, "Yes, he is." She extended the phone toward me, saying coldly, "It's her."

"Her?" Surprised and intrigued, I walked around and picked up the phone, saying to Candy, "Make my drink for me, will you? My usual."

She went back to the kitchen area, but then she stood there and watched me and listened. I put the phone to my face and said hello, and Liz's well-remembered voice said, "Who was that?"

"My hostess," I said, with a sweet smile toward Candy.

"She sounds like a bitch."

"Interesting analysis."

"I'm calling to invite you to a little party," she said.

"Oh?" Looking at Candy, I knew I didn't dare ask for a rain check on tonight's philander. "When?" I said.

"Tomorrow, around eight."

"That's fine," I said. "I'd like that." Candy glowered.

There were pencil and a note pad on the telephone table, and I took down the directions to Liz Kerner's house. There was no fence on the beach itself, so I should walk along there and turn inland only after I'd breached the Point O' Woods border. "I'll be there," I said.

"Don't overdress," she said, and we both hung up.

Candy suddenly started making my drink. "She sounded like a bitch," she said.

"That's funny," I said. "She remarked how sweet your voice was."

"Oh, I'm sure. Now look what you did, I'm burning the hamburgers."

Mend your fences while you still have some left. "After dinner," I said, "you and I, we'll go to Hommel's."

She flashed me a quick, lasciviously grateful smile, and went back to turning hamburgers.

3   3

WHEN SHE OPENED HER front door to me, Liz was wearing a white dress with a fitted bodice and pleated skirt and a narrow white patent-leather belt around the waist. I'd heard the fifties were coming back, and here they were. "This time," I said, "you really are overdressed."

"I beg your pardon?" Her frown seemed equal parts puzzlement and disapproval. Somewhere behind her a piano discreetly tinkled "Smoke Gets in Your Eyes."

"What's under that, I wonder," I said, and then Liz appeared all over again, behind this one, wearing a purple T-shirt dress with no bra. "Oh," I said.

"So there you are," Liz said, the Liz in purple. To the

non-Liz in white she said, "This is the riffraff I told you
about."

"You're the sister," I said.

Liz said, "They can't get them past you, can they? Come
on in, before we fill up with mosquitoes."

And so I entered the Kerner household. Too late, they
closed the door.

We were together in a small vestibule, the three of us.
Through an arched doorway was a section of party scene
painted by a member of the Royal Academy; the accom-
panying sound effects were polite conversational murmurs,
unobtrusive ice cube clinking, and the modest piano
segueing into "My Funny Valentine." Our three heads
were close together, the double Liz and me, and looking
from one to the other I said, "That's truly amazing." Except for differences of expression and hairdo the faces
were absolutely identical.

The non-Liz said, "But I thought *you* had a twin
brother."

How our thoughtless fibs return to plague us. "Oh, of
course," I said. "But I've never met any *other* twins before. Not as identical as you two." To get us away from
that subject, I thrust my hand out to the non-Liz and said,
"I'm Art Dodge, by the way."

She smiled, in the bland way that one does at parties,
and said, "I'm Betty Kerner." Her hand was cool and dry.

Then they brought me through into the next room, and
what a collection of store-window mannequins they'd assembled for their party. There were men present in cum-
merbunds, I swear to God. Most of the men appeared to
be named Frazier and most of the women Grahame. The
piano was being played by a hireling, a lanky black youth
with Belafonte good looks and a totally untrustworthy
smile; he was probably saving his money to buy a machine
gun. Two automaton black girls in black uniforms and
small white aprons circulated with trays of hors d'oeuvres,
while the bartender blockaded behind his white-cloaked

table was a beefy Irishman of about fifty who laughed heartily at all the drink orders, as though phrases like "dry vermouth on the rocks" or "two rye and ginger ale, please" were both witty and profound.

What kind of party was this to be hosted by two girls in their mid-twenties? There were perhaps forty people present, but only about a quarter of them were under thirty, and *they* were as stiff as their elders. There was no dancing. In fact, there was scarcely any commingling of the sexes at all; women stood with women to discuss department stores, Arthur Hailey novels, absent friends and other parties, while men grouped with men to talk transportation, taxes, politics and horses—breeding, not racing. I actually did hear one man say, as I was strolling past, "After all, racing does improve the breed."

"Quite the contrary," I said. "In point of fact, all our effort is the other way, to make breeding improve the race."

This being the most incisive remark any of them had ever heard in their lives, I was immediately absorbed into the group, where the man I'd contradicted thrust his hand out and said, "Frazier."

I gave him my honest grip and said, "Dodge."

Another man said, "Of the New Bedford Dodges?"

"Distantly," I said.

We chatted about horses for a while, then transposed to a critique and comparison of several North Carolina golf courses, during which I excused myself and headed for the bar. "Rum and tonic," I said.

"Ha ha ha," he said. "Got no rum."

"Make it vodka."

"Ho ho ho," he said, and made my drink.

Liz sidled up and said, "My usual, Mike."

"Ha ha," he said, gave me my drink, and made Liz's usual: one ice cube in a glass, vodka to the brim.

Waiting for it she said to me, with a head-nod toward the rest of the party, "See why I wanted you here?"

"I think you should have called the coroner."

"Here y'are, Miss Kerner."

"Thanks, Mike."

"Ha ha ha."

We strolled away from Pagliacci and I said, "If I'm going to hang around here, you'd better lay in some rum."

"Let's wait and see if your option gets picked up."

We stood in a quiet corner and observed the party. Betty, the twin, was in moribund conversation with a girl in yellow and a girl in pink. All three dresses, I noticed, ended just below the knee. I said, "You and your sister aren't really very much alike at all."

"She's noisier," Liz said. "What about you and your brother?"

"He's quieter." I was determined not to talk about my damn brother. "Is this your sister's party? It seems more her style."

"She isn't *that* bad," she said. "This is a political party. We want to sell the house."

"I'm afraid I don't follow."

"If you're going to sell a house in Point O' Woods," she said, "you don't exactly run an ad in the *Daily News*. We're a restricted community."

Looking around at the revelers, I said, "You can only sell to someone with a valid death certificate."

"Something like that. None of us actually own our houses, you know. The Association owns everything, and we have long-term leases. So what we're selling is the lease, and of course the Association has to approve the new leaseholder."

"Of course."

"You see the gent over there in the gray tie with the maroon polka dots?"

"I'm afraid I do, yes."

"He's our potential buyer."

He was one of the Fraziers: stocky, Republican, graying at the temples. "He seems absolutely perfect," I said.

"Doesn't he? Unfortunately, there's a problem."

"The wife?"

"Good God, no. That's her there, in the tweed."

Tweed, in August. The woman in question was a perfect Grahame. "What, then?"

"Family. They're a little outside the general circle."

"How awful for you."

"We're introducing them now, that's the idea of the party."

"Ah. And if they pass muster, you can sell. But why do you want to?"

She shrugged. "This was our parents' place. Neither of us wants it."

"Are you recently orphaned?"

"Last New Year's Eve. They were on their way to a performance of Handel's *Messiah* when someone tipped a piano off a terrace. It went right through the roof of the Lincoln. The chauffeur had a black key embedded in his shoulder but was otherwise completely unscratched."

"That must have been, um, terrible for you," I said. Sympathy is such a difficult mode to get just right.

But once again she shrugged, saying, "Death didn't change them that much. Fewer questions, that's all. Listen, why don't we go upstairs and screw?"

"What a wonderful party this is," I said.

She gave her glass a critical look. "Let me just get a fresh drink."

The houses of Point O' Woods are not summer cottages at all. They are perfect imitations of small-town houses, circa 1920. Brown shingle siding, white trim, full front porches, varnished wood floors. We did not clamber up a ladder to a sleeping loft, Liz and I, we walked up a solid flight of stairs to a solid second floor. Two bedrooms and a bath.

Unfortunately, that bath was the only one in the house, which meant a steady traffic of guests up and down the stairs. The bedroom doors were both standing open, and

Liz thought it unwise to try closing one. Therefore, we had at it in a closet full of dusty garments and chittering hangers. It was warm in there to begin with, and we'd soon created an atmosphere like that in a rain forest at midnight. Nor were matters helped much when Liz, writhing along midway in our progress, kicked over her fresh glass of vodka. Don't let anybody ever tell you vodka has no smell; in a closed closet it does.

Still, there was a good side to it all, which eventually climaxed with a lot of rucking and bumping amid the shifts and sneakers. Following which, we readjusted ourselves for public consumption and returned to the quieter side of the party, carefully closing the closet door behind ourselves. It really did look—and smell—as though some sort of debauch had taken place in there. "Poor old closet," I said. "Things will be dull for it once you sell."

"I wish I hadn't spilled that drink," she said irritably, but she was thinking of herself, not of the closet. Downstairs, she left me without so much as a thank you and headed straight for Mike.

I roamed a while, listened to three under-thirty males discuss the implications for the legal profession of no-fault auto insurance, eavesdropped on girl-talk about dog shows, had another vodka and tonic, and eventually found myself alone in a corner when Betty, the Liz who wasn't Liz, came over with her polite-hostess smile and said, "This party must be dull for you."

"Does it show?"

The smile became a touch more limpid. "No," she said, "you're carrying it off very well."

"So are you," I told her. Regardless of the white dress, regardless of the hostess smile and the tamed-down gestures, this face and body were so completely the same as the face and body I'd just been humping in the upstairs closet that I couldn't help a sense of familiarity, an easiness of discourse. Also, it was impossible to believe this one was as unlike her sister as she seemed; surely that throat could be made to produce the same low groans as Liz.

She raised one eyebrow. I've never been able to do that, and I've always envied people who could. "Don't you think I'm enjoying myself?"

"You've had better times," I told her, and reached out to pat a hand holding a glass containing what looked suspiciously like sherry. "And you will again," I said. Then I noticed Liz frowning in our direction from some distance away, and casually I removed my hand and placed it instead in my pocket.

But it seemed already to have done its work. The hostess smile was all at once much more honest, much looser. She said, "Do you like good times, Mr. Dodge?"

"Cozy times," I said, but it was all a charade and meaningless. Liz was too self-contained to break in on our chit-chat, but she was circling on the far side of the room, her awareness as intrusive as an electric current. You can't change sisters in mid-scheme. I've tried and I know; you lose them both. Blood is also thicker than oil, apparently.

The sister in purdah was saying something about ski lodges and roaring fires; following on my use of the word *cozy,* I suppose. "That's why I'm a winter person," she said. "I love the ice and snow, and then you come in and get all bundled up and warm." She hugged herself, and sipped sherry. "Are you like that?"

"Depends who I'm bundling with," I said.

She pretended to find me risqué, and took the opportunity to touch my wrist with her own cool fingertips. "Oh, you're perfect for Liz," she said. "She just loves fast people."

"And you?"

"Oh, I'm just a spectator." Her little smile was meant to be fatalistic, I suppose, but in truth it was smug.

"If you see something you like," I suggested, "just ask for it."

"Oh, I think I'll stay on the sidelines," she said, with a

depressingly flirtatious little smile. Then she said, "Do you know your eyes sparkle in this light?"

I wear contact lenses. "It's because I'm a romantic," I said. "And so do yours."

"Oh, I wear contact lenses. Liz doesn't, though; her eyes aren't as bad as mine." She gave me a coy look. "So we aren't exactly the same, after all."

"Two separate mysteries," I said, with low-voiced melodrama.

"That's exactly right. Isn't it that way with you and your brother?"

The brother again. "Oh, I suppose we're different in some ways," I said.

"Would I like to meet him?"

A comical thought entered my brain—casual, fanciful, not yet serious. "You'd probably get along fine with old Bart," I said.

"Bart, is that his name?"

"Mmm hmm."

"Why don't you bring him around some time?"

I smiled. "Maybe I will," I said. "Maybe I will." Then another ray from Liz's eyes struck my left temple a glancing blow, and I bowed my head to look at my drink and say, "I believe I need a refill."

We parted with mutual expressions of esteem, and Liz intercepted me at the bar. "My usual, Mike," she said.

"Ha ha ha," said Mike.

Liz tossed me a sidelong green-eyed glare. "Having fun with my sister?"

"She'd rather be in a ski lodge," I said. "Before a roaring fire."

"Or in one," she muttered, and Mike gave us our drinks.

I said, "Let's go back to the closet."

She gave me a flat look. "Screw you," she said, and went away.

I hung around a while longer, but she remained angry, and God knows there was no other reason to be there, so eventually I made my departure. I gave my hostesses separate farewells. "Drop in any time you're in the neighborhood," Liz said, with eyes much colder than her sister's winter wonderland. Betty, in her turn, said she was glad to meet me and asked once more after my dear brother Bart. Then I left.

This protected enclave of the well-bred well-to-do; they even leave their bicycles out at night, unlocked, safe from the teen-age chimpanzees who harass the proletarian communities. I stole the first bike I came to, rode it to the end of Point O' Woods, walked it with difficulty through the thick sand around the end of the fence, and then rode cheerfully down the central walk through Ocean Bay Park and Seaview and Ocean Beach. I had to abandon it then and walk along the beach to Lonelyville, but in Dunewood I found another untended bike—most unusual—and sailed along to Fair Harbor and the fair Candy, who had just had a raging fight with Ralph and wasn't speaking to anybody. Ralph and I went to Hommel's and drank, until Ralph asked me to go back to the house and try to soothe Candy. "She won't talk to me," he said. "Maybe she'll talk to you." So I went back to the house and soothed her.

4   4

THE NEXT DAY WAS WEDnesday and I was going to the city. Ralph decided to go in with me, so we took a morning ferry together, wearing shoes and carrying attaché cases. Ralph bought a *Times* at the Pioneer Market to read on the boat, and I spent the time trying to work up some fresh greetings. I didn't have a really good Get Well Soon, and it was also time to start thinking about Christmas. While the ferry wallowed across the Great South Bay, I doodled on a sheet of paper resting on my attaché case. "Get well soon—get well soon—get well soon—"

The voyage from Fire Island to Manhattan employs most of the transportation methods known to man. First the ferry to Bay Shore, on the southern coast of Long Island; then a cab from the dock to the railroad station; then a train on in to the city. "Get well soon," I wrote. "Get well soon." I was getting nowhere.

Then all at once a Merry Christmas dropped into my head, and I laughed aloud. "Ralph," I said.

He looked up from the bridal announcements; Ralph reads *everything* in the *Times*. "Mm?"

"On the front," I said, "there's a drawing of a cute priest. Barry Fitzgerald. He's smiling directly at us, with the caption, 'Merry Christmas.' And inside it says, 'you Jew bastard.' "

"Mmmmm," he said. "Won't that offend some people?"

"You really think so?"

"Not everybody is as sophisticated as you are," he said.

"Oh, go 'long with you," I said. I don't know why I sounding-board Ralph; he has no more sense of humor than a yak.

We separated at Penn Station, Ralph to cab downtown to the law firm with his homework, me to walk up into the bowels of the garment district. My office is on the fifth floor of a building so infested with third-rate garment manufacturers I think of the place as an outpatient clinic for bankruptcy court. The regular elevator ceased to function during the Harding Administration, and this time I shared the freight elevator with a rack of thin floral dresses accompanied by a pair of four-foot-tall PRs. *Hispanics*, they prefer to be called, but most people use the abbreviation: *spic*.

Gloria was at her desk, typing at her typewriter. "Look at the tan," she said.

"It comes from the Tabasco in the bloody Marys." I pulled the dress out from under my shirt and said, "Here's a little something I bought you."

"You bought me?" She held the dress away from herself with one hand, studying it without trust. "If I wear it to work, will I get arrested?"

"Think of it as a weekend dress. What's that you're typing?"

"A letter to my mother."

"Good. I was afraid it might have something to do with the firm."

"What firm?"

"No double-entendres," I warned her, and went back into my own room, which hadn't changed much in my absence.

My firm is *Those Wonderful Folks, Inc.*, and I do greeting cards. I create my own copy, farm out the illustrations, and am cheated by the printer and robbed by the distributor. My product, known as Folksy Cards, is distributed only in the Greater New York area, and pays just enough to make me ineligible for food stamps.

My favorite cards are framed and mounted on the walls in my office. It inspires me to be able to look up from the desk and see the earlier emanations of my genius. "Kiss me again—I'll turn the other cheek." "We'll have to stop meeting like this—roll over." "Love is—never having to say, 'How much?'"

In fact, they inspired me again. I no sooner sat down at my desk than I grabbed pencil and paper and wrote. "Get well soon—my doctor says you have it, too." That was two in one day, by God; taking a vacation really does help.

Whistling cheerfully, I turned to the stack of memos on which Gloria had listed the incoming phone calls of the last few days, and what an honor roll of complainers and spoilsports unfolded there before me. Even the landlord, for the love of Christ. Jack Mulligan, my sister, Ed Frazee, Linda Ann Margolies . . .

Linda Ann Margolies? I buzzed Gloria. "Who is Linda Ann Margolies?"

"A sexy voice on the phone. Young and cuddly."

"Get her."

"Mm hm."

"You're too cynical, Gloria," I said, hung up, and finished throwing away the rest of the phone memos. Three calls from my ex-wife alone. If these buffoons overworked Gloria, she'd up and quit. Then there were Dave Danforth, Abbie Lancaster, Charlie Hillerman. . . .

Hmmm, Charlie Hillerman. An illustrator with a very lewd style, he'd be perfect for the Get Well Soon. Unfortunately, I still owed him one or two fees for previous work, which was surely what he was calling about. Would he do just one more, prior to payment? It wouldn't hurt to ask.

Buzz. Gloria said, "Linda Ann Margolies."

"Fine. Get me Charlie Hillerman."

"You must be crazy."

"Just get him." I switched to the outside line, and said, "Miss Margolies?"

"Yes, it is." Gloria's description had been absolutely on the money: sexy, cuddly and young. "Is that Arthur Dodge?"

"Depends," I said. "What can I do for you?"

"I'm a graduate student at Columbia, Mr. Dodge," she said. "My master's thesis is on humor, and I'd like to interview you about Folksy Cards and your theory of comedy and, oh, all sorts of stuffy things like that."

"Well, you can't hope for too much from a first date," I said. (She had a nicely throaty chuckle.) "When did you want to get together?" Not that I was set on fire by the thought of a master's thesis on the theory of comedy—my own theory, which could quickly have been transmitted by telephone, is if they buy it it's funny—but the voice was intriguing. And, as John Ray pointed out back in 1650,

"A maid that laughs is half taken."

"As soon as possible," she said. "Could I come down there today?"

"Not today," I said. "Umm, how about next Wednesday?"

"What time?"

"One o'clock." Late enough for me to definitely be in town, early enough so I wouldn't have to leave for a while.

"Fine," she said. "See you then."

"Try to stay cheerful," I told her, hung up, and Gloria buzzed me. "Hah?"

"Hillerman."

"Ah." I pushed the button. "Hi, Charlie."

"So you're in town, are you?" He sounded dangerous, and I was recalling now that he's a large fellow for an illustrator. He comes from Oregon, and he's no stranger to woodchopping. "Just wait there," he said, "I'll be right over."

"No need, Charlie," I said. "I can describe the idea on the phone."

That bewildered him. "What idea?"

"The idea I'm calling about. It's a Get Well Soon, and what we want—"

"You want me to do *another*?" He became briefly falsetto. "You son of a bitch, you've been avoiding me with that out-of-town gag, all of a sudden—"

"Charlie, Charlie," I said, "what makes you talk that way? I *have* been out of town. You can ask Gloria."

"I was there yesterday," he said. "And I went to your apartment, talked to that freak you've got in there."

"You've got my home address, Charlie? That's wonderful; now we can see each other after business hours, too."

"You're in town *now*, you bastard, and—"

"Charlie, what are you upset about?"

"You owe me three hundred and fifty dollars, you son of a bitch!"

"That much?" With my free hand I opened my checkbook, which I keep edged in black.

"I'll take it out of your ass, Art, if I can't get it any other way."

"Charlie, you know how bad the greeting card business is in the summer. Don't act as though I'm not your friend, buddy, you've cashed my checks before."

"Some of them," he said. "And some of them I used to fix bicycle tires."

"That's good, Charlie, that's very funny. Listen, I'm looking at my checkbook right now, and—"

"The bank repossessed mine," he said.

"Charlie, you're really in top form today. You ought to write this stuff down."

"I'll tell you what I'm writing down. Never trust a dirty son of a bitch."

"That's a good rule, Charlie. Listen, to be serious for a minute, I can't pay you the whole thing right now, but I can send you a check for, uh, fifty bucks."

"A hundred," he said. "And don't send it, I'll come down for it."

"Sixty is the absolute best I can do," I said. "I have the landlord breathing down my neck."

"Eighty."

"Charlie, you can't get blood from a stone."

"I can get blood from *you*, Art. Eighty."

"Oh, very well. Seventy-five. But I don't know what I'll tell the landlord."

"You'll think of something. I'll be there in an hour."

"No violence, Charlie, okay? Fun's fun, okay?"

"I'll be as good as the check," he said ominously.

"Listen," I said, "on the trip down, be thinking about this one. 'Get well soon—my doctor says you have it, too.'"

"Have what?"

"Don't worry about it, Charlie. What we want is a girl, like a nice cross between a nurse and a hooker, okay?"

"You're a complete birdbrain, Art, you know that?"

"I have faith in you, Charlie," I said, and hung up, and went out to say to Gloria, "Now, how do you suppose Charlie got my home address?"

"Probably from your sister."

"That's a wonderful theory," I said, "only slightly hampered by the fact they don't know each other."

"Charlie was here yesterday when she called," Gloria said. "He's paranoid, he thought it was you on the phone, he grabbed it out of my hand and they had a nice long chat."

"Goody," I said. "Get her on the phone, will you?"

"Sure."

I went back to my office and made out Charlie's check. Seventy? No, I'd better not fool around; he'd sounded truly annoyed. If only all these people would remain calm until Thanksgiving; but they never do.

Buzz. "Your sister."

"Fine." I pushed the button. "Doris?"

"My goodness, you returned a phone call. To what do I owe the honor?"

"I think of myself as an only child," I said.

"That's your trouble, Art; you think of yourself all the time. Think about somebody else once in a while and—"

"The reason I'm calling," I said, "is to tell you I understand you had a nice chat with Charlie Hillerman yesterday."

"Who? Oh, that artist man in your office."

"That's the one. And Doris, I just wanted to say, if you ever give anybody my home address again, I will come personally over there to Red Bank and cut your vocal cords."

"Oh, that got to you, huh?"

"This is very serious, Doris. There are all kinds of wrong-headed people wandering loose in New York; you can't be too careful."

"If you'd behave decently to people, you wouldn't have to be afraid of them."

"What a wonderful concept. In the meantime, keep your mouth shut about my address."

"I will, if you'll answer my calls."

"I'm answering. I suppose it's Duane and the child support money again."

"I just can't talk to him, Art," she said. "If I even call him on the phone, he rants and raves so much it terrifies me."

A perfectly natural reaction, it seemed to me. "If you'd behave decently to people, Doris," I said, "you wouldn't have to be afraid of them."

"Oh, you think you're so smart. All I want you to do is call him and tell him this time I really will have him arrested and put away in prison for ever and ever. Really really really."

"Uh huh. I'll call him tonight."

"Don't forget."

"Of course not. I'm making a note of it now."

"And I'm sorry I gave out your address."

"Good. I hope I'm not. I have to hang up now, the other phone is ringing."

I hung up, and shook my head. The idea of me phoning Duane Cludder and ordering him to pay my sister her back child-support money was absurd on the face of it. Casting it from my mind, I turned to the accumulated mail stacked on my desk by Gloria, and waded through another sea of pettiness and cheap threats. And also a statement from my distributor, full of numbers out of some sort of accountants' fantasyland and accompanied by an insultingly tiny check. I buzzed Gloria. "Get me All-Boro."

"And two Excedrin?"

"Naturally."

The rest of the mail slid smoothly across my desk and into the wastebasket, except my Master Charge statement, which went into the center drawer of the desk. As I put it in, my eyes lit on my former glasses, worn until three years ago, when I'd purchased my contact lenses. I visualized myself putting them on, saying to Charlie Hillerman, "You wouldn't hit a man with glasses, would you?"

Buzz. "All-Boro."

"Right." I pushed the button. "Hello?"

"All-Boro Distributing. Who's calling, please?" It was the regular receptionist; I recognized her rotund voice.

"This is Those Wonderful Folks," I said. "Put that cheap filthy kike bastard on the line."

"One moment, please."

While I waited, Gloria came in with the Excedrin and the paper cup of water. I downed them, she went away, and Gossmann came on the line. "Hello, Art? Anything wrong, boy?"

"Not a bit of it," I said. "I was just noticing some pretty heavy returns on this statement you sent me."

"It's been a tough year, Art. Looks like people are moving away from obscenity."

"According to this statement," I said, "virtually my entire year's output has been returned from the retailers."

"We'll send them out again in the fall," he said. "Maybe tastes will change again."

"I sure hope so. In the meantime, I don't know, call it nostalgia, I thought I'd come visit my stuff."

"You what?"

"I thought I'd trot out to your warehouse this afternoon," I said, "and look at all my cards sitting there."

"Oh, you don't want to do that," he said.

"Just a little trip down Memory Lane," I said.

"It's a mess out there right now, Art. We're doing inventory."

"In August?"

"Sure, it's a slow time of year."

"Well, inventory's just counting, isn't it? I'll come help count. I'll count all my cards."

"Art, you'll just depress yourself. Besides, I think we're gonna send some out again this afternoon. They're probably loading on the trucks right now."

"Fast action, Joe," I said.

"Well, we got your best interests at heart."

"I'm glad. And I've got some other fast action you can do for me."

"Anything, Art."

"A revised statement," I said, "and another check, on my desk by next Wednesday. Or I go to the Queens D.A." He and I both knew that, since All-Boro's primary product was pornographic magazines and dirty books, the Queens D.A. would just love an excuse to subpoena the company's records.

"Aw, now, Art," he said. "We don't have to get nasty with each other."

"We don't? Next Wednesday, you unutterable prick."

I hung up, and looked around my desk. Time was fleeting. Not only would Charlie be here soon, a visitation I was looking forward to missing, but if I didn't manage to get out of town and grab an earlier ferry than Ralph, Candy was likely to have a relapse.

The Christmas card. I needed a Christian; how about Cal Knox? I didn't owe him any money at the moment. I called him, he loved the idea, and that was that. Anything to take to the island with me? I opened desk drawers, and once again noticed yesteryear's spectacles. Another thought occurred to me, a different usage than protection from Charlie Hillerman. I chuckled at the silliness of the idea, and put the glasses in my attaché case.

I N THE NEWSPAPER LIBRARY
on West Forty-third Street I read:

ALBERT AND ELIZABETH KERNER
DEAD IN FREAK ACCIDENT

Albert J. Kerner, prominent manufacturer and financier
who was chairman of the board of Laurentian Lumber
Mills, world's third largest supplier of wood and wood
products, and his wife Elizabeth Margaret Kerner, the
former Elizabeth Margaret Grahame, both died yesterday in a freak automobile accident in this city. Mr.
Kerner was 57 and his wife 53, and they lived here.

Mr. Kerner, well known in Wall Street and social
circles, inherited much of the family's company holdings, but in recent years had engaged in expansion, leading to the acquisition of several other firms, including a
television station in Indiana.

The couple are survived by their daughters Elizabeth
and Elisabeth.

Hmmmmmm.

"YOU MUST BE BETTY," I said, though I knew better.

"Not on your life," Liz said. "But I suppose you're Bart. Come on in."

I stumbled slightly on the threshold. Damn glasses, how does anybody see with them? All my perceptions were just slightly off; objects I looked at were either a bit too close or a bit too far away, or in any event slightly distorted. It was like living in a Dali painting.

"Watch your step," Liz said.

She led me into the living room. Without its party it seemed cozier, with comfortable chairs grouped around a stone fireplace. Portraits on the walls were undoubtedly Mom and Pop; he looked like the sort of fellow who makes illegal campaign contributions, and she looked like a Grahame.

I have never been in this house before, I reminded myself, and said, "Nice place you have here."

"Sorry," she said, "we already got a buyer."

"Oh, yes. Art told me you're selling."

She gave me a sardonic look; I wasn't being any fun. "I'll tell Betty you're here," she said, and left before I could thank her.

What was happening to me? I paced around the room, frowning inside my glasses. Usually I'm fairly good at casual chitchat, but just now I'd done a very good imitation of that entire party from the other night. All I do is put on spectacles and I suddenly become a baby Frazier; why?

I suppose partly it was the physical unease caused by the glasses themselves. If you're constantly afraid you might lean just a bit too far to the left and do half a cartwheel you really can't devote full attention to bon mots. And also there's a certain tension involved in facing a girl you've recently screwed in the upstairs closet and convincing her she's never met you before.

Well, probably it was all to the good. I hadn't thought in terms of a personality change when I'd decided to have a go at being Bart, but why not? It could only reinforce the physical changes I'd wrought.

An oval mirror in an ornate frame hung on the wall near the dining room arch, and in it I studied again the new face I'd made for myself. The glasses made me seem more serious, perhaps a bit older, and I'd combed my hair straight back to reveal the receding hairline I usually camouflage. I am thirty now, and for the last year the hair has been retreating from my temples like the tide going out. Never to come in again, unfortunately.

"Well, hello."

I turned around, and Betty had entered, wearing the same white dress and the same hostess smile as the other night. "Now," I said, "*you* must be Betty."

"Why, you don't look like your brother at all," she said, and through the artificial smile it seemed to me I detected disappointment.

"You look a lot like your sister," I said. I tell you, I'd never been funnier.

"Oh, she's prettier than I am," Betty said, adding artificial coyness and artificial demureness to her artificial smile.

"Not at all," I said. "You're a terrific-looking girl." I admit I wasn't being exactly brilliant, but you try complimenting a twin.

We chatted on in that sprightly way a bit longer, and

then Betty said, "Well, shall we go?"

"After you," I said, with a little bow. Christ!

Liz did not reappear, which was just as well. Betty and I strolled along the dark lanes past the quaint old-fashioned streetlights—imitation gas lamps, very pseudo-London—and did not hold hands. How to proceed? Glibness now would not only be out of character for the persona with which I'd saddled myself, but would also be inappropriate for this Senior Prom beauty tripping along at my side. I was here to ball her, not terrify her.

In point of fact, just why *was* I here? In order to get away from Candy and Ralph for a while, to some extent. And because the impersonation was a comic challenge that appealed to me. And because I'd suddenly realized I'd always wanted to fuck twins. And because they were rich orphans.

Let's not downgrade that final consideration. I've never been familiar enough with money to feel contempt for it, so I wasn't about to kick a girl out of bed for being rich. Money and those who possessed it had always held a certain appeal for me. My one descent into marriage, to a bitch named Lydia whom I'd met in college, had been based partly on the mistaken notion that my bride's family was well off. A publisher, I'd thought, is a publisher is a publisher; but not, it turned out, when the things published were four weekly newspapers in rural areas of New England.

So I was here to amuse myself by rubbing against a rich body. Which meant we were now in the seduction scene. Of course. I was the male lead in a Doris Day comedy. Simplicity itself. Turn off your mind, relax, and float downstream. "It's charming here," I said.

7

A<small>ND THE LADY WILL HAVE</small> the beef stroganoff," I said.

The waiter, a slender youth dressed like a musical comedy star, pocketed his pad and pranced away. "I've never been here before," Betty said, looking around in polite approval.

Neither had I. "I've always liked it," I said. "There's something . . . intimate about it."

She gazed out across the huge deck polka-dotted with tables, half of them occupied. "Yes, isn't there," she said.

So far tonight I had done everything exactly right, though often for the wrong reason. The boat, for instance. Feeling I couldn't spend the rest of the summer stealing bicycles every time I visited a Kerner sister, I had this afternoon made an arrangement with a local Fair Harbor teen-ager who possessed a motorboat. For fifteen dollars he would chauffeur me along the bay to Point O' Woods, wait for me to pick up my date, transport us here to the Pewter Tankard in Robbins Rest, and come back for us at eleven. At that time I would give him a prearranged signal as to whether or not he was to wait for me after returning us to Point O' Woods.

Well, I'd prepared all that only because the alternative —assuming no bicycles to steal—was a two-mile walk in each direction. I would not have been in love with that option in any event, but with these awkward glasses confounding me at every step it would have been impossible.

Thus, the boat. But now that I was in a seduction comedy, the boat had become the most quintessential of romantic gestures.

Similarly the restaurant. This was Friday, and my first three dinner choices in Ocean Beach had already been full when I called. But the Pewter Tankard, being slightly off the beaten track—it catered to boat people, and was accessible only by water—had been happy to take my reservation. Romance, again; I had found that little out-of-the-way restaurant, barely half full on a Friday night in August, where we could sit on an open deck built out into the bay and watch the distant lights of Long Island beneath a sky full of stars.

Betty sipped at her sherry, while I pulled gently on my rum and tonic. She said, "I understand you and your brother are in business together."

"That's right," I said, and prompted by her friendly inquisitive look I added, "We're in publishing."

"Oh, publishing!" she said happily, making the same mistake I'd made with Lydia. "Do you mean books?" More cautious than I'd been, you'll notice.

"Oh, nothing that grand," I said, in my modest way. "We have a small line of greeting cards. Like Hallmark, you know."

"Oh, really! That's fascinating." And apparently it was, since she went on from there to ask several hundred questions about the company. My answers were generally more descriptive of Hallmark than of Those Wonderful Folks, but the gist was there.

Meantime, nothing was happening on the food front. "Excuse me," I finally said to Betty, and snagged the waiter as he pirouetted by. He assured me our appetizers were scant seconds from delivery, but his manner struck me as shifty-eyed, so I ordered another sherry for Betty and another rum-and for me. "By Pony Express, all right?"

"Certainly, sir." And he gamboled off.

"You're very masterful," Betty told me. Her disappointment that I was not my brother seemed to have waned. In fact, she now said, "I bet you have the business head in the family, don't you?"

"Oh, we both do our share," I said.

Still, she pursued the subject, and I gradually permitted myself to admit that Art was more the clever intuitive member of the family, while I was the practical one who kept the company stable and afloat. "Liz and I are like that," Betty said. "She's just so clever and witty sometimes, and I'm the plain practical one."

"Not plain," I assured her. Reaching across the table, I squeezed her hand. "Anything but plain."

She squeezed back. "You *are* nice," she said.

Then it was back to the greeting card company, and now she wanted to know if we did all the "verses" ourselves, or did we accept work from "free-lancers." On the assumption that Mr. Hallmark doesn't do all his own writing, I said, "Oh, we buy most of our verses from professionals."

Something flustered and coy overtook her now, and she said, "You may not believe this, but I write verses myself."

My heart sank. "Do you really?"

"Oh, not for publication, just for family occasions. I don't suppose I'm good enough to be a real professional."

Nor did I. However, I now had no choice; it was required of me that I coax her, blushing and reluctant, to quote me some of her crap. Which at last, of course, she consented to do.

"I wrote this for my mother's fiftieth birthday," she said. "Mother, when I think of all/The things you've done for me,/I know no other mother could/Compare on land or sea./I think you're sweet, I think you're great./In short, I think you're nifty—"

"Oh, good!" I said. "Here come our drinks."

8   8

"GOOD MORNING, SWEET-
heart."

I must be awake; nobody could dream a headache this
bad. Cautiously—or incautiously, as it turned out—I
opened one eye, and a needle of sunlight struck straight
through into my brain. "Holy Mother of God!" I groaned,
and snapped the eyelid shut again over my charred eye-
ball.

A smell of coffee threatened my stomach with upheaval,
and a voice I recognized said, redundantly, "I brought you
some coffee."

This time I squinted, which was safer, and vaguely made
out her female form. Liz, or possibly Betty. Which one
was it? Come to think of it, which one was I?

"Do you want your glasses?"

Ah hah, a clue. Glasses = Bart. "Sweetheart" said to
Bart = Betty.

Sweetheart? Betty? What bed was I in? "Glasses," I
muttered, feeling sudden urgency, and waved a hand in the
air until my spectacles were thrust into it. I donned them
without sticking the wings in my eyes and blinked around
at a bedroom I knew from somewhere. Good God, there
was the closet, its door demurely closed. I was upstairs
once more in the Kerner house, and had apparently spent
the night.

Oh, really? I struggled to a sitting position, my back
against the knurled wood headboard, and looked fuzzily

around. This room was furnished with twin beds, in one of which I was roiling about and on the edge of the other of which Betty was sitting, cheerful and not at all hung over, crisp and cute in white shorts and a pale blue top.

She smiled at me. "Hung over?"

"I think it's terminal."

"I brought you some aspirin."

"Gimme."

She watched me struggle the aspirin down with gulps of coffee, and her expression was fond and indulgent and maternal, three of my least favorite mannerisms in a woman.

It was hard to think and swallow aspirin at the same time, but I forced myself. Last night: romantic evening, motorboat, Pewter Tankard. Betty had informed me she never drank anything stronger than wine, so I'd seen to it the table flowed with the stuff. Sherry beforehand, Moselle with the appetizer, Médoc with the entree, and stingers with dessert. (The wine limitation had fallen by then.) I did remember the stingers, but from then on memory faltered. There was a scene involving hilarious laughter and me failing to get out of a boat. There was something to do with whether or not we were going to steal bicycles. Beyond that, a veil covereth all.

At last I abandoned the effort and put the coffee cup on the night table between the beds, saying, "God, what a head."

"I guess you're just not used to wine."

"That might be it."

"You know, you look a lot more like your brother with your glasses off, and your hair tousled that way."

I whipped a guilty hand to my head, but could do nothing effective there, and permitted it to drop again to my side.

"Have you ever thought of trying contact lenses?"

"Oh, well," I said. "Glasses are good enough for me." They were hurting my nose.

"You're really very good-looking, you know," she said,

and when I looked at her it seemed to me there was something possessive, possibly triumphant in the set of her head
and the glint of her eye.

Had we? There are things you don't forget, aren't there?
Aren't there? I was naked beneath the sheet and thin blan-
ket. Speak, memory. Goddamn it to hell. But memory remained silent. And that is one question it is never possible
to ask a woman. They don't take kindly to the thought of
being forgettable. "I think," I said, "you should take cover.
I believe my head is about to explode."

"I'll massage your temples," she offered. "I do that for
Liz sometimes when she has hangovers, and she says it
helps just wonderfully."

"Anything," I said.

So she moved over to sit on my bed, remove my glasses,
and began stroking my temples with her cool fingers. It did
nothing for me in any medical way, but it did put her in
arm's reach, so I slid a hand around her waist. The smile
she gave me was very nearly as lewd as her sister's, and
she said, "Again? You'd better rest."

Ah hah, another clue. Again, was it? I stroked a breast
and drew her close and murmured, "It's the only known
cure. A medical fact."

"Now, Bart," she said, and we kissed. Despite my throb-
bing head I enjoyed it.

But when I tried to roll her into the bed with me she
pulled back, becoming at once serious. "Not in my father's
bed!"

"Your fa—" I glanced toward the other one. "Not that
one either, I guess."

"You can understand, can't you?" She petted my chest,
seeking forgiveness.

"Oh, sure. But—" How to phrase this, without tipping
the fact that our previous encounter wasn't on the tape?
"Last night," I suggested, "didn't we, uh? . . ."

She looked at me, with humorous shock covering the
true shock. "You don't remember!"

"Of course I remember." I sat up straighter, astounded that she could doubt me. "I remember *you*. But you know the condition I was in, and the dark, and . . ." I let it trail off, with a vague wavy gesture of the hand. "I just don't remember *where*," I said.

"You silly thing," she said. "On the porch."

"Ah."

"And the living room."

"Ah hah."

"And the bathroom."

"Ah?"

She giggled, and petted my chest some more. "You were just insatiable," she said.

I must have been. "I still am," I said, and petted *her* chest, while I looked around for some solution to our quandary. My eye lit on the closet; no, that would be going just too far.

"Oh, Bart," she said, and leaned forward to nibble my pectorals.

"Um," I said, and pointed to the floor. "You see that rug?"

"What a wonderful idea," she said, and bounded out of her shorts.

Even with twins, there are certain differences. Betty was a trifle thinner than Liz, and somewhat less imaginative. She was also a lot harder to bring off; in fact, I'm not sure I did. However, she seemed well enough pleased, and afterward, as I lay on the rug like a trout in the bottom of a boat, she wetly kissed my ear and whispered, "I'll make you a nice breakfast."

"Thank you," I whispered. She had whispered because it was romantic, but I did so because I didn't have the strength to talk.

She started away, then came back to whisper some more. "Now, if Liz comes in, remember we're going to keep it a secret."

A secret. Screwing? I wasn't up to any response other

than a bewildered squint in her general direction.

She was about to become hurt again. "Now," she said, no longer whispering, "you'll tell me you didn't forget our engagement."

"Oh, our engagement! Well, naturally I know about *that*. I just didn't know what you were talking about."

She considered me briefly, but finally decided to let it go, for which small kindness I hope she was given full marks in heaven. She left the room, and slowly I made it to a sitting position on the floor. I spoke aloud. "I'm engaged," I said, and then I giggled.

It wasn't until some time later that I thought of the world's third largest supplier of wood and wood products, and the several other firms including a television station in Indiana.

9   9

SUNDAY MORNING I TOOK the ferry from Point O' Woods to Bay Shore, stepped into a phone booth, and called the Kerner house. I knew it was Betty who answered, since Liz hadn't been around all weekend, but I said, "Hi, is this Liz?"

"No, it's Betty."

"Oh, hello. This is Art Dodge. Is my brother there, by any chance?"

"Oh, you just missed him! He just now took the ferry."

"Drat," I said. "Well, I'll call him tonight in the city. Is Liz around?"

"Not right now," she said doubtfully. She wasn't about to tell Art the hair-raising stories she'd told Bart, about Liz disappearing routinely for two or three days at a time. "Could she call you back?"

"Sure," I said, and left Candy and Ralph's number. Then I walked across Maple Avenue and took the Fair Harbor ferry, which wasn't at all in the same league as the boat from Point O' Woods.

Yesterday, after my hangover had ebbed a bit, and after Betty and I had committed sacrilege after all upon her father's bed, I'd called my Fair Harbor hosts to tell them not to worry, I was more or less safe and sound. Happily, it was Ralph who answered, and he'd understood at once. "Go get 'em, Art," he'd said, and I could just see him doing that little punching gesture.

Which left Candy still to be heard from.

She wasn't home, I'm glad to say, but the kids were there, spreading peanut butter and jelly on the kitchen counter. I took my damn glasses off, popped my lenses in, changed into bathing trunks, grabbed a towel, and headed for the beach. After a night and a day and a night of romping with Betty in a Liz-less house I was ready for some restorative rest.

But I wasn't to get it. I hadn't been lying there on my back twenty minutes when somebody kicked sand in my face. Squinting upward, I saw at first nothing but a blue-swathed crotch above tanned legs. Then Liz dropped to the sand beside me and said, "Hello, lover."

"Hello, yourself."

"Your brother came sniffing around," she said.

I glared, "After you?"

"Hah," she said. "You never saw a couple that belonged together like your Bart and my Betty."

Had I been that bad? Grinning in relief, I lay my head back on the towel and said, "Well, that's all right, then."

"So there you are," said another voice, and when I looked up this new crotch was swathed in yellow. It dropped down toward me, and there was Candy sitting on my left, baring her teeth across my chest at Liz. "And this must be your new friend," she said.

"Liz Kerner," I said, "this is Candy Minck, my hostess." And then, because one or the other of them would surely now say something that would blow the twin bit forever, with nothing I could possibly do about it, I rested my head back on the towel, closed my eyes, and folded my hands on my breast.

LIZ: "I recognized your voice from the phone. It's so distinctive."

CANDY: "You don't look at all the way I pictured you."

LIZ: "Really? You look exactly the way I thought you would."

CANDY: "Oh? How's that?"

LIZ: "Oh, I don't know. Sort of cute and matronly."

CANDY: "What a sweet thing to say. But Art has told us so little about you. Do you have a place of your *own* here, or do you just come over for the day?"

LIZ: "I have a little house in Point O' Woods. Not as . . . casual as yours, of course."

CANDY: "Yes, you have seen my place, haven't you?"

Opening my eyes, I cautiously lifted my head. Claws were dug into the sand on both sides of my rib cage. I said, "Where do you suppose Ralph is?"

Candy, her eyes still fixed on Liz, waggled impatient fingers toward the ocean. "Drowning." To Liz she said, "I want you always to feel free to drop in at my house just any time you want."

"That's so nice of you," Liz said. "It's so relaxing to be in a place where nobody cares about housekeeping and all of that."

"Say," I said, with a big friendly smile, "why don't we have a drink?"

"I thought you'd never ask," Liz said.

Candy was already on her feet, wiping sand from her

ass which just accidentally fell on my head. "We'll all go to *my place,*" she said.

So we left the beach and strolled along the boardwalk toward Candy's house. There was blessed silence for a minute or two, and then Candy said to Liz, "Do your people at Point O' Woods give you many days off?"

"Not many," Liz said. "Since I inherited my father's estate it's just business business business all the time."

"Oh, are you an orphan, poor dear?"

I said, "Liz has a twin sister. There's just the two of them left in the world."

"There's another one at home like you?" The idea seemed to daunt Candy slightly.

"You never know where you'll run into twins, ha, ha," I said, then pointed and said, "Isn't that one of the kids on the roof?"

"Wha?" Candy squinted, she shielded her eyes from the sun. "I don't see anybody."

"My mistake," I said. "For a second I thought I saw somebody there."

We walked on to the house. If only Liz had to go to the john, I would take Candy to one side, explain the twin scam to her briefly, assure her my intentions toward the Kerners were strictly mercenary and that my dishonorable intentions were still centered on her own sweet self, insist that my motive was Kerner investment in Those Wonderful Folks, and beg her connivance in the plot. The idea should appeal to her; Candy had a natural love of the underhanded.

Unfortunately, when we entered the house it was Candy who headed immediately for the john, while Liz stood at the kitchen counter, touching the peanut butter and jelly with a hesitant finger and waiting for her usual. I called after Candy, "And what's yours?"

"I'll make it when I come back."

Vodka-ice. Rum-and. "Cheers," I said, and we both drank.

"You have a true taste for the gutter, don't you?" Liz suggested.

"What, Candy? She's my best friend's wife."

"I took that for granted." She strolled around, looking at the furnishings. "It's hard to believe people still live like this."

"We are the people," I told her. "The salt of the earth."

She gave me a skeptical look. "You're more the nutmeg," she said. "But—" with another disdainful glance at her surroundings "—it's easy to see why you were attracted to Betty. The simple smell of soap would probably drive you mad."

I decided to ignore the crack about Betty; she couldn't possibly still be annoyed about the party. "The last time you were here," I said, "you seemed to find the accommodations, uh, satisfactory."

"I'll try anything once," she said. "I like new experiences."

I remembered she hadn't been home since Friday evening. "I'm sure you do," I said.

"It's too bad most of them become old so fast," she said.

"Don't I know the feeling."

We stood smiling at one another, me near the kitchen counter and Liz in the living room area, until all at once Candy marched between us, heading for the door, carrying what appeared to be my suitcase. We watched her kick open the screen door, rear back, and toss the suitcase out of the house. Underhanded, of course: It lofted up and over the railing and landed in the poison ivy.

Candy turned on me a smile that would crack granite. "I hope," she said, through her gritted grin, "you'll have a glorious time in Point O' Woods." Approaching me, she said, "And *that's* my drink, thank you very much." And plucked from my hand my rum and tonic.

Liz suddenly started laughing. "Oh, Art," she said, "what a beautiful face!"

"Well," I said.

Candy had taken a slug of my drink. "You get out of here, Art," she said. "Get out of here *right now*." From the look in her eye, she'd be picking up a steak knife next.

I backed toward the door, irritably aware of Liz grinning in the corner of my vision. "I suppose that goes for Bart too," I said, and before she could respond I quickly added, "Does Ralph know about this? Does he go along with this? He is, after all—"

"You leave Ralph out of this! I don't even want you to mention his *name!*"

"He'll just wonder why I'm not here."

"You don't think I'll tell him? You don't think so?"

I thought she was capable of any idiocy, given her present mood, so rather than reply I stepped outside, picked up the mop leaning against the wall near the door, and went fishing for my suitcase.

Meanwhile, Candy had turned on Liz. It's amazing how many coarse names she knew for female private parts. And while the pebbles Liz dropped into Candy's stream of invective were rather quieter, I wouldn't exactly say they were gentler.

I grasped my suitcase, hauled it up onto the deck, and went cautiously back inside. Candy was heaving so much in her little two-piece yellow bathing suit she looked like a belly dancer trainee, and Liz was also a bit red around the face. Neither, however, was speaking at this precise moment. "My attaché case," I whispered to them both, as though there were a sleeper nearby that I didn't want to wake, and I tiptoed to the ladder. Up I went, packed the last few items—including Bart's glasses—and carried the attaché case down.

Candy, though still panting, had developed now the beginnings of a puzzled frown on her foxy face. She said to me, "Who?"

Whoops. "All I can say, Candy," I said, "is that I did my best to ease your loneliness, and to be a true friend to you when you needed me."

"Why, you filthy son of a bitch," she said, "I'm going to cut your balls off!" And she went around the end of the counter into the kitchen.

"Come, Liz," I said, with dignity. "I know when I'm not wanted."

I crossed the room, opened the screen door, and a bottle of Firehouse Jubilee bloody Mary mix sailed past my head and into the poison ivy. Liz and I exited, and I closed the screen door behind me and spoke through it. "I'll tell Bart your decision," I said, "and I know he'll be just as hurt as I am that all our acts of kindness, our attempts to bring solace into the drab life of a trapped housewife, have been misunderstood and unap—"

An egg strained itself through the screen; some of it reached my chest.

"Mp," I said. I picked up my suitcase, and Liz and I departed.

We'd gone a block when the shouts started behind us: "Who? *Who*?" Fortunately, Liz was laughing too hard to hear it.

10   10

WALKING WITH LIZ TO Hommel's, toting my suitcase, I had leisure to think things over. What next, I wondered. I'd done my con and made it work, I'd screwed both sisters, I'd precipitated the break with Candy that I suppose I must have been angling for, so now everything was obviously finished. To repeat the twin gag would be insanity; I couldn't possibly get away with it twice. And while Liz was fun in her way she was hardly restful; I might as well have stayed with Candy.

So what I should do right now was take the next ferry/cab/train back to the city, move into my office (ah, the sleeping bag stored in the closet), and start hustling around for someone else to put me up for the rest of August. Also for another female, though that was at the moment secondary.

But I just couldn't seem to let go. I'd made the Art-Bart phone call to Betty the minute I'd gotten off the ferry, I'd risked severe physical impairment to drop Bart's name into my farewell scene with Candy, and now I was walking to Hommel's with Liz, my mind searching for a way to get invited to spend the rest of the summer at the Kerner house. Why?

Well, partly for the Laurentian Lumber Mills, I suppose. And maybe a tenny little bit for that television station in Indiana. I was, after all, engaged to an heiress, or at least Bart was.

And also for the sheer silly intrigue of it. I've never been able to quit when I was ahead, never known how to stop before I got caught, and I wasn't likely to learn now. So I went with Liz to Hommel's, watched a ferry depart, and waited to be invited home.

For a while it looked as though it wouldn't happen. Liz spent her first two drinks making remarks about Candy, some of which I thought were probably unfair, then devoted her third to class-conscious slurs of the citizens around us. It must be hard to be a promiscuous snob, but Liz managed.

Finally, partway into her fourth vodka-ice, she looked at me and said, "So what do you do now?"

"Swelter in the city, I suppose. I'll hate to break the news to Bart."

"Screw Bart."

"He's my brother."

"He isn't mine," she said, callously, I thought.

"Then there's my apartment," I said. I sighed, but was manful about it. "Well, I've camped in my office before."

"What's wrong with your apartment?"

I was just about to tell her it was sublet when I realized I was supposed to have been spending half of every week in the damn place. "Bart," I said. "It's just a one-and-a-half in the Village, there isn't room for both of us."

"He's in *your* place?"

That didn't make sense, did it? "Well," I said. Invention flowed through me, bred by necessity, and I said, "Bart doesn't have his own place yet. Not till after Labor Day."

"Why not?"

"He spent several years out on the Coast," I explained. (Of course! If a friend of mine expressed bewilderment about Bart in Liz's presence, this would explain it; he was a *long-lost* brother.) "He just came back the beginning of the summer," I said, "when he came into the business with me."

"Oh. Well, you want to come stay at my house?"

"Do I have to sleep in the closet?"

She showed me her sour grin. "I like being around you," she said. "You're a little funnier than most people. Like back at your lady-friend's house."

"I give all credit to my supporting cast."

"Uh huh." She downed her drink and signaled to the proprietor for another. "Can you get hold of that brat with the boat?"

"I can try." But should I plead Bart's case? No. Screw Bart, as Liz so correctly pointed out. Let him plead his own case, with Betty. "I'll be right back," I said, and headed for the pay phone.

A<small>ND</small> <small>THEN</small> I <small>WROTE:</small>
"Christmas comes but once a year—I'm glad you can do
better."

That was on the ferry, Wednesday morning, three days
after I'd moved in at Point O' Woods. I was old family
there by now, and I was sure Bart would do every bit as
well.

Betty had accepted my presence with her inevitable
artificial hostess smile, but of course the hypocritical little
bitch had to pretend Liz and I weren't screwing, so of
course *we* had to pretend we weren't screwing, so there'd
been a lot of tiptoeing back and forth as a result. At least
we hadn't had to enter any closets.

I was now in full uncontested occupation of Mom and
Pop's room. I had at first tossed my attaché case onto
Daddy's bed, to see if Betty would comment, and damn if
she didn't switch me over to the other bed: "It's closer to
the closet." An unintentional private joke, at which Liz
and I did *not* exchange looks. And also an indication that
Betty actually was the sentimental creep she pretended to
be; she was saving that bed for Bart.

And wasn't she, though. She insisted on calling Bart
right then on Sunday evening, inviting him out for his half-
week vacations. In desperation I gave her Ralph and
Candy's city number, praying there was no subtenant there
that I hadn't been told about, and apparently there was
not. After the third futile attempt, I said, "Why not call

him in the morning? He's bound to be in the office."

"That's just what I'll do," she said, and the three of us went out to dinner at Flynn's. During which I excused myself to go to the john, found a pay phone, and called Gloria at home. "Be there, bitch," I muttered, as I dialed, and damn if she wasn't.

Her husband answered, and when I identified myself he said, "Oh, yeah?" Then he covered the phone inefficiently —on purpose, I assume—and I heard him shout, "It's that bastard!"

Was no further identification necessary? And to think of the salaries I'd paid that ingrate, many of them on time.

"Hello?"

"Now you have to guess *which* bastard."

"Come on, Art, I'm watching television."

Ah, the married life. "Tomorrow," I said, "a lady will call asking for my twin brother Bart."

"Oh, for God's sake."

"Now, Gloria. All you have to do is take her number and tell her Bart is out at a meeting with his local distributor, and—"

"*Local* distributor!"

"And," I said firmly, "you will have him call back as soon as he gets in."

"How many felonies will I be committing?"

"None. A little white lie in the service of love, that's all it is."

"Bullshit."

"Gloria, remember how you hated working at Met Life? The bells going off all the time, twenty-two minutes for lunch?"

She sighed. "Bart, huh? Very original."

"It stands for Bay Area Rapid Transit," I explained, and went back to dinner with the ladies.

And so it came to pass that on Monday morning Betty called Bart, and an hour later Bart returned the call from the pay phone by the firehouse. Candy was discussed, and the unfortunate incident of the day before. Betty wanted to know if Bart thought Art had been adulterous with Candy, and Bart admitted he'd wondered the same thing himself. Betty preferred her invitation, and Bart was happy to accept. "We can be with each other three days a week," he said.

"And three nights," quoth Little Miss Hot Pants.

The intervening nights, however, belonged to Liz, who was no slouch herself. Bouncety bouncety; by Wednesday morning I was just as pleased to board that boat for a day's vacation at the office.

Liz saw me off at the pier. "I like a man who goes away for half the week," she said.

I bet you do, I thought. I said, "Have a nice rest," and patted her cheek. And wrote my new Christmas card on the ferry. Thus do we artists adapt the facts of our own lives to the purposes of our art.

12   12

THE GENTLEMAN WAITING in my outer officer was up to no good; I could tell it the minute I laid eyes on him. Gloria, with a now-you're-in-for-it look, waved grandly at the fellow and said, "There's a Mr. Volpinex here to see you, Mr. Dodge. He wanted either you or your brother Bart."

Whoops. Mr. Volpinex had apparently been my age when he'd died, several thousand years ago, and in the depths of the pyramid been given this simulacrum of life. The ancient chemists had dyed his flesh a dark unhealthy tan, and painted his teeth with that cheap gloss white enamel used in rent-controlled apartments. His black suit was surely some sort of oil by-product, and so was his smile.

"I take it," this thing said, extending its hand, "I am addressing Mr. *Arthur* Dodge?"

"That's right." His hand was as dry as driftwood.

"I am Ernest Volpinex," he said, and gave himself away. No *real* thirty-year-old would have reached into his vest pocket at that juncture and given me his card. So my first guess was right; he was the undead.

I took the card, but kept my eyes on its owner. "How do you do?"

"I am," he said, with the smile of a bone-grinder, "the attorney for the Kerner estate."

I sensed Gloria's ears cocking like a collie's at the phrase *Kerner estate*. Kerner had been the name of the girl two days ago, Bart was the person that girl had been looking for, and the word *estate* was well within Gloria's vocabulary. "Why don't we go into my office?" I said.

"Thank you very much."

And so we entered the office. I gestured to my guest chair, but Volpinex took a moment instead to read the cards mounted on my wall, so I sat at my desk and leafed through the call memos. Wastebasket wastebasket wastebasket . . .

I had transferred to the incoming mail and had discovered, to my pleased surprise, an actual amended statement and supplemental check from All-Boro, when Volpinex falsely chuckled, turning to face me, and said, "Very amusing."

"I keep them around to lighten my darker moments," I said. "Do have a chair."

"Thank you."

I didn't care for the way he made himself at home in that chair, settling in as though he'd just foreclosed on a mortgage I hadn't known about. He said, "May I smoke?"

You can fry. "Certainly."

He had a silver cigarette case and a black holder. The case was also a lighter at one end. If he hadn't used those two magic names *Bart* and *Kerner* I would have considered him some sort of overdone buffoon; as it was I watched him with respect, if not admiration.

Satisfied at last with his cigarette, he said, "We've been neighbors, you know."

What? "Have we?"

"You were staying for a while in Fair Harbor, and I've rented a place in Dunewood."

"Ah." Ah hah! With sudden conviction, I knew that *this* was my host at the party where I'd first met Liz. And wouldn't he also be the fellow she was with last weekend, while I was Barting Betty? Which was why Liz had suddenly showed up on that part of the beach.

And to think she'd been putting me down for my connection with Candy.

"You were staying," my saturnine friend continued, "with Mr. and Mrs. Ralph Minck, were you not?"

"That's right," I said.

"And so was your brother, known as Bart. Would that stand for Bartholomew, by the way?"

"No, actually his name is Robert. We were named after two famous World War One flying aces, Arthur Powerton and Robert Godunkey. But because we're twins and so on, I suppose the name just evolved into Bart."

"Ah," he said. "That's probably why I haven't been able to pick up much about him."

I permitted myself to look just slightly outraged. "Pick up?"

"I have a passion for being fair," he said, unruffled, smiling at me. "And I just don't believe it's possible to be fair if one isn't thorough. Don't you agree?"

"You've been checking up on my brother?"

"And yourself," he assured me. "And your—" his gesture around at my office was condescending "—company.

And even your hosts in Fair Harbor."

"My hosts?" What in hell was he after?

"Ralph Minck," he said. "Attorney, employed by a large firm downtown. Specialist in stock issue flotation and presentations to the SEC."

And recently promoted to a level where he could bring his paper work home. I said, "I don't quite follow what you're doing, Mr. . . ."

"Volpinex. I believe I gave you my card."

"Yes, you did. Now what do you want *me* to give *you*?"

"Quite simply," he said, "your assurance that neither your brother nor yourself is a fortune hunter."

I leaned forward over the desk, my forearms on my scattered mail. "Mr. Volpinex," I said, "you should go to bed earlier. Watching all those thirties movies on the 'Late Late Show,' letting them seep into your brain at three and four in the morning, it just isn't good for you."

"Thank you for your concern," he said, "but my own concern is exclusively with—"

"Another point," I said, raising one forearm to point a finger upward. A phone bill, sticking to my damp skin, came up with me, midway between wrist and elbow. I made a sound, shook it loose, and said, "Another point. What if *I'd* been watching the same movies, night after night? Then I would be brainwashed into believing that, guilty or innocent, my *only* possible reaction to such a charge was to punch you in the mouth. Luckily, my sleeping habits have been healthier than that."

"Very lucky," he commented dryly. "I'm a karate expert."

I gazed at him, utterly depressed. "Are you really?"

"Also kung fu. However, to return to the point, my own concern is exclusively with the Misses Eliz/sabeth Kerner. They are—"

"Excuse me, would you say that again?"

"Beg pardon?"

"The name part."

"You mean, the Misses Eliz/sabeth Kerner?"

"That's it. Thank you." I gave him a courtly gesture. "Proceed."

"Yes. Thank you. The young ladies in question are, as you well know, only recently orphaned. Their emotional condition is still unsettled. Were they alone and unprotected, who knows what advantage might be taken of them. Fortunately, however, they are not alone and unprotected."

"They have me," I said. "And my brother, of course."

"Please don't misunderstand, Mr. Dodge," he said, "but you and your brother are hardly on a social or, may I say, economic level with the Kerners."

"I thought this was a classless society."

"Did you really?" He frowned at me, trying to understand that, then shrugged and shook his head. "Setting that to one side," he said, with another gesture at my little office, "there is still the economic consideration."

"Of course there is. And I am, as you can see, a legitimate businessman, with a thriving company."

"Thriving? Your company might support one brother reasonably well, but two brothers would starve on it."

I couldn't have said it better myself. Nor would I have. I said, "My brother only recently entered the firm. In the fall we plan a major expansion."

"Bravo, Mr. Dodge. With two of you hawking your wares door to door I'm sure you'll do very well."

There was just something about his style. Here he was, a cockroach in a three-piece suit, telling me *I* was lower class. Not only that, he was a skinny swarthy thirty-year-old, and he talked as pompously as a fat fifty gray-haired WASP banker. Did he really think he *was* a Grahame or a Frazier?

Then I got it. A sudden conviction entered my brain, and I pointed at the slimy bastard. "You're after them yourself!"

"I beg your pardon?"

"One of them, I mean." I used my pointing hand to snap

my fingers, as an aid to thought. "Which one? Liz?"

His pinched-lemon face closed up even more. "I had suspected even before we met," he said, "that you were the sort to misunderstand professional ethics and automatically think the worst of your fellow man. Your insinuation is beneath—"

"We know each other, Jack," I told him. "We're sisters under the skin and you know it. I'm not—"

The door opened and Gloria came in, with two Excedrin and a cup of water. An invaluable woman. As I took my medicine she said, "Charlie Hillerman's outside."

"Tell him I went to Alaska to take some Christmas card photographs. Reindeer fucking, that kind of thing." Then my eye passed over my other unwelcome visitor, I suddenly remembered an odd incident from Charlie Hillerman's past, and I said, "No, wait. Tell him I'll be with him in just a minute."

"And give him a heart attack? Commit your own murders."

She left, and I went back to Volpinex. Now that I understood him, he didn't worry me any more. "You didn't come here," I said, "to find out if I'm a fortune hunter. Or my brother, him, too, if he was. You came here to find out if we're competition. And let me tell you something right now: we are. Both of us."

The pursed look remained on his face, but he got his ass out of my chair. "In your childhood," he said, looking down across the desk at me, "you should have heeded your elders' advice, when they warned you against judging others by yourself. I assure you, I will do everything in my rather considerable power to rescue those young ladies from you *and* your brother."

Straight out of a Victorian novel, but didn't he know he was lying? His parents must have kept him locked away in a dusty attic throughout his childhood (and who could blame them), where he had bided his time with the works of Harriet Beecher Stowe and Mrs. Humphry Ward.

But melodrama is contagious. Leaping up, driven to my feet by the force of the scene I was playing, and just for that moment meaning every ridiculous word I said, I said, "Speaking for my brother, Mr. Volpinex, and believe me I think I know my brother's heart, I'm telling you right now that all grasping attorneys and other vultures hovering over the Kerner inheritance had better watch their step pret-ty carefully, because Liz and Betty, in their hour of need and travail, have found their heroes at last! And good day to you, sir!"

13   13

WHEN CHARLIE HILLER-man came bulging in, after the slithering departure of Volpinex, I was hurriedly but calmly writing a check. "Okay Art," Charlie announced, coming over to lean over my desk and show me his biceps, "I figured it out you're always in town on Wednesday, and I'm here to tell—"

"Here you are, Charlie."

He took the check, and glared at it. "If you think you can fob me off with another partial pay—" He stopped, dead, and stared at the check.

"Not at all, Charlie," I said. "That's payment in full."

He sank into the chair lately defiled by Volpinex. "Holy God," he said. "Who do I kill?"

"Just the reverse," I said.

He frowned at me, his natural suspicion returning. Snapping the check with his finger, he said, "Is this any good?"

"Of course it is. Charlie, you remember telling me about the time you did the dollar-bill card for F&A?"

"Sure. 'If you want to sleep here, George, you'll need ten of those.' What about it?"

"You did such a good job the Treasury people came around," I reminded him. "F&A couldn't distribute."

He nodded, sulky at the memory. "And I never got paid."

"That's what you get for dealing for a schlock outfit, Charlie. Stick with me and you'll be okay."

"Huh," he said.

"The point is," I said, "I've got a Birthday you're perfect for."

His natural truculence was creased by a pleat of curiosity. "What is it?"

"I understand when you were born—three wise men left town."

"Not bad," he said.

"It's encouragement like that keeps me going, Charlie."

"What's the picture?"

"The card is a photostat of a birth certificate."

He frowned, not seeing it; in truth, it wasn't a very good idea. "Yeah?" he said.

From the bottom left drawer of my desk I took the photostat of my birth certificate I'd sent for when I got my passport; you never know when you might want to leave the country. Extending it across the desk, I said, "We'll use mine. That way, there won't be any lawsuits."

"Yeah?" He took the photostat and studied it, not charmed. "What do you need me for?"

"Well, I don't want it *exactly* mine, do I? You've got gray inks for the background, white inks for the lettering, you can make a couple minor changes. So it's sort of Everyman."

His stubby finger poked the stat. "John Doe in here?"

"No, that's too cute. We can leave my last name, it's common enough, something you find around the garage. Change the first name, let's see, something with six letters, hmmmmmmmm. . . ."

"Joseph?"

"Joseph Dodge." I pondered that. "Joe Dodge. Wasn't there somebody famous named Joe Dodge?"

"Was there?" Charlie in thought looked like a Bassett hound.

"How about . . ." I said, "how about Robert? That ought to fit."

"Okay."

"And listen," I said. "Change the birth time. You know, let's not give anything away to these astrology freaks."

He frowned massively at me. "What?"

"Just do it, Charlie," I said. "Think of it as a personal quirk."

He shrugged. "If you say so. Any particular date?"

"Oh, leave the date," I said airily. "No sense changing everything. Just make the birth time, oh, I don't know, say twelve minutes later. And then the rest you can leave just the way it is."

"So there's just the two changes, right? Arthur to Robert, and five seventeen to five twenty-nine."

"Right. When do you suppose you could have it?"

"When do you suppose I could get paid for it?"

"On delivery."

If he frowned any deeper his head would crack open like a coconut. "You been robbin' liquor stores?"

"I'm trying to maintain faith with my artists. When could you have it?"

"This afternoon. How much do I get for it?"

"Twenty-five."

"Wrong. Forty."

"For an hour's work? Even hookers don't get that much."

"Thirty," he said.

"I'm on a tight budget, Charlie," I said. "If I have to go above twenty-five I won't be able to pay you right away. I mean, if you're willing to wait—"

"I'll take the twenty-five," he said.

Buzz.

"Hah?"

"Linda Ann Margolies is here."

For just a second I was a complete blank. Linda what? Then my eye drifted past my desk clock, and I saw it was five after one, and it all came back to me: the Columbia gem, the master's thesis on comedy. "Right," I said, stuffing the rest of my pastrami-on-rye into a desk drawer, and hung up. I swigged down my coffee, underhanded the cup into the wastebasket, patted my mouth with the paper napkin, pocketed the napkin, got to my feet, and smiled a welcome as Gloria ushered in Linda Ann Margolies.

And when I saw her, I multiplied the smile by two.

Ah, yes, there are moments when I understand cannibalism. Food imagery kept filling my head as I looked at this lush morsel: home-baked pastry, crepes suzette, ripe peaches. If she were any shorter it would be too much, overblown, fit for a gourmand rather than a gourmet, but she was just tall enough to cool the effect slightly and thereby become perfect. Sex without loss of status, how lovely. "Come in, Miss Margolies," I said, and ignored the jaundiced lip-curl of Gloria in the background.

Gloria left us, I gestured the student into the Volpinex-Hillerman Memorial Chair, and she said, "I do thank you for your time, Mr. Dodge. I know you're a busy man."

"Up with the sun and on the run," I said, dropping back into my own chair.

She flashed a quick surprised smile. "Oh, yes! That's the one from the prune advertisement."

I was flabbergasted. "How in God's name did you know that?"

"Just part of my thesis," she said. Modest dimples parenthesized her modest smile. "I know them all."

"I bet you don't."

"I'd love to hear a new one," she said.

Frowning, I said, "Barbasol shaving cream. Woman in an evening gown holding a giant mock-up of the product."

But she was already nodding and grinning. "Is your can too small? Try mine for size."

"Wall Street Journal," I challenged her.

"I upped my income five percent last year. Up yours."

"Woman's clothing store, um, uh, Peck and Peck."

"There is a kind of woman," this calm marvel said, "who would like to have a chauffeur six times a day."

"Right," I said. "So I'm here to interview you about comedy, is that it?"

She laughed: modest, polite, friendly. "I've been doing my homework."

"I can see that. You sure you're in the right place, lady?"

"Don't downgrade yourself," she told me. "Folksy Cards is at the top of its field."

"The motto around this joint," I said, "is Don't Shit A Shitter. I know what field I'm in. Sex and violence tied to festive occasions."

Pencil and steno pad appeared from her knapsack-size purse. "The interview has started."

"Humor is like a fountain," I said.

"That's life. Are you a native New Yorker?"

I frowned at her. "What's that got to do with comedy?"

"There are theories about the humorist as the outsider," she said. "We can make it work both ways. If you were born and raised in New York City, you must feel isolated from the rest of the country: ergo, comedy. If you came from Kansas or somewhere, you feel isolated and rootless here in New York: ergo, comedy. I just want to know whether you go under Column A or Column B."

"I go with the West Lake Duck."

"Foreign or domestic?"

She was hard to shake. Shrugging, I said, "I grew up all over. You've heard the term Army brat?"

"Father a career man?"

"Right."

"Officer or enlisted man?"

"Another theory?"

"Of course."

"Enlisted man," I said.

"Of course," she said, and wrote something down.

I glowered at her. "What do you mean, of course?"

"Those tied in to the power structure," she told me, "don't need comedy. That's the theory, anyway. Parents alive or dead?"

"Ask me questions about comedy."

She gave me a sharp, and then a very soft look. "I'm sorry," she said, and she sounded like she meant it. "It's easy to get lost in words, and lose the faces. All right, we'll talk—"

"My father's dead," I said. "Coronary in a rowboat in Vermont, fishing, two years after he finished his thirty and retired. Mother hasn't been heard from since fifty-nine, when she ran off with the Danish xylophonist from the NCO Club dance band at Vogelweh, Germany, taking Dad's fifty-four Volkswagen but leaving behind her silver pumps."

Miss Margolies studied me for a long silent moment of uncertainty, and then said, "Was all that on the level?"

"You've just learned something else about comedy," I told her. "It causes paranoia."

She was too cool to be surprised. She nodded, her mouth smiling while the frown line remained between her eyes.

"All right," she said. "Let's talk about comedy. What is comedy, really?"

"Making people laugh."

"Below that," she said. "What is comedy really all about?"

"Acceptance," I said. "The comic makes them laugh, so they don't kill him."

When she frowned, she looked like a daughter in a television commercial, learning about deodorants. "I know about that, too," she said. "But there has to be something underneath it, something specific that makes this person or that person choose comedy instead of some other defense. So what is it?"

She was repeating herself, and boredom produces irritation. Taking a deep breath, I said, "Because the comic is a killer himself, that's why. The comic is the last civilized man to feel the killer inside himself. We're omnivores, little girl, and that means we'll eat anything that stands still, we'll eat anything that doesn't have flashing lights. 'Comedy instead of some other defense,' you said, and that's right. Comedy is surprise. I make you laugh, that means I surprise you, that means you'll keep your distance, you won't attack. Laugh meters should record in megadeaths, because that's what comedy is all about; I kill you for practice to keep you from killing me for real."

She nodded, watching her pencil skate across the surface of the steno pad. Smiling to herself she said, "Well, it works."

I frowned at her. "What works?"

Ignoring the question, she looked up at me again and said, "You're saying the comic is a killer among killers, and he uses comedy both to hide his deadliness for social reasons and to show his deadliness as protection. And of course in your greeting cards the sharpened teeth show very clearly in the smile, don't they?"

I said, "What works?"

She gave me a mock simper, the crowing of the smartass. "Ask the same question three times," she said, "and the third time you'll get the truth."

"Very cute," I said. But I hadn't agreed to this interview to be annoyed.

Her smarmy grin went on and on. "The last civilized man to feel the killer alive inside himself," she read, from her no-doubt perfect fucking shorthand. "Is that you?"

I walked around the desk, and her smile said she knew I would. I put her on the floor, and her smile said she'd known about that one, too. I played boy-girl upon her there, and twice I had the pleasure of seeing her look surprised.

15   15

SATURDAY AFTERNOON ON the beach at Point O' Woods—not exactly the Riviera. Older duffers sat around in shirts and pants and hats, discussing debentures, while their wives nattered under beach umbrellas. A few younger women paddled here and there in the shallow water, but there wasn't a bikini among them. Mostly they wore one-piece suits with little skirts, and some of them even had on white rubber bathing caps. There isn't a woman in the world who doesn't look as though she has fat thighs if she's wearing a white bathing cap and a yellow one-piece bathing suit with a little skirt, so there wasn't much to look at except the beach and the ocean and the cloudless sky and the pretty houses. But Bart didn't care; now that he was alive, he was having a great time.

Alive. Charlie Hillerman had showed up Wednesday afternoon with a doctored photostat that looked almost good enough in the original to pass for the real thing. A Xerox of it was perfect, absolutely perfect. And in the meantime I'd mailed off two dollars to Kings County with a request for another copy of my own certificate, so now Art and Bart would both be able to prove their existences.

And what if Bart actually married Betty? The possibilities were intriguing. Art might simply disappear, for instance, leaving his debts behind him. Or I might accept a settlement for a quiet annulment after I'd revealed the truth. Or Bart might be the one to disappear (killed by me), leaving Art to inherit. I could kill him with Daddy's gun.

Which had been a strange moment. Every once in a while in the turbulent life of man it becomes necessary to lubricate the ways, and on one such occasion in Daddy's bed I'd reached for the night table drawer, on the dim chance there might be some K-Y jelly in there. Pawing away left-handed, while the rest of me was occupied elsewhere, I suddenly became aware that I was clutching a gun. "Yike," I said, and lifted the thing out to stare at it. A revolver, shortbarreled, grayish-black metal, surprisingly heavy. "Good God," I said.

Betty, naturally, screamed; anyone would who found herself in bed with a naked man clutching a gun. The scream startled me, my hand flew open, and the gun dropped out of sight into the drawer again. I slammed the drawer, and would have stammered out something about the true object of my search except that Betty cried, "Be *careful* with that! It's loaded!"

"Loaded! Good Christ, what for?"

"We don't know how to empty it," she said, and looked at me hopefully. "Do you?"

"That's the first gun I ever touched in my life," I said.

"It was Daddy's," she said.

So much for Daddy's sex life. And, for a while, so

much for mine. But within a few minutes we both got back into the spirit of the enterprise again, and succeeded quite well after all without the help of the petrochemical industry. And I gave not another thought to the gun in the drawer. Of course, it didn't occur to me then that anybody was ever going to use it.

However. Apart from that one bad moment with the arsenal, Bart's life that week at Point O' Woods was as sweet as an Armenian dessert. Romp romp romp with Betty in and around Father's bed, late dinners out under the stars, and rest periods here on the beach. What could be better? Even Betty's insistence on wearing a one-piece yellow bathing suit with a little skirt couldn't dampen my spirit. Nothing could.

"Here comes Liz," Betty said.

"Mm?" She hadn't been around all week. Lifting my head from the sand—it was weighted down by both glasses and clip-on sunglasses—I looked off to the southwest, and here from the general direction of Dunewood came Liz. In a bikini, by God, a gleaming white one; suddenly I could hardly wait to be Art again.

But who was that with her? Squinting, I saw it really was Volpinex, the creature from the mummy case, slithering across the sand like an oil spill. His beach apparel was everything he'd worn in the office, minus the suitcoat and tie, and plus large dark sunglasses that made him look like a Greek millionaire's hatchet man.

Betty and I got to our feet, and Liz smirking as though at some private joke, made the introductions. *I have not met this man before.* "Glad to know you," I said.

He gave me a cold dry hand to shake (which I immediately gave back), and said, "I suppose your brother told you about me."

Surprise and shock suddenly lit my features. "Oh! You're the man who thinks I'm a fortune hunter."

His smile turned sour; he hadn't expected so direct a response in front of the ladies. His mistake had been in thinking I was another smart aleck like Art. Nevertheless, he was game, saying, "Not a fortune *hunter*." With a nod toward Betty, who was blinking in delayed comprehension at the both of us, he said, "A fortune *finder*, I would say."

"Ernest!" Betty cried, in outrage and astonishment, while Liz chuckled her dirty chuckle and said, "Ernie, you do have a knack."

"And a responsibility," he told her, his smile oozing around the words.

"Ernest," Betty said, "are you accusing Bart of, of . . ."

"Not accusing," Volpinex assured her. Lifting one finger, as though making a point he particularly wanted the jury to think about, he said, "I consider it a possibility only. But given my role in your affairs, it's a possibility I most certainly must take seriously."

All around us the sun shone down on the worthy Episcopalians. I said, "I think you right, Mr. uh. . . ."

"Volpinex," he repeated, rolling the word like a fetishist with a mouthful of leather.

"Well, Mr. Volpinex," I said, in my straightforward way, "I can't say I like your insinuations. I agree with your responsibility, but not your manner."

"That's right," Betty said. She looped an arm through mine and glared our defiance at the nasty man.

"I certainly don't intend," he said, with an ironic bow toward me, "to insult any honest gentleman present."

"My life is an open book," I told him. "I've lived the last seven years in California, and came here this spring because my brother wanted help in expanding his business. We may not be rich, but we are honest and hard-working. I invite you to study my past history as deeply as you want, and you will find nothing, I guarantee it."

"I must say I hope you're right," he said, trying for sarcasm but failing to hide his discomfort. He had come after me as though I were Art, and instead had found himself face to face with Horatio Alger. *I'd* give him Victoriana, and what exactly would he do about it?

Withdraw. "Well, it's been nice chatting with you," he said.

"You're going to feel terrible, Ernest," Betty said, "when you find out how wrong you've been."

Volpinex glanced sourly at our linked arms. "Yes," he said. "I know what a loyal heart you have, Betty. But do remember that I am loyal, too."

I said, "And I'm sure Betty appreciates you for that."

He gave me a quickly calculating look. He knew I was too good to be true, but was it possible I was true anyway? The question still in his eyes, he turned away. "Well, Liz," he said, with an unsuccessful attempt to take her hand, "we really ought to be going."

"I can hardly wait," she told him, "to see you with the other brother." Then she turned her mocking smile on me, saying, "You really are an Eagle Scout, aren't you?"

Betty said, "Now, Liz, don't *you* start."

"I meant it in sincerest admiration," Liz assured her and to Volpinex she said, "Come along, Ernie, you know it gives you a rash to be in the presence of goodness."

Volpinex showed us all something that might have been a grin, and followed Liz away in the direction of the Kerner house.

Betty said, "Now do you see why I want our engagement to be a secret? The world is full of suspicious minds."

"He's only doing what he thinks is his duty." Bart, I was surprised to see, was magnanimous in victory.

She hugged my arm, giving my knuckles a graze of warm crotch. "Won't they be surprised," she said, "when we turn up married?"

"Yes," I said, "I believe they will."

Sunday morning. Betty said, "Bart, I think I'll go into town with you."

"That's wonderful," I said.

She gave me a conspiratorial smirk. "We'll leave Liz alone here with Art."

"Sneaky of us," I said.

Liz had returned this morning, probably in anticipation of Art's arrival. Could she actually have spent last night—not to mention Wednesday and Thursday and Friday nights—coupled with that creep Volpinex? Had the woman no standards at all? There was no telling from looking at her, of course. Briefly I considered probing more deeply while in my Art persona, but quickly abandoned that idea. Art, after all, had not seen Liz and the ferret together. Also, Liz was far too sharp for me to get cute with.

Anyway, I now had a much more serious problem to deal with. Betty was coming to town with me? How could Art spend the next three days with Liz if Bart was stuck in Manhattan with Betty? For the first time I found myself wishing I actually were twins.

All right. Every problem can be dealt with, if we but try. I managed to get away from Betty briefly, and phoned the Minck household. Let Ralph answer, I prayed, and let it not be Candy.

Well, it was neither. It was a snot-nosed brat. "Child," I said. "I wish you to take down a phone number, and if you take it down wrong I shall come to your house tonight with a hatchet and chop off your feet."

"I'll get it right," the child said defensively. "I always do."

Slowly I read off the number from the phone in front of me, then demanded the child read it back. Only when it was read back to me with no numbers transposed or misinterpreted did I move on. "I wish you, child," I said, "to go to your father at once, tell him it's important, and tell him to call this number and ask for Bart. B. A. R. T. Got it?"

The child, upon reading it back, turned out to have it.

"Good, child," I said. "Your father must call this number within half an hour. *Not* your mother—your father. Got that?"

The child said yes. We both hung up. I went off to the kitchen and prepared myself a drink containing alcohol. Then there was nothing to do but rejoin Betty on the front porch and wait.

Twenty minutes. I was becoming fidgety, I was having trouble concentrating on Betty's heartwarming tales of college days at dear old Bennington. I was on the verge of losing my sweet disposition. What the hell was I doing all this for anyway? The card racket wasn't major money, but it was keeping me housed and fed. Screw the world's third largest supplier of wood and wood products *and* the several other firms *and* the television station in Indiana. Let the money go, let Volpinex have both sisters and whatever else he wanted; why should I strain myself when the whole scam was certain to fall apart sooner or later anyway?

Phone. Ting-aling-aling; what a cheerful sound.

Through which Betty kept talking, paying no attention. "Dear," I said. "Wasn't that the phone?"

"Hm?"

Ting-aling-aling. "The telephone," I said. "I think it's ringing."

She'd been halfway through a story as fascinating as the

road from Cairo to Aqaba and the interruption made her irritable. "Now, who could that be?"

"Someone who wants to talk to you," I suggested, and for the third time the phone went ting-aling-aling.

"Oh, well." At last she got off her ass and went inside and I heard her say, "Hello?" Yes, yes, yes. "Just a minute." Ahhhh. "Ba-art?"

"Mmm?"

"It's for you."

"Really?" Already on my feet, I strolled into the house and crossed the living room toward the phone she was extending in my direction. "Who is it?"

"I'll ask,' she said, and dipped her head toward the receiver.

Christ. "Never mind, it's okay." I took the phone away from her and said, "Hello?"

Ralph's voice. "Art? Is that you?"

"Oh, Art!" I said. And I mouthed silently at Betty. *It's Art.* She nodded hugely, understanding.

"The darn kids got it wrong again," Ralph was saying. "They thought you said Bart."

"Oh, that's a shame," I said.

"Well, at least they got the phone number right."

"Well, sure," I said.

"You think so? You'd be surprised how those kids can louse up a message."

"If you say so," I said.

"Art? Is there something wrong?"

"I'm really sorry to hear that," I said. Betty was mouthing *What is it?* I gestured at her to wait.

Ralph was saying, "What? No, I didn't mean there was anything wrong with *me,* I meant was there— Uh, is everything okay there?"

I said, "You sure I can't help?"

"I'm fine, Art," he said. "Listen, you're all confused."

"Well, okay," I said, sounding doubtful.

"You wanted me to call you, right?"

"Then I'll give you a ring tomorrow," I said.

"Oh, I get it. There's somebody there right now, and you can't talk."

"Sure," I said.

"You and your girls," he said, with a little chuckle of envy. "Okay, I'll talk to you later."

"Any time at all," I said.

"So long."

Would he ever get off the goddamn phone? "That's right," I said.

"Well, uh . . ." For the love of *Christ*, Ralph! "So long, then." And he finally hung the hell up.

"The thing is, Art," I told the dead phone, "when I came back East it was to be helpful." I waited; the phone said *buzzzz*. "Well, sure, kid, I realize that." *Buzzzzzz*. "Fine. Then I'll see you Wednesday." *Buzzzzz*. "So long."

I hung up, and Betty said, "What was *that* all about?"

"That was Art," I said.

"Well, I know *that*. What did he want?"

"He can't come out this week. There's some tax problem, auditing the company books, something like that. I really don't know enough about that side of the business yet, so Art has to handle it himself."

"Oh, that's too bad," she said. "Liz will be disappointed."

"So's Art," I said, and I meant it. "But he says I should just stay out here all this week. There wouldn't be room for me in the apartment with him there."

"Well, we'll stay in my place," she said.

Another complication? "What place?"

"In Manhattan."

"Gee," I said, "I do hate to waste these summer days. It's so much nicer out here."

She gave me a coquettish look. "But we have a special reason to go to the city," she said. "Don't you know what it is?"

I didn't, and I hate uncertainty. Life is tricky enough

as it is. "Some special reason to be in New York?"

"Do you know who I'm going to be by Wednesday?"

"*Who* you're going to be?"

"I'm going to be Mrs. Bart Dodge," she informed me, then abruptly flung her arms about me and kissed me on the ear and neck. "Isn't that going to be wonderful?"

"Fabulous," I said, which was the simple truth.

She released me, and I saw there were stars in her eyes. "Do you think your brother could be our best man?"

"Gee, what a great idea," I said. "Of course, he might be too busy this week, but I'll sure ask him."

17

ART WAS THERE IN SPIRIT. Like the tremulous virgins in Victorian novels, I went through my wedding in a daze. Betty ran the whole thing; all I had to do was sit back and let it happen.

And wonder, from time to time, just what the hell was going on. What did Betty want with me anyway? I knew why I was marrying her, but why was she so hell-bent on marrying me?

And I mean *determined*. From the moment of our arrival in Manhattan Sunday afternoon, when she browbeat the Kerner family doctor into backdating our blood tests to Friday, until the moment of our legalization in a judge's chambers in Weehawken, New Jersey, on Tuesday evening, Betty drove forward like a piranha fish through a cow, undeflected by cartilage or bone. Was Bart really that lovable?

Well, what other explanation was there? I'd been too busy with my double life to pay much attention, but apparently I'd bowled the girl over right from the beginning with my plodding semidistracted amiability. I'd never realized such depths of passive charm resided within me. Nor was it likely to be generally as provocative as Betty found it. Hers had to be a very special taste: if I was in truth the most exciting bachelor she'd ever met, the moneyed class in this country is in serious trouble.

In any event, Betty set to with a will and got us married. "You just relax, sweetheart," she said, giving me a quick kiss and a brisk shove into a handy easy chair, "and I'll take care of all the details. And if there's anything you want, just ask Nikki or Blondell or Carlos."

"Yes, dear," I said.

Nikki or Blondell or Carlos. The Kerner family home in Manhattan, an eight-room apartment on Fifth Avenue in the sixties, with windows and terrace overlooking the park from a safe seven stories up, was *exactly* my idea of the life of the rich, starting with the three servants just mentioned. We'd been roughing it at Point O' Woods, doing our own cooking, dressing ourselves, all of that lower class raggle-taggle. A local girl from Bay Shore, a stout blonde teen-ager who seemed to be molded out of wet white bread and who occasionally answered to the name Francine, ferried over twice a week to do the laundry and sweep the floors, but my God even dental technicians have cleaning ladies.

Well, the apartment in New York was more like it. The rooms were spacious and expensively furnished, and the things hanging on the walls were, I discovered with my fingernail, paintings and not prints. There were three phone lines, reflecting the former occupancy of Kerner père and his far-flung business interests, and there were four bathrooms, reflecting his tendency to produce daughters. And while the three servants lived in, they were hardly underfoot; they had quarters of their own, beyond the kitchen. Nikki, and Blondell, and Carlos.

The last-named, Carlos, was the chauffeur who'd had the piano key inserted in his shoulder during the New Year's tragedy. A short and stocky forty-year-old with a flat sullen Indian face and an accent like a briar patch, he went out of his way to assure all and sundry that he was Mess-kin and not Poor Ree-kin. When not driving, which was most of the time—his trip out to Bay Shore to pick up Betty and me from the ferry Sunday afternoon had apparently been his first excursion in the family's new Lincoln in several weeks—Carlos was vaguely a handyman, terrace gardener, sometime butler, frequent bartender, and general layabout. We viewed one another from the outset with mutual distrust.

Blondell, a great round black mammy of the sort I'd thought had been made illegal by the Supreme Court decision of 1954, was the cook, of course. She was also not an American citizen, which perhaps explained her continuing existence in a form that had to be rated a debit to her race. Hailing from an obscure Caribbean island named Anguilla, she carried a British passport, but the language she spoke could hardly have been less English. Her accent, even more impenetrable than that of Carlos, was like wayward breezes: soft and unpredictable. Since as Bart I wore glasses, and Blondell loved intellectuals above all things, she and I got along from the beginning.

Nikki's accent was French. She was the maid, her manner was saucy, and her presence made me revise slightly my opinion of the late Albert J. Kerner. She had Candy's boniness, and some of Candy's foxlike facial features, but softened in her case by a more honest lewdness. Her uniform skirts were short, and she seemed to find an incredible number of work tasks that required her to bend over in front of me, showing me what she would have called her *derrière*. I called it an ass, and I wanted to bite it, but of course with the wedding so close that was impossible. Perhaps Art, in a few days? . . .

Well. That was for the speculative future; in the specu-
lator's present I was about to become a gushing groom.
The waiting period in New York State was too long, so on
Tuesday Carlos drove us to Jersey City where we took out
our license, and where Charlie Hillerman's birth certificate
passed with flying colors. Then some sexual extravagances
in the backseat of the Lincoln during a run out to Far
Hills for dinner with an old college chum of Betty's plus
the chum's new husband; these were the only people in on
our little secret.

I must say I liked their house. This was the foxhunting
section of New Jersey, where Jackie Kennedy used to hang
out, and the house did the neighborhood proud. A great
sprawling stone creature four stories high, it stood amid a
park of imported trees, dotted with tennis court and arbor
and swimming pool. The stables were out back. Inside,
there were warm wood tones and expensive antiques and
the comfortable aura of money gouged from generations of
peasantry.

The owners, Betty's chums, were named Dede and
David. Dede was a cool ash blonde such as American men
are supposed to go crazy for but which I have always suspected would be an inept lay, and David looked like one of
those junior Washington lawyers who get sent out for
coffee. He was in fact an attorney with the family firm in
Philadelphia, and this house—Windy Knob they called it,
which made my teeth jar—was also a family fixture, having
been most recently occupied by an aunt who was now de-
clining on the Côte d'Azur.

Having seen Betty mostly in sexual encounters recently,
I'd forgotten just what a crashing bore she could be in
company. The modulated voice, the standardized conversation, the social smile. How proud her etiquette teacher
would have been.

Not that Dede and David helped. They'd gone to the
same etiquette school, and with no trouble at all the three
of them recreated that Point O' Woods party at which

Betty had first entered my life. David talked with me about the stock market, Young Republicans, sailing, and men's shoes, and by God if Bart didn't join right in. Art would have behaved badly here, of course, either with smartass remarks or by falling asleep, but Bart was of a more placid nature. Men's shoes: I'd never known they could be that interesting.

Dinner was early, since our wedding was scheduled for nine. In a two-car caravan, Dede and David following in their V-12 Jaguar, we roared northeast to Weehawken, where we cooled our heels for twenty minutes in Judge Reagensniffer's quarters while Hizzoner finished dealing with his evening's quota of traffic offenders and wife beaters. David spoke to me about imported automobiles.

At last the judge entered. A sharp-faced skinny geezer with thinning white hair on his bony pate, he probably wasn't a day over eighty-five, and had the brisk spryness that comes from years and years of uninterrupted bad temper. He looked at us, sitting around on his sagging brown leather furniture, and snapped, "What do you people want?"

"I'm Elisabeth Kerner," Betty told him, her smooth surface unmarred by his cantankerousness. "We have an appointment here to be married."

"Ah!" His sour face creased in a bony if fatherly smirk; he'd known for a long time how to behave with the gentry. "Of course, Miss Kerner," he said. His little eyes surveyed us all. "And this would be?"

"My fiancé, Robert Dodge. And these are our witnesses."

Introductions were made. The judge offered to shake my hand, and I found myself gripping something that seemed to be made of coat hanger wire and sausage casings. Then the forms were gone through, Betty pulling envelopes from her purse, the judge sitting at his massive old wooden desk, people signing things right and left.

There was one form for me to put Bart's name to, which

I did while leaning over the desk. Finishing, I looked up and saw the judge glowering at me in sudden distaste. "Well, young man," he said, "what do you have to say for yourself?"

"I beg pardon?"

He frowned, looked puzzled, glanced around at the others, and suddenly flashed a wide insincere smile, saying to me, "No last-minute doubts, eh?"

"No, sir," I said. Not of the marriage, anyway.

"Fine, fine." He went through the forms one more time, gave us all a swift keen look of disapproval, and rapped out, "Bailiff!"

The door popped open and a worried-looking gent popped in. "Yes, sir, your honor?" He was about thirty, covered with a layer of baby fat, and with dandruff sprinkled like monosodium glutamate on his black-clad shoulders.

Having called in this flunky, the judge seemed unsure what to do with him. "Mm," he said, hefted the marriage papers in his hand, dropped them on the desk, and pointed vaguely toward a far corner, saying, "You just be, um, present."

"Yes, sir, your honor."

So the bailiff went off to stand in the corner, like something from a New England ghost story, while Judge Reagensniffer married us. First he got up and drew a slim volume from the shelves of lawbooks behind his desk, and then he spent an endless period of time arranging the four of us in some precise pattern in the middle of the room. "A bit to the right. You come forward a step; no, not that much." Was this a judge or a photographer?

Well, the arranging finally came to an end, the judge stood in front of us flipping pages in his book till at last he found the right place, and then, one finger in the book to mark his intention, he said, "I usually preface these ceremonies with a few introductory remarks."

A spectral throat-clearing took place in the corner. We all jumped.

"Marriage," the judge told us, "is a frail bark on the stormy sea of life. It is not to be undertaken lightly. And those who do, and who don't watch their steps, can't expect to be treated lightly either. I'm the same man in these chambers that I am on the bench. I'm willing to listen to explanations, but I firmly believe in the letter of the law." He fixed us with his bird-eyes. "Well? Anything to say to that?"

We all made uneasy movements. This wasn't quite the ceremony any of us had had in mind. Finally, to break the awkward silence, I said, "Your honor, we still want to get married."

"Married," he said, as though it were a new and possibly interesting word. Then he blinked, looked at the book impaled on his finger, and said, "Ah, yes, married. Those who enter upon the married state take unto themselves a strong partner, a companion through the shoals and rapids of life. Two are stronger than one, a companionship, a giving and receiving of strength. And for there to be a conspiracy, no overt act needs to take place. Only the intention of the individuals to conspire together. Is that clear?"

Not to me, Jack. This time it was Betty who worked at getting us back on the right track, saying, "Your honor, we intend to conspire together and love together and remain together forever."

"Yes, indeed," the judge said. "A permanent bond." He hesitated; was he going to say a *life term*? No, he fell the other way. "So we might as well get on with it," he said, opened his book, and with no more preamble went directly into the wedding ritual. He read it briskly, almost angrily, as though explaining our rights to us before passing sentence, and we made the appropriate responses in the appropriate locations. Betty looked misty-eyed throughout, and I did my best to look solemn and trustworthy.

". . . I now declare you man and wife. Bailiff, take them away."

And so I was married. Bride and groom were kissed by the witnesses. Hands were shaken. I passed a sealed envelope to the judge, making sure Betty saw me do it. Everyone was pleased by that, but then again they probably all thought the envelope contained money. Its sole content, however, was a card from Those Wonderful Folks that had turned out to be even more apropos than I'd thought when I'd selected it yesterday afternoon. On the front an old man in a wheelchair is saying, "I'm not too old to cut the mustard." Inside he finishes, "I just can't seem to find the hot dog."

18

WHEN LIZ ARRIVED THE next afternoon at two-thirty, I knew at once I was in trouble. "Well, you've made yourself at home," she said, coming out onto the terrace where I was enjoying the sunlight, the view of the park, a rum and soda, and my marital status. Dropping into a canvas chair, she waved generally at the park and said, "Next you'll want to graze your sheep on our lawn."

"Well, hello," I said, in my witty Bart manner. "Betty didn't tell me you were coming to town."

"Betty didn't know." She shrugged, looking vaguely irritable and discontented: normal, in other words. "I just thought I'd come in and see Art in his natural habitat."

"Ah," I said.

"He takes long lunches."

"Oh?"

"I called the office," she said. "His secretary said he was still out to lunch."

"Well," I said, "they're business lunches. You know, with artists and distributors and so on."

She frowned at the blue sky. "Maybe I'll go down there and hang around, see what the office looks like."

"You never know how long he'll be gone," I said. "Why not wait for him to call?"

She picked at the canvas of her chair, looking mulish, then frowned at me and said, "What about you? Shouldn't you be at work?"

On my honeymoon? Well, I wasn't to mention that; Betty still insisted on keeping our marriage secret, even from Liz, and for reasons of my own I was happy to oblige. Once again invention came when needed. With no more devious intention in my mind than to offer an acceptable answer to Liz's question, I fell once again into a useful arrangement. "Art and I have had——" I gave a little shrug "——kind of an argument. I haven't seen him for a while."

Her attention had been caught; I could see in the sudden glint in her eye and curve in her lips the hope of hearing something amusing. "An argument? You two?"

"All families argue." Bart would never amuse Liz, the best day he lived.

"I thought you and your brother were very close."

"Don't you and Betty argue sometimes?"

The eye-glint turned steely for a second. "We're not talking about me and Betty." Curiosity returned, and she said, "But what do you find to argue about?"

What, indeed? Searching for subject matter, poring over the personality differences I'd established between us, I said, "Oh, I just think sometimes Art gets a little careless with, um, business ethics."

"Business ethics?" She found the phrase hilarious, but struggled to keep a straight face for my sake.

"He doesn't treat the artists well," I said primly. Then I leaned closer to her, lowering my voice and looking toward the terrace doors as I said, "I haven't said anything to Betty about it. I didn't want to upset her."

"You have a lot to learn about Betty," she said.

Less than Liz thought. "Will you keep my secret?" I asked her.

She shrugged. "Why not?" And, since the threatened diversion had not after all arrived, she changed the subject without a backward glance, saying, "What's that you're drinking?"

"Rum and soda."

"Isn't that Art's drink?"

"I thought I'd try it," I said, grinning sheepishly at the glass and cursing myself for a fool. "I suppose it means I wish he and I were friends again."

Liz was the perfect partner for a parlor psychology conversation; it put her right directly to sleep. "Yeah, that's probably what it means, all right," she said. "But who I want to be friends with is me. Would you see if you can find Carlos, tell him to make me my usual?"

I'd been looking for an excuse to go inside, and here it was. "I'll do it myself," I said, and absolutely bounded to my feet.

She squinted up at me in the sunlight. "You know what I drink?"

Did I? I couldn't remember if Bart had ever been introduced to Liz's drinking habits or not. "I'm not sure," I said.

"It's an easy formula," she said. "One glass, one ice cube, vodka to taste."

"Coming up," I told her, reflecting that Bart was apparently not worth being given the line about a big wet kiss, and hurried inside.

All right. Many things were lined up against me, including the fact that I didn't actually have a twin brother, but here and there were some small factors on my side—prin-

cipally, at this point, the Kerner's telephone system. Not
only were there three separate lines, there were also exten-
sions all over the apartment, including a long-corded one
in the living room. Already I had seen Nikki several times
carry that phone out to Betty on the terrace to answer an
incoming call. So Liz would stay where she was, and there
just might be some hope after all.

The kitchen was empty. The extension there was a white
wall phone, and like all the others it had a row of plastic
buttons on the bottom for selecting which line you wanted
to use. It also had a long cord, so one could tuck the receiver in between ear and shoulder and hold a conversation while walking around.

Fine. I picked up the receiver, tucked it, and pushed the
button for the first line. It immediately lit up, as would the
same button on all the other phones in the apartment,
showing that this line was in use. Unfortunate, but un-
avoidable. Quickly I dialed the number for the second line
and then, while the phone company did its mumbo, jumbo
of clicks and computer notes, I walked across the room to
the cabinets and picked out a glass. I was turning toward
the refrigerator when simultaneously the receiver said,
"Bdrrrrrrrrp," in my ear and all the phones in the house,
including the kitchen phone, said, "Ting-aling-aling." No,
I'm a liar; the phone in Betty's room would not be saying,
"Ting-aling-aling." At her special desire and request, it
would be giving a really sickening birdcall, all tiny whistles
and trills. If I was going to live around here very long, I'd
have to give that phone poison some day.

I opened the freezer door and carefully selected an ice
cube, and Nikki came bobbling in to answer the phone.
"—the sleeves as soon as—Hold on," I said to the phone,
and to Nikki I said, "I'm on the phone to my tailor. Catch
that on one of the others, will you?"

"We," she said, and headed away again.

"Later," I told her derrière, and crossed the kitchen
again to the cabinet containing the liquor. I got the vodka

out, the phone rang a second time, and Nikki answered: "Kairnair rezeedonce."

"Liz Kerner, please." I opened the vodka bottle while Nikki told me to please wait on.

Time passed. Click. "Hello?"

"Liz? You're in town?"

"Oh, it's you," she said. "Where'd you have lunch— Philadelphia?"

"Copenhagen," I said, that being the name of a local restaurant. "What are you doing off-island?"

"Slumming. Why don't you come take me out tonight?"

Because Betty and I were going to a special honeymoon dinner tonight at The Three Mafiosi, one of New York's hundred-dollar-a-plate restaurants, that's why. "I'm afraid I can't baby," I said. "Why didn't you call me earlier?"

"You've got a date."

"When the cat's away, you know."

"The rats will play."

I said, "I don't think that's quite the way that goes. Listen, I tell you what, I'll cut it short, all right?"

"Come on over here, I'll cut it short for you."

"Honey," I said sweetly, "I'm answering *your* call." And it occurred to me the simplest way out of this morass might be to get Art into arguments with everybody. Art on everybody's shit list, good old Bart hanging around all by himself. Could Bart put the make on Liz?

But she said, "Yeah, you're right. I guess I'm just in a bad mood from the drive in."

"You drove in?" It seemed to me I'd seen Carlos lounging around the apartment all day.

"A friend drove me," she said. "A friend of yours."

"Mine?" Candy? Dear God, did Liz know all?

"Ernie Volpinex."

"Oh!"

"He met your brother, you know. *That* was some—" Then she cut herself off, saying, "Just a second. Hold on a minute, will you?"

"Sure," I said, thinking fast. She'd just reminded herself of Bart, ergo of the drink. I was taking too long.

"I'll put you on hold."

"Ah," I said, suddenly understanding what she would do, and the instant I heard the two clicks I said, in the most guttural voice I could manage, "Menches con carne conquista malatesta bergonez."

"Carlos!" There she was, on the other line.

Still guttural, I said, "Hallo?"

"This is Miss L," she said, and she sounded as offensively arrogant as the man from the finance company. Oh ho, I thought, so that's the way you speak to the lower orders. "Mr. Dodge is wandering around in there someplace, making me a drink. Give him some help, will you?"

"Si," I said, listened to the clicks, and in my own voice said, "And as in uffish thought he stood, the Jabberwock, with—"

"What?"

"Oh, you're back," I said.

"What time tonight?"

That was brisk. I said, "Why don't I come by for you, say, eleven-thirty?"

"That late?"

"This girl's important to me," I said. "Her brother's maybe going to invest in my—"

"Spare me. All right, eleven-thirty. Your place?"

"No, I'll come over and get you." Then, just in time, it occurred to me to say, "What's your address?"

"Why, you creep," she said, "she's sleeping over! You're coming here because you're going to leave her there!"

"I should know better than to try to put one over on you," I said. Argument after all?

No. "That's what I like about you," she said. "You're a breath of foul air. Eleven-thirty." And she gave me the address.

"Right," I said, hung up, and carried her drink at a brisk trot through the apartment, slowing to a friendly walk as I stepped out onto the terrace.

"Well," she said, "that took long enough."

"Carlos said you sent him to find me."

She sipped from the drink and watched me sit again in my previous chair. She said, "What happened to you?"

"Call of nature, first," I told her, with my sheepish good-guy grin. "Then I got kind of turned around, I'm still not used to this apartment."

"Your brother called," she said.

"He did? Did he mention me at all?"

"Uh huh. He said you were a goody-good and a bleeding heart and he was sorry he took you into the business."

I looked at her. "Now I wonder," I said, "why he'd say a thing like that."

19

By eleven o'clock Betty was sleeping the sleep of the drugged; and that's what she was. The label on the prescription sleeping pills in her medicine chest had said to take one capsule one hour before retiring, so it was the contents of two capsules I'd mixed with the sauce on her *coq au vin* when she retired briefly to the ladies room in the restaurant. That was shortly before nine; when at ten-thirty she was still wide awake and raring to go I was beginning to get worried.

But then she flopped all at once, with huge yawns and an inability to keep her eyes open and a weaving unsteadiness in her walk. I got her into the Lincoln waiting outside, Carlos drove us home, and I half-carried her into the apartment and through to our bedroom. Liz had gone out somewhere before we'd left, and had apparently not as yet returned; if she stiffed me, after all the trouble I was going through, I'd never forgive her.

I undressed Betty, who folded sleepy arms around my neck and mumbled, "Screw me, lover." She stayed awake for it, but was gone before I was off the bed.

Hurriedly I dressed, while my mind went scouting the terrain ahead. I couldn't maintain both halves of this charade much longer, that was clear. The joke was long since accomplished, so where was I now and what were my goals?

Money. A poor man among poor men is reasonably content, but a poor man among rich men begins to itch. The people inhabiting these Fifth Avenue apartments and Point O' Woods cottages and Far Hills estates were dull enough to dry quicksand, but their way of life was precisely what I had in mind for myself. Chauffeurs, tennis courts, terraces, stables out back. French maids, by God. *Money*. Like the tiger who has just had his first taste of man-meat, I now knew what I was hunting.

So. I'd dropped two lines into the water, one labeled *Art* and the other *Bart*, and damn if the Bart line hadn't hooked a big one. Betty and I hadn't had a direct talk about money yet, but tonight on the way to the restaurant she'd handed me her American Express card and said, "You might as well use that until we get new ones." Meaning it was all mine. Whatever Betty had I had, and she had the world.

So it was time to cut the other line; Art had to go. Bart would have been simpler to get rid of, naturally, but it could still be done. This evening at dinner I'd told Betty about the brotherly falling out, so now both sisters knew there was trouble. Typically, Liz had done her best to stir up the trouble a little more, while Betty had given me a serious look, like the social director at a resort hotel, and

asked me if there was anything she could do. I'd assured
her there was not.

So my next move was to precipitate a break between
Art and Liz. That shouldn't be impossible, given the
naturally nasty tongue of both principals. Then, with Art
no longer seeing Liz, I could settle down peacefully as
Bart with my little Betty and live happily ever after.

As to Art, probably the best thing to do was mothball
him. Three years ago eight of my artists had gone to court
against me, trying to gain control of Those Wonderful
Folks, Inc., in lieu of the back payments I owed them.
They'd lost, naturally, but now I could make them a very
similar deal. They'd take over the firm, the copyrights,
debts, office furniture, accounts receivable and all, in lieu
of payment. We'd do it legally, with lawyers and signatures
and possibly even handshakes, and that would be the end
of it. Art Dodge would simply have grown tired of his
company, would have sold it to get out from under his
debts, and would have moved on. I might even bruit it
about that Art had told me he was going to England for a
while.

Changing clothing now, with Betty dead to the world on
the bed, I went over my options again and again, and
among my other emotions I was surprised to find a growing sense of relief. The game had been fun at first, but as
the stakes had risen it had become steadily less fun and
more nerve-wracking. It might be difficult to go around
pretending to be drab old Bart for the rest of my life, but
nowhere near as difficult as pretending to be *two* people.
The stunt was over, and good riddance to it.

20   20

AT ABOUT TWO IN THE morning, just after I'd ordered another round of drinks, Liz took a sheaf of documents from her purse, unfolded it, extended it across the table toward me, and said, "Take a look at that."

We were in a bar on the upper East Side, surrounded by advertising executives and television commercial actresses. For the last three hours or so I'd been under a considerable strain, trying to get Liz to join me in an argument. There was something strange about her tonight, muted and distant and almost mournful; whatever it was, it made her impervious to irritation. In fact, the only time she'd shown anything like her usual self was when she'd told me that Bart, after my phone call this afternoon, had said he was keeping away from me because I was nothing better than a crook. "You do bring out the best in people," I'd responded, and she'd looked away and said, "I wish I did."

What the hell was the matter with her? Was she onto me? Was that the purpose for these lies to the "brothers"? But it didn't feel like that; I wasn't sure exactly what Liz would do if she found out the truth about the con I'd been pulling, but cryptic remarks and withdrawn silences and an inability to get mad seemed unlikely modes of response.

And now this document. I've been served with subpoenas before, and I was hesitant to reach across the table for this thing. "What is it?"

"A proposal of marriage."

"Ha ha ha," I said.

"Go on and take it," she said. "It won't bite."

I looked more closely at her and her grim face. What was this minor key melody she was singing? What was so serious? Reaching out at last to take the papers from her, I said, "Am I going to love this?"

"That's up to you," she told me, picked up her drink, and looked pointedly away.

I moved my own rum and soda to one side, unfolded the papers, saw they comprised a legal document of some kind, a contract or some such thing, and began to read:

We the undersigned, Elizabeth Anne Kerner and Arthur Drew Dodge, desiring a clear understanding between us prior to the solemnization of our marriage, have contracted and sworn with one another as follows:

What the hell? I looked up at Liz, but she was still gazing away, watching something on the far side of the room, the way a cat will look sometimes at an empty doorway. I said, "What is this thing?"

She gave me a quick cold look. "Just read it," she said. "It's self-explanatory."

"And on the level?"

"Do I look as though I'm joking?"

She didn't. But Christ on a crutch, *both* of them? First Betty gives me the most incredible rush of my life, and now Liz chimes in with the same damn thing, though of course in her own lovable style. I know I'm not a sad sack when it comes to women, but how irresistible can one man be?

More to the point, what was the story with this contract or whatever it was? Bowing my head, skimming the introduction again, I proceeded to read the thing word for word, beginning to end.

Incredible. Here in seven pages was a full-fledged contract outlining the financial and personal agreements between Liz and me which would become a part of our marriage bond, and which would be effective as of the date of our marriage. On the first page, following the preamble and some bits of legal boiler plate, Elizabeth Kerner's assets were listed, turning out to be well beyond my previous dreams of avarice, and then my own financial situation was overestimated. So far, so good; their research may have produced my correct middle name, but the bookkeeping down there at Those Wonderful Folks had defeated them.

Onward. Beginning on page two, it was proposed I be given a subsistence of two thousand dollars a month for the period of the marriage, plus the salaries of two male servants not to exceed sixteen thousand per annum, plus unlimited use of the Kerner residences wherever situated. The subsistence and servant salaries might be increased from time to time at the pleasure of Elizabeth Kerner, but would not be decreased.

Moving right along, through clauses dense with extraneous words, Liz and I both renounced exclusive sexual or social privileges between us, agreeing—in legalese—that we could both do what we wanted where we wanted when we wanted with whom we wanted and no questions asked. I, however, was alone in guaranteeing not to do anything in public that might bring embarrassment or disgrace on Elizabeth Kerner, her family, or any business firm with which she might have a connection. "Says here," I said, "you can embarrass me, but I can't embarrass you."

"That's right," she said.

"Ah." Reading on, I found that next we both declared ourselves to be at the present time unmarried to anyone else—hmmm—and to be aware of no impediments to the proposed wedding.

Okay, where was the nitty gritty? At the end, of course. In the event either of us should ever want a divorce, the other agreed not to contest the action in any way, and I was called on to acknowledge that all financial arrangements between us would cease at the first filing of divorce papers. In the event of my predeceasing Liz, it was agreed that any legal interest I might have in the Kerner fortune or assets would be inherited by Liz, with none of it reserved for any other of my possible heirs or assigns. In the event of Liz checking out first, I agreed to make no demands on her estate, neither for a continuation of the monthly subsistence nor for any rights of inheritance, but acknowledged my wife's desire that her total estate should go to her sister Elisabeth.

Anything else? Yes. Prior to the fact, I acknowledged paternity of any children that might be born to Liz in the course of our marriage and for one year after any divorce or separation. I held Liz and the Kerner family and all business firms connected with them blameless in the event of any lawsuit against me from outsiders, or in the event of any other social, sexual, financial, or other hassle that might come at me from the non-Kerner portion of my life. In the event of my being kidnapped—Jesus *Christ*!—it was my clear understanding nobody from the Kerner family or firms would pay any ransom. I would not use my position or any of my income—whether from the Kerners or not—to start, abet, contribute to, or otherwise deal in any business or firm which was in direct or indirect competition with any Kerner firm. I would leave all marriage announcements, from wedding plans to divorce and including any other possibility in between, to Liz. And I was signing this agreement of my own free will, prompted solely by my affection for Liz and our desire not to have financial or other extraneous questions interfere with our love for one another and our prospects for a long and comfortable united married life. Liz had already signed the last page, in what I thought of as a crabbed and greedy hand.

I put the document down next to my drink. Liz looked at me. "Well?"

"Well," I agreed. I sat there nodding, tapping the contract with my fingertips and trying to think.

Liz said, "Aren't you going to say anything?" Her lips were tight, her voice just slightly hoarse.

"Well, I don't know what to say," I told her. "I've never been proposed to before."

"It's either yes or no. I won't haggle over details."

"There's nothing in here," I said, tapping the papers, "about love."

"About what?"

"The point is, why me? Why not, for instance, that fellow over there with the sideburns?"

"You're the man for the job," she said.

"Why?"

She shrugged. Behind her hooded eyes, she peered through chinks in her armor. "You're easy to be around," she said. "We understand each other."

Perhaps. I nodded, slowly, and tapped the contract some more. "Volpinex put this together?"

"He's my attorney."

"Mind if my attorney looks it over?"

"Yes. You decide now."

Tap-tap-tap, my fingertips on the contract. "What's the gimmick? What's it for?"

"If I'm single by the end of this year," she said, "it will cost me over three million dollars."

"Taxes," I suggested.

"My father," she said, "thought because he was Episcopalian the fix was in, and he wouldn't have to go till he was ready. He didn't leave us protected."

"I see." And I saw a lot more than that, too. I saw, for instance, why Betty had been so hot to get married. Even at the time, I'd thought Bart was a bit stodgy for the terrific results he was getting, and now I understood. In a very modern sense, Betty had had to get married.

But why hadn't she told me the truth? She'd talked about love, but she'd never mentioned three million dollars.

Nor had she presented me with a contract. Which merely meant she felt safe, she didn't think she had to protect herself from Bart the way Liz was protecting herself from me.

But what about all the secrecy? Why had Betty insisted on keeping the marriage a secret from Liz? Was there something else happening, something beyond the money, some feud or finagle between the sisters? I said, "What about Betty?"

"What about her?" Liz seemed surprised by the question, but not upset.

"Does she have to get married, too?"

"You don't have to worry about Betty," she said inaccurately. "Just about us."

"I'm trying to get the overall picture."

"Screw the overall picture." She was doing some table-tapping of her own now; I could see she was becoming increasingly edgy. "Make up your mind, Art," she said. "And do it soon. This is a one-time offer, and the deadline's getting close."

Well, of course, there wasn't any question. I already had my access to the Kerner fortune, no strings attached, through Bart's marriage to Betty. I'd only stalled along here for information's sake, not because I thought for a second I could or should marry Liz.

Of course, on the other hand . . .

What other hand? I already had everything, I didn't need anything more, and this whole charade was wearing itself out anyway. I would mothball Art and live for a while exclusively as Bart, as planned. Toward which end, nothing could be more helpful than this contract; all I had to do now was become insulted, righteous, *what kind of boy do you think I am?*, growing anger, a scene, and me stalking away into the night. Then Art would be safely out of the picture, and Bart would loll peaceably in luxury.

"Art? It's now or never."

The alternative? No alternative. Impossible. And unnecessary, goddam it. Bart was married to Betty, wasn't that enough?

"Art?"

And it wasn't. Don't ask me why, it just wasn't. I *wanted* to marry Liz, I *wanted* to go on being Art, I even wanted to run this gauntlet some more. I'd rather do anything than live twenty-four hours a day as Bart, married twenty-four hours a day to Betty.

"Art?"

Shit. I raised my head and smiled across at my bride-to-be. "I think this occasion calls for champagne," I said. "On you."

21   21

Mᴏ DREAMS WERE FULL of mirrors, and when I awoke the room was backward. Or I was. Sunlight hummed beyond the curtained and draped windows, making an underwater glow in which I saw my clothing scattered about the carpeted floor. My head ached, and the air conditioning made my shoulders cold. Groaning a bit, though mostly in comfort, I wriggled down deeper under the covers, and beside me Betty murmured and moved, rubbing her warm hip against my side. I touched her near breast, she sighed and reached for me, and soon we were in marital conjugation, all legal and aboveboard.

Later, my headache came back, and my eyes seemed to be burning. I flopped onto my own side of the bed, damp with exertion, and Betty, fully awake now, rose up on one elbow to give me a lewd look and to say, "I must admit you make a first-rate fiancé."

"You mean husband," I said. Then I realized I was seeing her far too clearly, and I blinked. No wonder my eyes hurt; my contact lenses were still in. But that wasn't right; as Bart I was a glasses wearer. I'd have to get into the bathroom and make the switch before she noticed anything. In the meantime, I tried squinting, like your average four-eyes without his specs.

"Husband?" Betty echoed, looking at me. "Let's not rush things, lover."

I stared at her, forgetting to squint. Betty? This wasn't Betty, this was Liz!

Holy jumping Jehosephat! I won't say it all came rushing back to me, but a lot of it did, and I could fill in the rest. Liz and Art: we had toasted our engagement in champagne, and then some more champagne, and then some more champagne. Then a cab had brought us here, I had come upstairs, I had entered this room and this bed and this woman, and all the time I had planned to leave right afterward, make my exit as Art, wait ten minutes or so, and then re-enter as Bart, who would tippy-toe to Betty's bed and sleep the sleep of a husband. Instead of which, I had fallen asleep. Asleep.

And now it was morning. What time? Was Betty awake? How was I going to get Art out of here without leaving as Bart? With this head and these eyes, how was I going to do *anything?*

Betty—that is, Liz—was frowning at me. "Something wrong?"

"Bladder," I said. "I'll be right back."

"You're so romantic," she said.

The sisters had separate rooms and separate lavatories, but shared a room with a tub. I hurried out of Liz's sharp-eyed presence, closed the lavatory door behind me, and pushed the lock button. Now what? Around me were toilet, sink, towels, mirror. Mirrors. "I could use you next door," I told my reflection, and hurried through the next room past the tub and on into Betty's lavatory, where my reflection recurred, but had nothing to say for himself. I paused, took a deep breath, considered my naked body in the mirror without noticing anything that might excite Betty's suspicions, and pushed open the door.

Betty was sitting up, looking bleary-eyed and prodding the heel of her hand into the top of her head. "Oh, there you are," she said, her voice fuzzy. "I have a horrible headache."

"Good morning, sweetheart." Squint, I reminded myself. You are Bart, and you are not wearing your glasses. "How are you this morning?"

"I *told* you," she said crossly. "I have a headache."

"Oh, you poor thing. Wait right there, I'll get you some aspirin." And I turned around and headed right back into the john, closing the door behind me.

Betty was going to take a few minutes, I could see that already. Bare feet sprinting on the tiles, I headed through to Liz's lavatory, reassured myself the door was locked, and turned on both faucets at the sink. Then I went back the other way again, closing the sliding doors at both ends of the central room with the tub, so that the water running couldn't be heard by Betty. Panting slightly, I got aspirin from the medicine cabinet, put water in the toothbrush glass, and returned to Betty, who was half-propped up against the headboard, frowning into the middle distance. "Here you are, my darling."

"Did I drink that much last night? My head feels just terrible."

"Maybe there was something wrong with the *coq au vin*," I said. Then I remembered it was the *coq au vin* I'd spiked with the sleeping capsules, and wished I'd kept my mouth shut.

But maybe not. Looking at me, squinting even worse than I was, Betty said, "You know, you could be right. I thought there was some sort of, I don't know, bitter taste or something in the sauce."

"It was probably turning," I said. Sitting on the edge of

the bed, I solicitously fed my bride the aspirin and water. "You'll feel better soon now," I promised her. "Why not nap for a while, an hour or so?" Long enough for Art to get the hell out of here.

"Lie down with me," she said. "You've spoiled me, I can't sleep alone any more."

"Yes, dear," I said. Would she be soon asleep? Was the drain working properly in Liz's sink? Was Liz even now calling to Art through that locked door and wondering what on earth was wrong? My own headache thundering away, but a fixed smile of compassion on my face, I slid into bed next to Betty. "Put your head on the pillow now," I said. "Close your eyes. Try to nap."

"Yes, love." She murmured and moved, rubbing her warm hip against my side. When I remained unresponsive, she took my hand and placed it on her near breast, then sighed and reached for me.

"Darling," I said, "you should try to—"

"Silly boy," she whispered. "Cure me, lover."

So all right; *that* was marital conjugation.

My headache never went away. Later, I flopped onto my own side of the bed, very damp with exertion, and Betty sleepily stroked my belly, saying, "Oh, I feel much better already."

"Bladder," I said.

Her half-closed eyes opened. "What?"

"Go on to sleep," I soothed her, and stroked her cheek, and kissed her forehead. "I'll be right back."

Another romp through the facilities, pausing only to turn off the water in Liz's sink. (The drain was in excellent condition.) Then on into the bedroom, where Liz was pacing back and forth in a pale blue peignoir, her arms folded beneath her breasts. "You do take long enough," she said.

"I thought I might as well wash up," I said. "I'm sorry, did you—?"

"Tell me about it later," she said, and zipped into the

bathroom with every indication of urgency.

Well, that's the way it is in the morning, particularly if you've been putting away many gallons of champagne or other liquid the night before. In fact, come to think of it . . .

Down the hall from the bedrooms, toward the living room, was another lavatory for the convenience of guests. I found it very convenient, streaking down the hall in nothing but my skin, relieving myself, then washing up in the guests' sink and drying with the guests' tiny towels. Why do guests get such tiny towels?

I had made the initial run without meeting any of the servant population of this apartment, but on the return trip I emerged from the guests' john to find Nikki prancing by with a watering can in her hand. Surveying my nethers with pleased surprise, she said, "Ooo la la!" I hadn't known they really said things like that.

I looked at her, saw her roguish eyes and her twitching tail, and firmly ordered myself away. Not even counting the physical demands to which I'd already been put this morning, there was the increasingly desperate need to reduce my presences here to one before either of the sisters caught wise. "Later," I said, and trotted off down the hall.

At the end, Betty's door was on the left and Liz's was on the right. Betty's was just slightly ajar; looking through the crack, I saw that she was not only awake, she was sitting on the edge of the bed. And from the concentrated way she was staring toward the closed bathroom door, I knew what she was waiting for.

God almighty, was there no end to this? I'd been awake less than half an hour, and already I'd been through an exhaustingly full day. I ran on into Liz's room, took two deep breaths, and Liz came out of the bathroom. "Not dressed?" she said.

"I thought I'd shower." Quickly kissing her surprised face, I waved gaily, said *"Hasta la vista,"* and scampered off.

I couldn't lock the lavatory door behind me, but I could certainly lock the tub room door, and did so. The far side door I daren't lock from Betty's side, since she might notice, so I had to leave it closed but vulnerable. In the meantime, I'd switched on the shower, and to the merry splash of water I went back to Betty, who jumped up from the bed the instant I appeared, ignored my "Why, darling, you're still awake," and zoomed into the john.

And now at last I had a minute by myself to collect my wits and try to work out an answer to this mess. I couldn't very well keep playing bathroom games all day long. Somehow or other I had to get Art out of this apartment. Putting it simply, Art had to make an exit while Bart stayed here. Putting it even more simply, I had to be in two places at the same time.

My current situation was that Bart was naked here in Betty's bedroom while Art was naked over there in the shower. Therefore, my first order of business was to get Art out of the shower. Then I had to put Bart somewhere out of sight for a while until I could get some clothing on Art. Then Art could start to depart, but would dart back to where Bart was hidden apart so *he* could hop a cart back to his sweetheart. Smart?

I was still chewing on that one when Betty returned from the bathroom and looked at me in surprise. "Aren't you going to get dressed?"

"Fart," I said.

"What?"

Then I leaped to my feet. "A shower," I said loudly. Everything was happening twice. "I'm going to take a shower."

I started to run by her toward the john when she said, "Liz is in there now."

My heart bounced off the floor. "In where?"

"Taking a shower."

Liz was in there? If Liz was in there, she had to know the truth, or anyway be damn close to it. Two thousand a

month: a mental image of bills with little wings flying out
a window. Husband to Betty, unbound by extra contracts;
a mental image of a huge lumber mill with wings flying
away over a mountain. I said, "Are you sure?"

"I heard the water running."

"Oh," I said. Oh, the water running, that was all right.
In fact, I almost said something about that being Art in
there, not Liz, when I realized there was no way for me
to know such a thing.

But now what? If we were all going to wait here for Art
to finish his shower, we were all going to get very very
dirty.

"Here," Betty said. She was extending something toward me.

"What? What?"

"Don't you want your glasses?"

"Oh!" Another goddamn detail. I took the glasses
and put them on and then I really did squint. Lenses and
glasses make the best combination since ice cream and
pickles. "Maybe," I said, trying to look at her like a man
who could see and who didn't have any other problems
either, "maybe he's out of, I mean, maybe she's out of
there by now. I'll go, uh, I'll go check." And I scampered
away to the bathroom, cracking my naked hip against the
doorjamb on the way by. Oh, my poor eyes.

Close the lavatory door. Open the tub room door, enter
a room which was by now full of steam. My glasses immediately fogged. Wrenching them off, I turned off the
water, hurried back to Betty, put the damn foggy glasses
back on, peered over them at her, gave her the falsest
cheerful smile I've ever worn, and said, "All clear now.
See you in a few minutes."

As I started to shut the door again, she called, "Do you
have enough towels?"

"Plenty. Plenty."

"If you don't there's some in the cabinet under the—"

"Plenty plenty plenty."

Shut lavatory door, but leave unlocked. Into still-steamy tub room, close door, lock it. Remove glasses, place on counter opposite tub, turn shower on again, cross room, slam nose into other door.

Ouch. Damn, I forgot it was locked. Unlocking it, I slid it open, saw that Liz's lavatory was unoccupied, stepped in, slid the door shut, opened the bedroom door, and stepped out to see Liz, dressed, patting her hair at a mirror on the wall. "You must have been very dirty," she commented.

I closed the lavatory door. "Now that I'm your property," I said, "I'll have to take very good care of myself."

She gave my reflection in her mirror a sour look, then turned to offer a repeat performance to the original. "I wonder what I would have done," she said, "if you'd refused to sign."

"You would have loved me more," I suggested, "but you wouldn't be marrying me." I knew it was true when I said it, and I felt a small twinge, but nobody gets everything in this life. You decide your priorities and you make your choices. I'd decided long ago that any cake I had would be eaten.

Liz was frowning at me, thinking it over. "That's right," she said. Then, turning away, she said, "You want some breakfast?"

I was hurriedly gathering up my clothing, still scattered here and there on the floor, and throwing it onto my body. "No, I'd better got out of here," I said. "I wouldn't want to run into Bart."

"You want me to drop you any place?"

I hopped around on one foot, pulling on a sock. "Don't bother. I'll take a cab downtown."

"Where will you be today?"

"That's hard to say." I could only find one shoe; then the other turned out to be under the bed. "I'll call you tonight," I said.

"Be sure to get that blood test."

"I'll call my doctor as soon as I get to the office." Shirt on and tucked in, I went toward her to kiss her good-bye. But she turned away, studying her hair in that damn mirror again. Standing behind her, looking at her reflected face, I said, "Does this mood go away?"

"We'll find out, won't we?" she said.

"Right. Well, don't bother to see me out, I can find my own way."

She didn't say anything. She was brooding at herself in the mirror when I left the bedroom.

Betty's door was now entirely closed. Down the hall I went, feeling very nervous, and ducked into the guest bathroom again without seeing anybody. Closing the door, I sat on the toilet and leaned my ear close to the keyhole, so I'd hear when Liz walked by.

It took a while, and once again I had leisure to think. I visualized Liz entering the lavatory, hearing the shower running, going in there and finding the room empty, turning off the water, and then meeting Betty in the middle. "Where's Bart?" "Who?"

I'm too greedy. I shouldn't have signed, I should have kept to my original plan and made Art disappear. Look what was happening this morning, and this was only the beginning.

And we were rapidly reaching the point where exposure would mean a lot more than a simple loss of income. We were moving into Felonyland now: bigamy, fraud, God knows what else. I could even wind up in jail at the end of this; both of us, Art and Bart, serving concurrent sentences.

Sounds in the hall, somebody going by. Once they were past me, I opened the door a crack and peeked out, and it was Liz moving away down the corridor. Looking at her, I found myself wishing it was Betty I could give up, and not entirely because of the two grand a month.

Oh, well, stick with the possible. Once she was out of sight, I nipped out of the guest's john and sprinted back down the hall toward the bedrooms again. And all I needed now was for Betty's door to open, for Betty to come out and find me running along here, for Betty to begin asking. . . .

It didn't happen. Into Liz's room, across it, into the lavatory, through it into the steamier-than-ever tub room. There were large storage drawers under the counter, some of them empty. Yanking my clothing off, I jammed it all into an empty drawer, added my contact lenses wrapped in toilet paper from Liz's john, and stepped into the shower spray just long enough to get wet. Then I turned the water off, got a big soft golden bath towel from a shelf, put my glasses on, and returned to Betty, who was standing in front of a mirror on the wall, dressed, patting her hair. Turning a sweet smile toward me, she said, jokingly, "You must have been very dirty."

"Now that I'm yours," I said, "I'll have to take very good care of myself." Twice, everything twice.

"Do you want breakfast?"

"Yes, I do," I said. "For some reason, I'm starved."

22

W HAT A DAY. I TOLD Betty I wanted to go to the apartment I allegedly shared with Art, because I wanted to get the rest of my things from there. She offered, naturally, to go with me, but I managed to talk her out of it. Once out of the apartment, I headed for Dr. Osbertson, the quack who fails to cure my flu every winter, and received my second blood test in

less than a week. From there I went to my apartment; the
freak who was subletting was away, but had left traces of
himself behind. Apparently his hobby was blowing up
pizzas. Picking my way through the swamp, I packed a lot
of junk that could be Bart's, and toted it all away to the
office, where the usual turmoil and trouble from my other
life awaited me. I let it keep on waiting while I called
Ralph out at Fair Harbor, but unfortunately got Candy
instead. "Ralph Minck, please," I said, but she recognized
my voice, made a few formerly unprintable suggestions,
and hung up on me. And through it all I kept thinking, *I
have to get rid of Bart, just for a little while; I have to get
him out of town, I have to make him go away, go away,
go away.*

When I was a kid, the Saturday afternoon movie would
occasionally show a treasure-hunting underwater diver
caught in the clutches of an octopus. Fighting and strug-
gling, bubbles rising up, seabed roiling, octopus arms
waving all over the place. For the first time, I understood
exactly what that diver was going through.

Over the next hour I dealt with the mail, the telephone
messages, crap from illustrators, threats from the printer,
filthy language from the landlord. "I'm getting out of this,
prick," I told the landlord, while my mental image-screen
showed dollar bills with little wings flying *in* the window.
And through it all I was thinking, *Bart away.*

I tried to be smarter than that. I tried to reason with
myself, convince myself of the insanity of even *planning*
to marry Liz. Stay with the old plan, take the lumber mills
and run, don't be so greedy, don't be so stupid, don't be
so crazy. I told me, I really did, I can't claim I didn't warn
me, but none of it did any good. In my brain, or whatever
that is behind my eyes, I was already committed, I was
thinking only, *Get rid of Bart.*

The only distraction was a pair of phone messages from
Linda Ann Margolies. Regretfully I dropped them into the
wastebasket; I had liked that girl, but one more complica-

tion would finish me forever. Or should I just return her call, talk for a minute, see if she knew any new jokes?

No. I phoned Ralph again instead, and this time I got him. "Listen, Ralph," I said, "could you do a little job of research for me? On the QT."

"Sure. Trouble at the firm?"

"No trouble. In fact, and this'll probably surprise you as much as it does me, I'm thinking of getting married."

"No kidding! Well, you old son of a gun. Anybody I know?"

"You never met her," I said. "She's got a place at Point O' Woods."

"Rich, huh? Trust you."

That was something nobody was likely to do. I said, "She's the one I'd like you to look up. Also her lawyer."

"Her lawyer? You aren't pulling something funny, are you?"

"Of course not. I'll tell you the situation, Ralph. I'm in love with this girl, and she's in love with me, but her lawyer's out to get her for himself, because she's rich. Anyway, that's what I think."

"That's unethical," Ralph said. He sounded shocked.

"Exactly what I told him to his face," I said. Then, speaking to Ralph in what I took to be his own language, I said, "He brazened it out. But I just don't trust him."

"What's his name?"

"Ernest Volpinex."

"What firm is he with?"

"I have no idea. No, wait, I think I have his card. Unless I threw it away." I made a fast search on my desk, but it wasn't there. "Sorry, I don't have it any more."

"That's all right. I can look him up."

"Fine."

"What do you want to know, exactly?"

"Well," I said, "he told my fiancée she had to get married this year or she'd have a great big tax bite next April.

She's an orphan, see, her parents both died last New Year's Eve."

"Before or after midnight?"

"I have no idea."

"Well, what's her name?"

"Elizabeth Kerner. What I want to know is her financial position. How much did she inherit, does she really have that tax problem, what her general situation is. And about Volpinex, I want to know what kind of bird he is. I think he's a crook, and I'd like to know his reputation in his field, and any scandal or anything like that in his past."

"You want to turn your girl friend away from him, is that it? Move her to a different lawyer."

"I'd like to move her to you, Ralph, if you'd like a client."

"How much is this alleged tax bite?"

I knew why he'd asked that question. He wanted to know how rich she was, so he'd know how much he wanted her as a client. So I told him the simple truth: "Three million dollars."

"Ah," he said, calmly but promptly. "I'll look into it right away for you, Art. I'll find out everything I can."

Thanks, Ralph, I appreciate it."

"Anything for a friend."

"You're true blue, Ralph."

"It's nothing. And congratulations on the coming nuptials."

"Thanks, Ralph. This time it's the real thing."

We chatted a bit more, and then we both hung up. I sat there a moment, quiet, my hand resting on the phone. *I have to get rid of Bart.*

THE TELEGRAM ARRIVED
at nine that night. Good old Joe; it's a blessing to have
friends you can rely on, particularly when they live in
California and you need a telegram from California.

Betty and I were having dinner for two on the terrace,
bathing in the warm August air and watching the lights of
taxicabs on the Park Drive. Liz was out somewhere, foul-
tempered and door-slamming, and Art hadn't been heard
from all day.

"Now what?" I said, and extended the yellow form
across the coffee and peach melba toward Betty. Nikki
had brought it out to us, wiggling her rump, and now stood
beside the table, giving me her lewd looks and awaiting
further orders.

Betty took the telegram, frowning past it at me. "What
is it? That's all, Nikki."

Nikki turned like a Buckingham Palace guard, but more
interestingly, and pranced back indoors. She moved like
someone with good pelvic muscles. I said, "It's a telegram.
Trouble of some kind."

Betty cautiously lowered her eyes to the words on the
yellow paper, reading them by candlelight. I knew what
they said. Not only had I just read it myself; earlier today
I'd written it. And what it said was:

BART,
CALL ME TONIGHT OR TOMORROW. SERIOUS
SITUATION.

JOE GOLD

"Who's Joe Gold?"

"An old friend of mine in Los Angeles. Makes a living writing record liner notes."

"You know the strangest people," she said, and handed the telegram back to me. "What's it all about?"

"I don't know. I suppose I better call."

"Do you still have business affairs out there?"

"No. I told you, I sold my interest in the car wash before I came back East."

"Then what could it be?"

"I just can't think of anything. I ought to call."

"I suppose so," she said doubtfully. She frowned in mistrust at the telegram in my hand, a legitimate telegram legitimately sent from Los Angeles by a man legitimately named Joe Gold. "I suppose so," she repeated, then picked up the summons bell on the middle of the table and shook it.

Nikki responded immediately to the tinkle—an eavesdropper, apparently, among her other qualities. "Yes, madame? I should clear now?"

"The telephone for Mr. Dodge."

"Yes, madame."

While she was gone, Betty said, "Why would he send a telegram here?"

"He must have called the office, and Art gave him this address."

"Then why wouldn't he call here?"

"I don't know." I did not, in fact, have a good explanation for that, and trusted the question would eventually become lost in the onrush of events. For my own purposes, a telegram established the California connection much more realistically than a telephone call, but that was hardly something to mention to Betty.

Nikki came back with the long-corded phone. "I wish he'd given his number," I said. "How do I get information in Los Angeles?"

Betty's take-over qualities came promptly to the surface, as I'd hoped they would. "Give me the phone," she said. "Nikki, pencil and paper."

"Yes, madame."

While Nikki pogoed away once more, Betty dialed L.A. information, then asked me, "What's his address, do you know?"

"Vassar Drive, in Hollywood."

"Vassar?" Her lip curled slightly. "Those people out there. Yes, operator. In Hollywood, a Mr. Joseph Gold on Vassar Drive. Yes, I will."

Back came Nikki, with pad and pencil. She started to give them to me, but I shooed her over to Betty. She started then to leave again, but I said, "Nikki, wait here a minute. We may want something else." If she was an eavesdropper, I didn't want her near any of the extension phones in the next few minutes.

"Yes, Mr. Bart." The words, the manner, and the look were all directly out of *The Story of O*, and not for a minute did I believe that coincidental.

Betty, her hand over the receiver mouthpiece, said to me, "Is he Jewish?"

"I really don't know," I said.

"He probably is." Then, into the phone, "Yes, operator?" She wrote down some numbers. "Thank you, operator." Hanging up, she said, "Nikki, give all this to Mr. Dodge."

"Yes, madame."

Ignoring Nikki's dance routine, I glanced at the phone number on the pad, saw that Betty had gotten it right, and dialed it from memory. Ring. Two rings. Three rings. Come on, Joe, you said you'd be home, it's only six P.M. there. Four ri— "Hello?"

"Hello, Joe?"

"Hey man. You got it, huh?"

"Yeah, I got it. What's it all about?"

"I must say," he said, "your relationships with women get more baroque all the time."

"Good God!" I said. I sounded shocked, and I'm sure I looked stunned. Nikki and Betty both watched me, with curiosity and apprehension.

"I never did like Lydia," Joe was saying, "even when you were married to her."

"When?" I asked. I was hunched tensely over the phone.

"But at least," Joe said, "that was your ordinary tag-team unfaithful modern marriage."

I said, "Do you think she meant it?"

"What you're into now," he said, "I shudder to think."

I said, "What do the doctors say?" Both women on the terrace with me reacted predictably to the noun.

"There must be an easier way to get laid," he said. "Or to break off with a woman, or whatever the hell you're doing."

I said, "Good God, Joe, that was over a long time ago. I never gave her any—" And stopped, as though I'd been interrupted.

Joe was saying, "Don't you have any massage parlors back there?"

"Yeah, I can see that," I said reluctantly. "But what am *I* supposed to do?"

"Have you considered onanism?"

I gave Betty a helpless look, shaking my head. "Joe," I said, pleading to be understood, "you don't understand. I have commitments back here now, I can't just—"

"Of course," he said, "as Marx once pointed out, the bourgeoisie had to invent adultery to keep from dying of boredom."

"I realize that, Joe," I said desperately.

"Or was it Lenin? One of those commies."

"Well, how long would it be for?"

"The point is, maybe what you need is a hobby. Jigsaw puzzles, for instance."

"The thing of it is, Joe," I said, being confidential with him, "I've got a girl now, back here in the East."

"I don't doubt it for a second."

"It's, uh, it's serious, Joe. If I came out, I'd have to—"

Again I appeared to be interrupted. Both Nikki and Betty looked shocked at this suggestion that I was being asked to go to California. Meanwhile, Joe was saying, "Maybe you'd like to grow plants. Vines and things. Tell them all your little secrets, and watch their leaves fall off."

"Joe," I said, "how can I explain that to my girl?"

"If anybody can, Art," he said, "you can."

"I see what you mean," I said, but I didn't sound happy about it. I said, "The doctors really think so, huh?"

"They sure do," Joe said. "They think you're a nut."

"Thanks, Joe," I said. "I'd appreciate that. Be better than a hotel."

"Do you get the impression," he asked me, "that we're talking at cross-purposes?"

"I don't see how I can promise anything," I said.

"Go ahead and promise, baby."

I nodded slowly, listening. Logic, duty, friendship, my own moral sense, all were clearly conspiring to make me agree to something about which I was extremely reluctant. "You're right, Joe," I said.

"Why, thank you," he said.

"I'll work it out somehow at this end," I said, "and I'll get out there as soon as I can."

"Don't you dare," he said.

"Sure, Joe, I know," I said, "and I appreciate it. So long."

"Is it soup yet?" he asked me, and I hung up.

Betty said, "You're going to California?"

"It's—" I stopped myself, glanced at Nikki, and said, "You can take the phone back now, Nikki."

"Yes, Mr. Bart." Off she went, no doubt to hide behind

the draperies and listen to me tell my tale.

Betty was showing understandable impatience. "For heaven's sake, what is it?"

"A girl," I said. "Her name's Lydia, we used to go together when I lived in L.A. For a while, we even talked about getting married."

"And?"

"We broke up," I said. "I hadn't seen her for two or three months when I left. In fact, that's part of the reason I was so glad when Art called and wanted me to go into the card business with him. I was ready to come back."

Her impatience was not appeased. *"And?"*

"She tried to kill herself."

"Bosh," Betty said, sitting back, and suited the old-fashioned word with an old-fashioned expression of disbelief and contempt. "It's a silly ploy to get you back."

"I don't think so, I really don't think so. She drove her car off a cliff, up on Mulholland Drive. I mean, it wasn't a sleeping pill thing or head in the oven, one of those tries with rescue built right into it. She really did try to kill herself."

"Well, what are *you* supposed to do about it? Go back and marry her?"

"Go back and see her," I said. "Her doctors think she's idealized me or something, that if she sees me as I really am, if we have a talk and she sees the reality of it, she'll snap out of it. She made another try in the hospital, tried to drag herself to the window."

Sympathy for this unknown victim of heart's blight finally began to seep into Betty's expression, mixing with the impatience and the annoyance there. "Don't they have her under restraint or something?"

"They can't leave her like that forever." I reached across the table, taking Betty's hand in both of mine, and gazed sincerely into her eyes. "Betty," I said, "this thing is ghastly. I wish I didn't know a thing about it. But I do know, and how can I turn my back? What if I refused to go out there, said it wasn't my problem, and—"

"It *isn't* your problem."

"What if she tries again, a third time? What if she makes it? Could I have that on my conscience the rest of my life?"

"She might try it anyway, even if you do go out."

"But at least I'll have done what I can. Betty, how could I face myself if I didn't at least make the try?"

Her arguments were failing, and she knew it. "This is so inconvenient," she said, looking away at the darkness of Central Park. "I'm not sure I could get away now."

"Betty, you can't come with me. Don't you see what a shock that would be to her, rubbing her nose in it, I show up with—"

"You mean you'll go out by yourself?"

"Just for a day or two," I said. "Joe offered to let me stay at his place. You have the phone number, we can be in constant contact."

Briskly dismissing that, Betty said, "She wouldn't have to know I was anywhere in the state. We could stay at the Bel Air, I could visit friends while you were at the hospital, there wouldn't be any problem."

"You may think I'm silly," I said, "but I couldn't do that. It would just be on my mind all the time, as though I were flaunting my own happiness in the face of her misery. Let me do this my way, Betty. It won't be for long, and once it's over it'll be over for good."

She frowned. "How do you know she won't do it again a year from now? An annual event, like the tulip festival. Lydia's leap."

"Even if it happened," I said, "I wouldn't feel obligated any more. Once is all I owe her, but I do owe her that. And besides, you wanted our marriage kept a secret. How could we travel together, stay at a hotel, visit your friends out there, do all of that and keep the secret?"

She glared out over Central Park, with its viaduct of taxi headlights and the dim lamps gleaming uncertainly along the blacktop paths. She considered arguments, rejected them, went back to them, thought out the potentials and the implications, and at last irritably shrugged her shoulders and said, "All right. Do it your way. I suppose I should be happy I have such a straight-arrow husband."

"And I'm delighted," I told her, squeezing her hand, "that I have such an understanding wife."

24   24

T HE NEXT PLANE TO LOS Angeles was not, as I'd already known, until nine-thirty the following morning. Betty and I rode out together to Kennedy in the Lincoln, Carlos at the wheel. A good if arrogant driver, Carlos delivered us to TWA's concrete-bird terminal earlier than anticipated, and we had a cup of coffee together before saying good-bye. "I'll call you from Joe's place the minute I arrive," I promised.

"I'll be waiting."

"And remember," I said, "you be sure to call me if there's any problem at all. You've got Joe's number?"

"I have it," she assured me.

"Good." And if she called, Joe would tell her I was at the hospital or out to dinner or whatever the time of day suggested, and would then call me, and I would then call Betty. Considering some of the scrambling I'd already done this month, the Bart-in-Hollywood device was child's play. Miniature golf.

At last the moment came for departure. "Our first separation," I said, clutching her to me.

"Hurry back," she whispered, and just slightly ground her hips.

"Oh, I will. I will."

We kissed good-bye, I clutched the first-class ticket paid for by Betty's American Express card, and off I went through the anti-hijack screening process. Passengers Only Beyond This Point. She stood on the other side of the private guards, watching me with her friendly and efficient smile. Bye-bye, Betty. I waved and waved, and walked away down the long red tunnel.

Out of sight. Good. The men's room was just over there. Fortunately, Betty had reminded me to buy a paperback book for the plane ride, so I had reading matter to take me through the following twenty minutes in a toilet stall for which I had paid a dime. Then, leaving the book behind for the next customer, in case the toilet paper should run out—it really wasn't a very good book—I hefted the small canvas bag I'd packed for my California trip, left the men's room, and joined a group of passengers deplaning from—or so their conversations suggested—Detroit. We all walked together back down the red tunnel to the main terminal area, where I tried to turn the round-trip ticket in for cash. (My expenses had been hellish this month.) Damn them, they wouldn't give me money, only a credit on Betty's American Express. "In that case," I said, "I'll take the flight after all."

"I believe it's already left, sir."

"I'll catch up," I said, took my ticket, and went away.

25   25

Two DAYS IN A ROW," Gloria said when I walked in. "Summer must be over."

"When I'm with you," I told her, "there's always summer in my heart." Then I went on inside to see what new outrages had been laid on my desk through the wonders of the postal service and the telephone.

Not many. I'd grown used to weekly accumulations, Wagnerian in scope and volume, while one day's output barely showed up on the seismograph. Linda Ann Margolies had not made any more calls, which I regretted. Nor were there any from Liz, though there was one from Ernest Volpinex. Oh, really?

Click. "Gloria, get me that fellow Volpinex, will you?"

"Right."

On to the mail. Wastebasket, wastebasket, wastebasket . . .

Buzz. "Volpinex."

"Thanks." Click. "Volpinex?"

A female voice said, "One moment, please."

I considered hanging up. Didn't Gloria know better than that? She should have insisted on the other secretary producing *her* boss first.

Ah, screw it. Volpinex wasn't likely to appreciate such subtleties anyway. Unless, of course, he had it in mind to keep me waiting. The clock on my desk has a sweep second hand, which I now stared at; I would wait exactly one minute, then hang up.

Forty-two seconds: "Mr. Dodge?" Volpinex's voice, like curdled molasses.

"That's right."

"*Arthur* Dodge?"

"Come on, Volpinex," I said.

"I suppose you know why I'm calling."

"Dumb supposition," I told him. "If I knew, I probably wouldn't call back."

He chuckled slightly. "I must admit I like you better than your brother," he said.

"That's why you called? Sorry, I'm already engaged."

"As a matter of fact, *that's* why I called. Your engagement, the contract you signed."

"What about it?"

"I drew it up, of course."

"Of course."

"Not willingly."

"Of course."

"I spoke against you as strongly as I could," he assured me.

"Speak for yourself, John Alden," I suggested.

"Nevertheless," he said, "Elizabeth insisted. You were the only candidate she would consider."

I chuckled deliberately into the phone. "Put your own name in nomination, did you?"

"In order to protect her, yes. I know you won't consider that selfless of me, but in truth it was. Particularly when it's Betty that I've always been the most fond of."

I burst into sudden honest laughter. "That's footwork, Volpinex!" I told him. "Now you're out to be my brother-in-law."

"I'm used to your cynicism," he said. "And to be honest with you, I—"

"Oh, yes, do," I said.

"I hold as low an opinion of you," he said, "as you do of me. But whatever may happen between myself and Betty, there is still the fact that I am your fiancée's attorney. And a brother-in-law status in the future is not entirely inconceivable."

"It is to me," Bart told him.

"Don't count too highly on your brother's prospects," he told Art. "I've seen Betty through this sort of infatuation before."

"Have you now."

"Yes, I have. Still, the point is, in one way or another you and I will have to reach some sort of accommodation. Whether we can rise above our personal dislike or not, we'll have to construct a viable procedure for dealing with one another."

What did he want now? I asked him: "What do you want now?"

"A truce," he said. "Possibly productive, but at least not harmful. To either of us."

"Fine," I said. "You don't knife my back and I won't knife yours."

"Possibly we could go into greater detail," he said. "Would you be free for lunch?"

It was not yet eleven. I said, "Today?"

"Or tomorrow. The sooner the better."

"All right, today. Where?"

"At my club," he said, and gave me its name and address. He had, of course, gone to one of the correct New England universities—educational standards are not what they used to be—and it was that university's club at which we would lunch. "Twelve-thirty," he suggested.

"Fine," I said, and we both hung up.

Now what? Did Volpinex really think I'd help him beat my brother's time with Betty? If he did, he either had too high an opinion of himself or too low an opinion of me. And if that wasn't what he wanted, what were the alternatives? "A viable procedure for dealing with one another." How much was that, in American money?

Well, I'd find out soon enough. Right now, it was time to reestablish contact with sweetheart number two. Back to the phone I went, and dialed.

"Kairnair reseedonce."

"Hello, Nikki, this is Art Dodge. Is Liz there?"

"Meez Leez? I go see." There was a click as she put me on hold, and I spent the next minute or two going through the rest of the telephone message memos. Nothing from Ralph yet, but it was far too soon anyway; I'd only put him to work on Liz and her lawyer yesterday. As for the rest, it was wastebasket, wastebasket, wastebasket . . .

"Hello?" A voice as snotty as ever.

"Hello, there, my bride-to-be," I said. "How's my little dove this fine morning?" I'd very nearly said *pigeon*, but switched in the nick of time.

"You were going to call me yesterday." She sounded imperious and annoyed, very like her tone when she'd thought she was talking to Carlos.

It was time to start fine-tuning the relationship. Casually I said, "I was busy."

"When you're supposed to call me, you—"

"*Supposed* to call you?"

There was a brief pause, and when she spoke again anger had been replaced by cynicism. "A little rebellion, eh? A sop to your self-respect. Okay, Art, you showed me how manly and independent you are."

"I don't want to be independent," I said. "When do we get married?"

"What's your hurry?"

"No hurry, I just want to know when."

"Some time after Labor Day," she said.

"After Labor Day?" Impossible. I could keep Bart in California four or five days, maybe even a week, but no more than that. *After* Labor Day? Two weeks, maybe longer? No way.

Then, making it worse, Liz added, "We have till the end of the year, so why rush? Besides, we ought to wait till your brother gets back."

"Bart? Back from where?"

"Los Angeles. He left this morning, some old girl friend tried to kill herself."

"Old girl friend!" I expressed outrage. "What do I care about old girl friends?"

"You asked," she pointed out.

"Why that dirty son of a bitch!" I yelled. "He's supposed to be my partner, he's supposed to help me in this goddamn expansion, he hasn't been around the goddamn office all week, and now he's in *California?* The son of a bitch, I'll throw him out of the company, I swear to Christ."

"You do that." She didn't sound very interested. "You

want to come to the Island with me tomorrow?"

"Fine," I said.

"I'll take you out to dinner tonight. That is, if you don't have to stay up with a sick housewife."

"I'll come to your place around seven."

"Good."

"About our wedding date, I've always—"

"Don't push it, lover," she said, and hung up.

Damn.

26   26

V OLPINEX SAID, "I'VE never had much of a sense of humor, myself."

"You surprise me," I said.

We were having lunch at a snowy table by a tall arched window. This dining room on the third floor of the club, hushed and half full, overlooked Park Avenue swarming with taxis. A new office building across the way, a dull slab gridwork of glass and chrome, formed a great segmented mirror in which I could see Volpinex's club reflected like a dream of the landmarks commission: Victorian brownstone elegance shimmering on a surface of functional blah. I had waved my hand near the window early in the meal, hoping to see myself across the way, but the reflection didn't offer that much detail.

"I've always thought of comedy," Volpinex went on, "as a mark of unreliability. A fellow in my fraternity was always telling jokes, and then he hanged himself."

"I won't do that," I promised.

He brooded at me. "No, I don't suppose you will."

"Chilly in here," I said, and buttered a roll with a cold silver knife.

Volpinex always surprised me; in memory he tended to become older and fatter, but in life he was invariably a slender healthy thirty-year-old. My contemporary, in fact, and about my size, but probably in better physical shape: a karate expert, for instance. Born of Count Dracula, out of a White House aide. It was his humorlessness, the determined flatness and bullshit of his speech, that made him seem fat and fifty.

Speaking out of that train of thought, I said, "Comedy keeps people young."

"In the sense that it's childish, yes."

"Besides," I said, "I've always heard that comedy is what separates us from the animals."

"Parrots tell jokes," Volpinex said, "and hyenas laugh."

"What do *you* think separates us from the animals?"

"Nothing," he said, and the conversation paused while the waiter brought Volpinex's oysters, my mussels, and our half bottle of Chablis. The tasting ritual was accomplished with deep and solemn pleasure on all sides, and the waiter went away. Volpinex said, "I do, however, appreciate that humor can be a salable commodity."

"Anything can be sold," I said.

He gave me a thin glinting smile. "Including yourself, for instance."

"There's always the possibility," I suggested, "that I signed the contract not because I love money but because I love Liz."

"I suppose that's a joke," he said, his smile fading. "You've never been audited," he said, dipped an oyster in the blood red sauce, and ate.

I squinted at him. "Say again?"

"By Internal Revenue," he explained. "They've never audited your tax returns."

"They'd need a microscope."

"You strike me," he said, "as the sort of person who

would commit fraud for the sheer pleasure of it. Claim your dog as a dependent, that sort of thing. A tax audit might very well finish with you in Danbury."

He meant the Federal prison there. In true Volpinexish language, the Feds call it a Correctional Facility. I said, "What are you getting at? Free legal advice?"

"Should you marry Elizabeth Kerner," he said, "your economic position would alter significantly. It wouldn't surprise me in the least if the IRS then took an interest in you."

I ate a mussel. I drank a bit of Chablis. I said, "Did you really get me here to make stupid threats?"

"Threats? We're merely discussing possibilities."

"No, we're not. We're discussing fantasies in your head. You're telling me you have friends at Internal Revenue, and they'll lean on me if I don't get away from Liz."

Nothing changed in his cold dark face; I got a sudden whiff of hair oil. "The comedic mind is often paranoid," he said, and sipped at his wine. "I've noticed that before."

This echo of a comment I'd made to Linda Ann Margolies startled me; had she been a setup, working for Volpinex? No, that *was* paranoia. Volpinex had no need to infiltrate me with Mata Haris. I said, "I'm going to marry Liz. There's nothing to talk about."

"According to your ex-wife," he said quietly, "comedians make unsatisfactory husbands."

I ate my last mussel. I drained my wineglass, and a silent waiter at once refilled it and withdrew. I said, "Look, Volpinex, whatever dirt you could find on me you've already showed to Liz, and she brushed it off. The income tax threat doesn't scare me because once I'm married to Liz I'll use her accountants to defend myself." I gave him the tightest grin I had in stock, and said, "I'm coming into the family, sweetheart, so just relax and enjoy it."

He couldn't answer at once. Our appetizer plates were being removed, a half bottle of Médoc was being tasted and approved, and our entrees were being delivered; lamb chops for him, rare sirloin for me. I finished my white wine while all this was going on, started in on my steak, and Volpinex said, "You have just touched on my real objection to you. And to your brother. Family. Who are you people, where do you come from? You are barbarians at the gates, and it is my duty to repel you."

Could he possibly believe all that? But the humorless man makes no distinction between truth and falsehood; words to him are simply tools, effective or not effective. I said, "What about you, Volpinex? That's no fine old Point O' Woods name you carry around. What cave do *you* come out of?"

"While my ancestors enjoyed the Mediterranean breeze," he told me, "yours were chained to the oars. Civilization has declined since then."

I cut meat. "You don't expect me to pull my forelock and shuffle out of your life," I said. "So what's the point?"

"I want you to understand my antipathy," he said. "You have labored under the belief that we are a pair of opportunists together, that I am somehow similar to you."

"You're different, all right," I said. "I know when I'm kidding."

"You don't think I'm serious about family?"

"Liz's mother had the family connections," I said. "But old man Kerner was a lumberjack out of Canada, with no more family than a hooker in front of the Americana Hotel. He had the one thing better than a family tree—a money tree."

"You have neither."

"They're on order," I said.

He studied me, saying nothing, and for a while we both merely ate. Every time I glanced at him he was still brooding at me, watching me like a highway engineer looking at a mountain. Tunnel away, bastard, this mountain is here to stay.

Finally he said, "Let's discuss this from a different angle."

"It's your turf," I said.

"You are not quite the standard fortune hunter," he said, "some money-mad chauffeur out to make a quick killing. You are better than that, more educated, more intelligent, more talented."

I put my fork down and stared at him. "Now you're trying to sell me an encyclopedia."

He ignored that, saying, "If you're honest with yourself, you'll admit you enjoy the life you already have: the freedom, some sense of adventure and experiment, the opportunity to employ your talent."

"And the bill collectors," I said. "They're my favorites."

He nodded, thoughtfully. "The money Elizabeth offered you has gone to your head, and why not? It's a lot of money. But it isn't what you really want."

"What I really want is a fire engine and a set of soldiers."

"What you really want," he told me, "is the life you're living now, but with a somewhat firmer economic cushion."

"Like two thousand a month."

"No," he said. "*Earned* money. The product of your own labor."

"As a psychiatrist," I told him, "you make a great stand-up comedian."

He plowed ahead; he was thin, but he talked fat. "I have clients," he said, "with available venture capital. You own a business with rather strong potential. A larger and more diverse line, national distribution of your product, and you could be quite well off. I believe I could authorize an investment of, oh, say, thirty thousand dollars."

"You really are something, Volpinex," I said. "First threats, then bribery." And I couldn't help wondering how he'd narrowed it down to just that figure.

"I had already assumed," he said, "that you would choose the worst possible interpretation of that offer. Nevertheless, it still stands."

"And nevertheless, I'm still going to marry Liz. Give it

up, Volpinex. Nothing is going to keep that marriage from taking place." I saw no point in mentioning that Folksy Cards would never survive expansion, or that thirty thousand dollars was fifteen months pay from Liz. What did I need with his venture capital? I had a couple ventures of my own going.

His look was now as cold as the air conditioning. "I had hoped we could find an accommodation," he said.

So he'd shot his last bolt, finally. "I tell you what," I suggested. "Try the routine on Bart. He might go for thirty thousand dollars. Or Betty might be more impressed by scandal than Liz."

His expression clouded. "Your brother has lived a much cleaner life than you have," he said, and I could hear a certain frustration in his voice.

Of course. A standard background check covers only two areas—credit and police blotter. Bart would come up blank on both, and the conclusion to be drawn was not that Bart Dodge had in fact no real-world existence, but that Bart Dodge was a very clean-living guy. It is, as they say, very difficult to prove a negative.

"Bart always has been a boy scout," I said, and drank some of the Médoc. It was delicious.

27

27

AFTER LUNCH, VOLPINEX invited me to play squash. "I've never played," I said.

"You'll pick it up. Come along, I'll lend you a sweat suit."

Squash turned out to be a game combining the worst

qualities of tennis and handball. In a bare high-ceilinged room the two of us stood in our sweat suits facing the same wall, holding the kid brothers of tennis rackets in our hands. A small hard rubber ball was to be hit against that wall with this racket by player number one. Player number two was to hit it on the rebound, and player number one on *that* rebound, and so on.

What the game consists of mostly is running back and forth in an empty room, occasionally crashing into a side wall. I understand the upper class is nuts over it.

Volpinex told me the rules of the game, and I began to understand its appeal for a certain kind of intellect, since it's about as complicated as fifty-two-pickup. "I see," I said. "I hit then you hit then I hit then you hit."

"That's right," he said, bounced the ball, and whammed it with his racket at the opposite wall. It hit, and caromed back on a beeline for my head. I flung myself away to the right, heard the *fwizzzzz* of its passage, and turned to see it thud into the opposite wall and head back my way again.

But with less determination. It bounced before it reached me, and only hurt my hand moderately when I caught it. A rather hard little rubber ball. I said, "This thing goes pretty fast, huh?"

"Good players in a fast game," he told me, "will get rebounds up to a hundred miles an hour."

"Wouldn't do a fellow's forehead much good," I suggested.

He offered me his thin smile. "You do have to keep out of the way," he said. "Go ahead and try it."

All right, bastard. I'm fairly good at pool, I should be able to work out the angle between where I was standing and that creep's nose. I chose a spot on the far wall, bounced the little ball, and swung as hard as I could.

The ball went some damn place. It hit the wall, but nowhere near the spot I'd chosen, and it came back out at an angle that had nothing to do with Volpinex's nose.

And Volpinex was off like a mechanical rabbit. He shot

past me, flung himself in front of the richocheting ball, swung his racket, sliced the ball on the fly, and here the damn thing came again. Off the wall and straight for my left eye, faster than ever.

"Jesus!" I shouted, and practically fell on my ass scampering out of the way. The ball whizzed by, and I turned to speak severely to Volpinex, only to see him running again, at an angle across the floor, racket at the ready.

What in hell was all this? *Whump* went the racket against the ball, and here came the ball, a buzzing little V-2 rocket aimed at the London of my stomach. By screeching to a halt and sucking in my gut I gave the little devil room to fly, but it was gone so fast, and coming back again from the wall so soon, that I didn't have time to do anything else but duck again, reeling away toward the side wall, off balance to the front, running like mad to try to get my body back under my head.

Whump I heard behind me, and *thock* as the little round bastard shot off the wall again. I didn't even look for it; I just hit the wall and shoved myself backward hard. As quick as a subliminal message on a movie screen, the ball came spinning in from the corner of my right eye, *zze-thuzz*ed off the wall in front of me, and rocketed away somewhere to my left.

I followed it, running for my life. Volpinex was loping to intersect the damn thing. He was swinging; I was veering to my left because that was where I'd guessed he would go next. *Ying*, went the ball, very loud, as it brush-burned my right earlobe. I was running as though a husband had come home unexpectedly, and I was watching Volpinex's eyes. Let *him* watch the ball.

It was coming in behind me, I knew that, and he was coming in from the front. At what I judged to be the last second, I launched myself across Volpinex's path, leaping out low and straight, parallel to the floor, as though I were making a flat dive into a swimming pool. I caught him at shin level, me in hurtling motion and him in a flat-out dash, and the two of us went tumbling about on the floor like planes colliding above the clouds.

I rolled and rolled, until I was away from all those extra legs and rackets, and then lunged staggering to my feet, gasping for breath and staring all around for that goddamn rotten ball.

There it was, on yet another ricochet. But its speed was lessening now, it was bouncing across the floor in long innocent skips, as though it wouldn't hurt a fly. Running diagonally after it, I snapped it out of the air, clutched it in both my hands, and let my momentum carry me on to the nearest wall, which I thudded into like a mail sack.

For a minute I just stayed there, leaning forward into the wall, my hands clutching the ball protectively at my middle. My throat was painfully raw from gasping, my right side felt as though I'd broken my ribs against that murderous bastard's shins, my left side had a crick in it from all that running, my legs were trembling, my earlobe burned, and generally speaking I was a mess.

"Had enough for today?"

I rolled till I was sideways against the wall and could see Volpinex standing there, smiling at me. He wasn't even out of breath, the bastard. And I had no doubt he really was some sort of karate genius. I panted at him.

"Perhaps it's too fast a game for you," he said. He patted the racket into his other palm: plong, plong. "You don't want to get into games that are too fast for you," he said. "You should get out of such games, as a safety precaution." And he turned and walked away, across the room and through the little door on the far side and out of sight.

Oh, I had a lot to say to him, it was just I didn't seem capable of speech yet. So I just hung against the wall, going *hee-haw* through my open mouth, and glared daggers at that closed door. None of them stuck.

A<small>ND THEN I WROTE</small>, "T<small>HE</small> front of the card shows a yawning grave. Inside, the card says, 'Drop in any time.'"

That was at three o'clock, back in my office, shortly before Bart called Betty from L.A. Sucrets had eased my throat, Excedrin had dulled my aches and pains, and Mediquik had stunned my stinging earlobe. My ribs appeared to be intact, though there were spreading bruises on my right side, and I was seated in relative calm at my desk. After phoning the *Daily News* to reassure myself that Bart's flight hadn't crashed or been hijacked, I dialed Betty's number.

"Kairnair reseedonce."

"Hi, Nikki, this is Bart." I shouted a bit, like someone calling long distance. "Is Betty there?"

"Hold on one moment, pleeze."

So I held on one moment, massaging my sore ribs. Get even with Volpinex, I have to get even with Volpinex.

"Hello? Bart?"

"Hi there, sweetheart!" I shouted. "Well, I'm here!"

"Oh, I'm happy you called," she said. "That was nice of you."

"Yep," I said. "The flight was easy, Joe met me at the airport, and here I am."

"Did you see that girl yet?"

"Heck, no," I said. "I just got here. Joe has the doctor's phone number, so I'll call him next and see what I'm supposed to do."

"What's the weather there?"

"Hot," I said, telling her what this morning's *Times* had told me, with its national weather map. "Hotter than New York. I bet it's a hundred."

"Really? That must be awful."

"Well, it's air-conditioned where I am, and Joe's car is air-conditioned, so it isn't too bad. Boy, it's funny, you know? It's only noon here."

"You're probably suffering jet lag," she said.

"I wouldn't be surprised."

"You know," she said, "Art's really mad about you going away."

My, how news can travel fast. I said, "Art is? What for?"

"He told Liz he was going to throw you out of the business because you came to help but then you didn't do anything, and now you've run out on him."

"Well, that dirty rat," I said, with honest outrage. "He told me himself I should take a few days off, while he was doing that auditing business."

"All I know is what Liz told me."

"Well," I said, "I'll get back there in a day or two, and straighten things out with that brother of mine."

"Maybe you shouldn't be involved in that business of his anyway," she said. "Wouldn't it make more sense if you were my business manager, with a salary and everything?"

"You mean, live on you?" I sounded *really* boy scout when I said that.

"Of course not. I have a business manager now, so you'd just take his place."

"Oh," I said. "Well, that might be all right. Though I don't like the idea of getting somebody else fired for no reason at all."

"Well, he could still be my lawyer, but you'd be my business manager, that's all."

"Lawyer? You mean Volpinex?"

"Oh, no, he's not *my* lawyer. I have somebody of my own."

Which was good news. I said, "But your man is lawyer and business manager both?"

"It's always been more convenient that way."

"Well, I think it would probably be better management to have two different people for those two different jobs."

"There, you see? You're already talking like my business manager."

I laughed boyishly. "I guess I am," I said.

29   29

WHEN WE CAME IN from the beach, around six o'clock, I said to Liz, "Well, what do you want to do tonight?"

"I don't know about you," she said, "but I've got a date."

"Ha ha," I said. "Anybody I know?"

"Ernie Volpinex," she said, and headed for the stairs.

I frowned after her. "Wait a minute, wait a minute. Is that on the level?"

She turned on the second step and looked at me. "Have I ever lied to you?" Then she started up again.

"Hold on, there," I said, and followed as far as the foot of the stairs. When she turned to look down at me without curiosity, I said, "We're supposed to be engaged, aren't we?"

"Clause seven," she said. The sexual nonexclusivity clause.

"So you're going out with Volpinex."

"That's right."

"I see," I said, controlling my sudden anger, and stepped a pace back from the stairs.

Her lip curled a bit. "I'm sure you do," she said, and went on up to the second floor.

So. I detected Volpinex's fine Mediterranean hand in that, goading Liz to test my obedience to the contract. The bastard was going to be an ongoing pain in the ass, was he? Or in the side.

Had he told Liz yet how he'd squashed me? She'd noticed my bruises last night and I'd just muttered something about an accident, but Volpinex would go into more detail than that. I take badly to humiliation, and that was the weapon he was turning against me.

What could I do to him? Wandering out to the kitchen, making myself a drink, I tried to think of some way to get back at him, make him lay off.

"I could kill him," I muttered aloud, surprising myself as much for the thought as for voicing it out loud in an empty room.

Kill him? No, that was merely one of those extravagant thoughts we all have sometimes. But what else was there? Carrying my drink out to the back deck and the late afternoon sun, I sat in a sling chair and brooded over the problem of Attorney Volpinex. I sipped at my drink and sopped up the last of the sun and after a while I snoozed.

When I awoke it was twilight, and the mosquitoes were growing interested. I went inside to a dark house and switched on some lights. Liz had gone, without saying anything, and Betty was having dinner with family friends. I had the house to myself.

So I got sloshed, which I very rarely do, and watched bad comedy on the living room television set until I passed out. I awoke around eleven with a splitting headache and an urgent desire to become sober; an hour later I was on my fifth cup of coffee and was watching *The Ladykillers* when Betty came in, looking cute but dated in her white frock. "Hi, there," she said. "All alone?"

"Liz had a conference with her lawyer."

"Oh, dear," she said, and sat on the other end of the sofa, half-turned toward me, her face and knees all giving me sympathetic study. "I know she's my sister," she said, "but I must admit she can be a trial sometimes."

"And a judgment others." On screen, Herbert Lom dispatched Cecil Parker on the cottage roof with Parker's own cane. Trundle trundle trundle down the tile.

Betty continued to study my profile. "I've never seen you like this," she said. "You know, quiet and serious."

Quiet and serious. I frowned at the television screen, unable to think of an answer to that, and suddenly realized I was being quiet and serious.

"It's strange about twins, isn't it?" she said.

I turned away from Alex Guinness's manic smile. "What's strange?"

"They're so alike, and yet they're so different."

Ah hah—profundity. It had been a while since I'd been Art in Betty's presence, and with my other problems to think about it was hard to reach for the right responses. Bart, of course, would simply have agreed with her yin-yang statement by adding a platitude of his own, but what would Art say?

Wonderful. I'd forgotten how to make believe I was Art.

In the meantime, Betty had filled my silence with more words of her own. "Like Liz and me," she said. "I know we look alike, but inside we're so different it's hard to believe sometimes that we're even related."

"I'll go along with that," I said. Discreet mayhem continued on the television screen.

"I bet it's the same with you and Bart," she said, and when I glanced at her again there was some sort of tiny glint in her eye. And was that the ghost of a playful smile manifesting itself around her lips?

And what have we here? My curiosity piqued and my

interest aroused, I said, "You think we're that different?"

"Well, I don't really know, do I?" Now it was her turn to look at the television screen, and the expression of innocence glued to her face was about as realistic as a Dacron wig.

"You've seen us both," I said.

A sidelong look. "Not the same way."

I reached out my left hand and used my forefinger to tap a knee. "You interested in a scientific experiment?"

She faced me, the innocent look tilted askew by a crooked grin. "Whatever do you mean?"

"I'd like to know if *you're* really different," I said.

"I'm sure you'd just be disappointed," she said, but the open smiling mouth and the sparkling eyes were saying, *Come and get it, come and get it.*

So I went and got it.

30   30

S UDDENLY, IN THE MIDDLE of the proceeding, the thought came to me, *I am cuckolding myself!* This was so startling that for a minute I wasn't at all sure it would be physically possible to go on. However, I rallied, and I don't think Betty noticed the slight sag in my narrative.

But the thought did not go away. God knows I've applied the horns to other men's brows, and I've always suspected the existence of some antlers of my own from my marriage to Lydia, so I know the appropriate state of mind for each of the potential roles, but what was I to think when playing both roles at once? Has such a thing ever happened before? Maybe somewhere in the *Decameron*, but what about real life?

As to Betty, this little bitch was supposed to be the *good* sister. Married four days, and straight into bed with another man, by God. Well, maybe not exactly another man, but certainly not her husband. Or in any case she didn't *know* it was her husband.

Just what sin was this, anyway? She was trying to commit adultery, God knows, but in truth she wasn't succeeding. On the other hand, she didn't know that. Was it a sin of intent? Can a sin that involves an action be a sin of intent?

And just who was I, in all this? For the first time, the twin brothers did both exist, simultaneously and in the same corpus, both thinking away at top speed. I was both sinned against and sinning, in identical proportions.

And as if that weren't enough, not only was Betty wildly different from her sister, a fact I'd already known, she was also very different from the Betty who slept with Bart. This Betty was rather more demanding, more vocal, and more readily satisfied. What madness was I into here? Doesn't *anybody* have a solid reliable personality you can count on?

Betty, who as Bart's bride always followed sex with a relaxed and boneless dreaminess, turned out in this version to be a toucher and a commenter and a nibbler, darting this way and that on my chest like a kitten on a shag rug. She consoled me for my rib bruises—I did my usual muttering about an accident, when asked—and complimented me on my belly button, which she apparently found of abiding interest.

So did I. Some of her other activities were also interesting, and soon we were at it again.

After that one, Betty loomed over my supine body, resting her forearms on my chest and smiling down at my face as she said, "Isn't it amazing?"

"Amazing," I agreed, though I had no idea what she

was talking about. Perhaps just twin-ness, the idea of distinction within identity.

"Sometimes I wonder about you two," she said, grinning knowingly at me.

"You do?"

"Yes," she said, and then she chilled my blood. "I've never seen you both at the same time," she said, and laughed at her idea. "Wouldn't that just be too awful? Then you'd be Bart, and you'd know everything."

"I don't think I'd like that," I said. "I'd rather be me."

"Mmm, you." She kissed my chest, while I searched frantically for a change of subject. But she switchéd all by herself, lifting her head again to say, "Well? Is there any difference?"

"Vive la différence," I told her, stroking her cheek. And then, since a certain curiosity on my part would surely be considered normal at this point, I said, "What about me? Am I different?"

She was smirking, grinning, giggling at me. "Close your eyes," she said, "and I'll tell you."

So I closed my eyes. I felt her leaning down over me, I felt the warmth of her breath in the cavern of my left ear and the trembling of her lips around my earlobe. "YOU'RE BETTER," she whispered.

31   31

WAS THAT A THOUGHT-
ful look in Betty's eye when she saw me off at the ferry? Was she remembering last night's joke, about never having seen the two of us together? Would that thought return to

her? "See you soon," I said, as the ferry started away from the dock.

Standing there in the sunlight in her white tennis shorts and yellow-and-white striped blouse, she smiled through her frown and called, "See you." And was her frown caused only by the sunlight?

Too many problems. I went into the cabin to sit down and try to think, and they all kept crowding in on me.

Liz, for instance. She had not come back at all last night, and still hadn't returned. I'd seen on the schedule that this ferry was leaving just after one o'clock, so at twelve-thirty I told Betty I was going back to the city, and I handed her a sealed envelope containing a note for Liz. "When you're ready to get married," the note said, "call me at the office."

Betty had said, "Do you have to go?" We'd started the day with another sexual encounter, but since then by unspoken mutual consent we'd returned to our previous friendly distant relationship.

"I can't stay here like a lapdog," I'd told her, "waiting for Liz to come back whenever she feels like it."

Betty had sympathized, had agreed, had promised to turn over the note, and now I was on the ferry, a nearly empty Sunday midday ferry, and I was heading back to the city with a full cargo of problems. Liz, and the contract, and Volpinex. Betty and her budding suspicions. My own continuing bewilderment about my attitude toward last night's fornication.

Ferry to cab, cab to train. On the train I wrote, "If I were twins—we'd want you all to ourselves." But no, that was the wrong image for Folksy Cards; I crumpled the piece of paper and threw it away.

Manhattan. I couldn't very well go to the Kerner apartment, so it was the sleeping bag in the office after all. Walking north from Penn Station into the garment district, deserted today, I found myself brooding over and over on the same phrase: "It's all done with mirrors, it's all done with mirrors."

Sure, mirrors. I remembered that bathroom morning at the Kerner apartment when I'd tried to recruit my reflection. Fat chance.

And then it dropped into my head, or popped up, or whatever the right image. John Dickson Carr. Years and years ago in some summer cottage somewhere I'd come across and read a mystery novel by John Dickson Carr, and in it the guy. . . .

Adaptable? I tried to visualize the whole thing, my outer office, my inner office, the hall door. Why wouldn't it work? No reason I could think of, not one.

"All right. All right." I said it aloud, and a twitching moustached old woman festooned with shopping bags looked up from the litter basket she was rifling and backed away from me as though *I* were the crazy one. I grinned at her, though probably not in a way she found reassuring, and said, "So she wants to see us both at the same time, does she? She'll *see* us both at the same time."

The woman fled, shopping bags aflutter. Cupping my hands around my mouth, I shouted after her, "It's all done with mirrors!"

32   32

AMIRROR IN THE GARment district? Easiest thing on earth: I picked one up on the way to the office.

In the same building, in fact. The service elevator doesn't run on Sundays, and the other elevator doesn't run ever, so I climbed the stairs, stopping off at the floor below mine to break into Froelich's Frocks by inserting my Master Charge card between the door and its frame.

Thousands of frocks. Another time, I probably would have picked up something nice for Gloria, but today I had no room in my head for nonessentials. I needed a mirror, approximately seven feet high and two feet wide, and freestanding. Come on, come on; the models have to look at themselves somewhere.

Right. In a rear room where half a dozen mirrors of exactly the right type, freestanding in their own frames. I picked one up, found it weighed a ton, and carried it upstairs anyway. Placed it in position, stepped back, stepped forward, squinted, frowned, studied.

Yes.

33   33

W<small>HEN</small> R<small>ALPH</small> <small>CALLED</small> at ten o'clock Monday morning, I was still groaning and creaking and waiting for Gloria's latest dose of Excedrin to start to work. A night in the sleeping bag on the office floor had done very little good for my body, and nothing at all for my disposition. Ralph identified himself, and I said, "Now what?"

"You wanted me to find out about your fiancée." He sounded surprised and hurt at my manner.

"Oh, that's right. Sorry, Ralph, I had a bad night."

"I'm sorry to hear that, Art. The wedding's still on, I hope."

"Not that kind of bad night. What have you got?"

"Well, in the first place," he said, "there are two Elizabeth Kerners."

"They're twins," I said.

"They're twins," he said. "They— Oh. You already knew about that?"

"Right. They spell the name differently. I'm interested in the one with the Z."

"All right," he said, and proceeded to tell me things I already knew about the late parents of my girls. The family was as rich as I'd been led to believe, and their business holdings were even more extensive than I'd guessed, in both this country and Canada. There were several collateral branches of the family, uncles and aunts and cousins, but while they tended to have some ownership of Kerner subsidiaries, the controlling interest in the entire empire had been retained by old Albert himself, and had now passed on to his two daughters. "They're suing one another, you know," Ralph said.

"Who is?"

"The girls. Elisabeth and Elizabeth."

"Suing each other? For what?"

"You didn't know about that?"

"Ralph," I said, "just answer the question."

"They're suing one another for control," he said. "Their marital status has something to do with that, something in their father's will. I couldn't get exact details without seeming too nosy. I'm an attorney, after all, not connected with the case."

"You're doing fine, Ralph," I told him, and he was. "Anything else?"

"The one with the Z—that's your girl friend?"

"Fiancée."

"She's been in some scrapes," he said doubtfully.

"I'm sure she has."

"I hope you know what you're doing, Art."

I glanced across at the mirror, next to the closed outer-office door. "I hope so, too," I said.

"Do you want details? About the scrapes?"

From the way he said it, I knew I didn't. "No, I don't think so," I said. "What about Volpinex?"

"The attorney?" he asked uselessly. "He only represents one of the sisters, of course."

"I know."

"The one with the Z, your girl friend."

"I know, Ralph. Give."

"Well," he said, "he's a bona fide member of the New York Bar."

"I thought he might be," I said, "but I need something even worse. Is he a crook? A pervert? A member of the Progressive Labor party? A government spokesman?"

"Afraid not," he said. "He's a junior partner in the firm of Leek, Conchell & McPoo, and they think very highly of him."

"They're wrong."

"Nevertheless. He was married once, but—"

"She divorced him? Extreme cruelty?"

"She died," he said. "Automobile accident, while they were on vacation in Maine."

"He killed her."

"Ha ha ha," Ralph said.

"He did, Ralph."

Ralph said, "Art, be careful with silly things like that. You can say them to me, but some people have no sense of humor."

"That's hard for me to believe, Ralph."

"A remark like that, meant all in fun, could nevertheless be construed as libel."

I hadn't meant it all in fun, but what was the point dragging on the conversation? I said, "Ralph, do you have anything negative about the son of a bitch at all, that I could use?"

"Sorry, Art," he said. "He may be as big a crook as you think, but if so he's covered his tracks."

"He would," I said. "He's a smart crook."

"They're the toughest to get something on," Ralph said seriously.

"You may have something there," I said. "Well, I do appreciate everything you've done for me, Ralph."

"What are friends for?" he asked, reasonably enough. "Oh, by the way, Candy told me to be sure to pass along her very best wishes on your impending marriage."

"She did, did she? That's sweet of her."

"She's a good old girl," he said complacently, and then we said our good-byes and we both hung up, and I sat back to contemplate for a while the look that must have been in Candy's eyes, the little crooked smile on her feline lips, when she'd sent to me through Ralph those best wishes.

Some time in the future, when I had all this twin business sorted out, I really had to take a pass through Candy's life just once more. For old time's sake.

34   34

At QUARTER PAST THREE, I began my rehearsals.

I'd sent Gloria home early, I had the mirror positioned just inside the inner office door, and I stood in the doorway in front of it practicing my moves. Half-blind with my lenses out and my glasses held at waist-level in my right hand, I told my reflection, "I'll think it over and we'll talk tomorrow." Then I stepped back, pulling the door shut toward me with my left hand while my right hand came up in a single robotlike gesture that slipped my glasses onto my face and continued up to tousle my hair backward from

Art's hair-forward style to Bart's hair-back appearance.

Last night, before inserting myself in my sleeping bag here, I'd made another Bart-from-Los-Angeles phone call to Betty, telling her I was coming back to town today. She wanted to meet me at the airport, of course, but I explained I was still troubled about the rift with Art, and that I wanted to take care of that before I saw her or did anything else. "I'll take a cab in from Kennedy," I'd told her, "and go see Art at the office. Why don't you meet me there?" We set the time at four o'clock.

And by three forty-five I was ready. At first my little Balinesian dance had been stiff and uncoordinated, but practice had made it perfect, and now my movements were smooth and assured. The mirror was angled right, the door was open just so, everything was ready. All I needed was my audience.

Nerves. Opening night jitters. I left the office, walked down past the freight elevator and back up the hall, down to the elevator and back to my office, fidgeting, scratching, constantly checking the time. Was Betty the kind who would show up early, or late? Would I still be able to do my glasses-and-hair gesture with this new aching stiffness across my shoulders? Would I be able to coordinate the movements of two hands, two feet, and one mouth while twitching like a sandpiper?

Every once in a while, the freight elevator would grind into motion. I would dash back to my office, stand just inside the door, try to calm my heart and my breathing, and listen to the groans and complaints as the elevator puffed its way upward.

To a different floor.

Ten minutes to four, five minutes to four, three minutes to four.

I stood by the elevator as it went downward after yet another false alarm. The stairs were next to it, with the door propped open in violation of the fire laws. I'd told Betty to take the freight elevator, but would she come up the stairs instead? I cocked an ear, trying to hear approaching footsteps.

Whinninninninninninne. The elevator was coming up again. This time pretending disdain, I strolled casually back to my office and was barely out of sight when the damn thing *greek*ed to a stop at this floor.

I'm on! I shut the outer door, crossed the office to the inner door, stood facing the doorway and the mirror. My lips and mouth were dry, and I worked at producing a little saliva, so I'd be able to speak. With my left hand on the doorknob and my right hand clutching the glasses, I looked into the mirror, past my own reflection at the corridor door. Silently I rehearsed my line: "I'll think it over and we'll talk tomorrow. I'll think it over and we'll talk tomorrow. I'll think it—"

The corridor door opened. Betty walked in.

Now, let me tell you what Betty saw. She entered the room, and she saw Bart with his back to her in the doorway opposite, in conversation with Art. She could clearly see Art's face, spectacleless and with hair brushed forward, beyond Bart's right shoulder. She saw Art's lips move, and she heard Art say, "I'll think it over and we'll talk tomorrow." Then, as it seemed to her, Art pushed the door closed in Bart's face, forcing Bart back a step. Bart moved back, turning, lifting his hand to his head in a distraught manner, and finished turning to blink through his spectacles, lower his hand again from his brushed-back hair, and say, "Betty!"

"Darling!" Betty responded, combining the joy of reunion very delicately with a sudden concern. She hurried across the room to me, saying, "Was there trouble?"

I'd previously decided my best manner at this juncture would be a slight vagueness, a distraction caused by a combination of jet lag and the argument with Art. It was a happy decision, as it turned out, because a numb befuddlement was about all I was capable of at that moment. The mirror, Artless, was just the other side of that door. An

entire Artless room, in fact, was just the other side of that
door. How on earth could I have hoped to get away with
such a juvenile stunt? "Trouble?" I echoed. "Trouble?"

"I saw Art just now," she said, gesturing toward that
rather special door, "and he—"

"You did? You saw him, eh?"

"Of course. And it didn't look to *me* as though you two
were getting along."

A great flamingo-wing smile spread across my face. I
couldn't help it, I just couldn't help it. "Quite the contrary," I said. By God, it had worked! "I think," I said, "I
think everything's going to be all right."

"But he was—I saw him—"

"I know you did, my love," I said, and gave her a great
big kiss. I didn't even *care* that she wasn't faithful to me.
"Don't worry about Art," I told her, "that's just his manner. He can't come down off a mad all at once. Believe me,
I know him, things are fine now. I'll call him tomorrow
and we'll be buddies again."

"If you say so," she said.

"Listen, let's get out of here," I said. "Give him a chance
to sulk and get it over with."

She frowned in the general direction of the closed door.
Was she thinking of going in there, arguing with Art on
my behalf? No. She shook her head and said, "Well, you
know him better than I do."

I might have disputed that, but I didn't. Instead, I held
the door for her, we left the office, and we rode the in-
terminable freight elevator down down down.

As we were leaving the building, Candy was going in.
She looked grim, and she brushed by us with hardly a
glance. I admit I was startled, but I don't think anything
showed.

Oh, but what if she'd arrived first? What if she'd been
the one to get out of the elevator and open the office door
to see the twin charade? What if Betty had walked in
second, to find one brother, one mirror, and one strange

woman, instead of the well-rehearsed playlet about Art and Bart? A close call, that.

Carlos and the Lincoln were out front. Betty and I got in, and as we started away it seemed to me that from the corner of my eye I saw Candy appear again in the building entrance, staring, perhaps frowning, toward our car. But I didn't look back.

35   35

LIZ CAME TO THE OFFICE Wednesday morning. Gloria tried to announce her, but Liz barged on in and said, "Okay, I'm here. Let's go get married." Gloria did a discreet double take, and withdrew.

Slowly I looked up. "No," I said.

This was two days after Betty had seen Art and Bart both at the same time, and I'd spent the intervening hours assessing my situation and coming to some firm conclusions. Such as that I definitely was not going to marry Liz.

Bart had been born on August fifth, twenty-three days ago, during my initial conversation with this bitch, and from then on I'd had practically no time to myself. August was damn near over by now, and I hadn't even *seen* it. I'd started a con for the hell of it, and then I'd spent the next three weeks scrambling around like a cat in a full bathtub, going going going every second.

All of which had now come to a screeching halt. After Monday's mirror routine, Betty and I had spent a pleasant evening together on the town (on her), and a pleasant night together in her apartment (ditto), with the lights firmly off so she wouldn't recognize any of Art's bruises on Bart's body. Then on Tuesday morning I'd kissed her good-bye and gone off to be reunited with my loving brother. And for the first time in weeks, I was faced with an entire day to myself, a day in which I was neither Art with Liz nor Bart with Betty, a day without schemes, phone calls, split-second timing, near misses, or jerry-built explanations.

Tuesday, August twenty-seventh; a date to resound in history. Maybe I could get some Central American republic to name an *avenida* after it. *El Bulevar de la Paz del Agosto 27.*

What a day. I basked in my solitude in the inner office, I took Gloria to lunch and paid her share, I returned a call from my sister Doris and was both sympathetic and understanding, I sent off partial payment checks to three of my illustrators, and I wrote another card: "The front of the card, with no illustration, says, 'Things ain't been the same since you went away.' The entire inside, left and right panels, is covered with a drawing of an old house bursting with a huge party: Roman candles over the roof, half-naked girls hanging out windows, a beer truck on the lawn with a hose extending in through a window, etc. etc."

Etc.

And through it all, that whole long peaceful riverboat of a day, I considered my alternatives. Now was the time to decide once and for all what it was I wanted, and what I didn't want.

What I didn't want. I didn't want anyone to catch on to the twin gimmick. I didn't want to lose my entree to the Kerner money. I didn't want to go to jail, or to be hounded by a rich family with a grudge. I also didn't want friend Volpinex to do any more cute stunts with squash balls, nor with karate moves, nor anything else.

What I did want. Money. Every creature comfort I could think of, and others as they occurred to me. An Alfa Romeo. Unlimited air travel. Stables out back. Another Alfa Romeo. A separate room just for my clothing, and more clothing than would fit in it. Soft women on hard beds. Winters in Palm Springs or Palm Beach or Palma; I'm not picky. Summers in air conditioning. Nights under the stars, under the sheets, under the influence, and under the protection of money. Money. A Jaguar, a Rolls-Royce, and another Alfa Romeo. And money.

All of which seemed clear enough. I should marry a Kerner sister and live happily ever after. *One* Kerner sister. Marry one Kerner sister, stop the twin game at once, kick sand over my trail, and go whistling off into contentment and joy.

Greed, that's my big problem. I'd had this worked out once before, even with the details of unloading Folksy Cards and mothballing Art, creating disruptive arguments to explain his disappearance while Bart wallowed in the luxury of his married state, whirl without end, amen. And then Liz had come along, with the siren song of that bloody contract, two grand a month, money *and* freedom, and I just couldn't stop myself. I'd signed, I'd signed, and I'd been moving with the speed of a Gilbert and Sullivan chorus line ever since.

So it was time to stop. I'd had two days to tie myself to the mast; sing, damn you, nobody gets *me*. And when Liz came stalking in, arrogant and sure of herself, to say, "Let's go get married," my answer was an immediate and irrevocable, "No."

"Bullshit," she said. She dropped into the other chair, crossed her ankles, gave me a jaundiced look, and said, "How much?"

"No much," I told her. "The deal's off."

"We have a contract."

"Which doesn't go into effect until the marriage ceremony."

A frown line formed vertically between her brows. "I don't have time for crap, Art," she said. "We made a deal. You can't hold me up for more money, I won't give it to you."

"And I wouldn't take it," I said. "I'm through, Liz. I don't like you and I won't marry you."

The frown grew more intense, and then softened a bit. In a different tone she said, "I pushed you too hard, huh?"

"You and Volpinex," I agreed. "That's part of it."

"What's the rest?"

"You're using me. This marriage business is just a dodge."

"You're just a Dodge yourself," she said, and grinned at me.

"You know what I'm talking about."

"The tax problem? I told you that right from the beginning, why get upset about it now? Sam isn't your *real* uncle, you know."

"Not the three million," I said. "The lawsuit."

A sudden stillness settled on her face and body. Carefully she said "Lawsuit?"

"Between you and your sister. That's the main thing it's all about; this tax evasion thing is just secondary."

"Who told you about the lawsuit?"

"What does it matter? I won't be used that way."

She leaped to her feet, and in a very cold way she was blazing. "I want to know who told you about the lawsuit. Was it Ernie?"

"I wish I could say yes," I told her. "I'd love to see you two at each other's throat. But if I lied to you he'd wriggle out of it somehow."

"He's smarter than you are," she said. "Who told you? Not Betty."

"Bart told me."

"Bart!" She looked around, and I saw her registering the fact that my famous brother wasn't here. Except in a way: haggard-eyed, he looked at me from the depths of Froelich's mirror, tucked in a far corner of the room. "How would *he* know?" Liz demanded. "And where is he, anyway?"

Ignoring the second question, I answered the first: "Betty told him."

"Don't be silly. Why would Betty talk to your brother about something like that?"

"Because they're married," I said.

That was my first bombshell, and it was wonderful to watch the bicycles and fence parts and human bodies *whooommm* up into the air when it hit. Liz actually staggered back, hit the chair she'd been sitting in before, and dropped into it again. Bull's eye.

By God, this time I was going to do it. Spread trouble and strife, cut Art loose from the rest of them, and *disappear*.

"Why that little—" Liz was whispering, mostly to herself. "That little bitch," she whispered, and then gradually focused on me again and said, "Are you sure of that?"

"Absolutely. Some couple from Far Hills stood up for them. They were married in New Jersey."

"How long ago?"

"Last week some time."

"That bitch," Liz repeated, and glowered past me at the wall. Bloody thoughts moved behind her eyes, like a jungle at night.

"You people are too much for me," I said. "Maybe Bart can put up with it, but from now on I'm. . . ." And my voice trailed away, because I'd attracted Liz's attention again. Her brooding gaze shifted to me, and she said, "We can be in Connecticut in less than two hours. We've had our blood tests more than four days, and there's no waiting period there after you get the license."

"You're not listening, Liz," I said. "The deal's off. I think you people stink, and I don't want anything to do with you."

"You don't have to have anything to do with me," she said. She was hard and urgent and brisk. "We're talking about a strictly business proposition, you don't ever have to lay eyes on me again after today, but today we're going to get married."

"Absolutely not."

"You want more money, isn't that it? What's your price now?"

"No price," I said. Certain flutterings were taking place in my brain, but I ignored them. "I'm not trying to get a better deal, I'm telling you it's *no* deal."

"But *why?* It's strictly business, a marriage in name only, you never have to *see* me again. Once this legal business is settled, you can get a divorce, an annulment, if you want."

"No."

"What, is there some supermarket cashier you're crazy for? If you want another woman, that's no—"

"There's no other woman. I just don't want the deal." I leaned forward across the desk, spreading my hands, saying, "Come on, Liz, the woods are full of bachelors. Two thousand dollars a month and options on your bed—with terms like that you could enlist an army."

"Bums off the street?" Her lip curled, then straightened again as she said, "It won't do, Art. The man has to be presentable, he has to be *possible*. Not so much for the tax people, but for the court. You know the kind of life I live; the people I see at home are too rich and too straight arrow for a deal like this, and the people I meet when I go out I couldn't bring into court with me. I've been looking all year, believe me I have, and you're the first real possibility I've come up with."

"What about Volpinex? He'd marry you in a minute."

"Not me," she said. "I wouldn't go near him, he terrifies me."

"Terrifies *you?*"

She'd come in with a canvas shoulder bag, and now she pawed into it and said, "All right, I believe you, you really want to call it off. But I can't afford that, Art." She had brought out, I saw, a checkbook and a pen, and now she paused and gave me a look of urgent sincerity. "I pushed you too hard," she said. "I could tell you that was Ernie's idea, and it was, but that wouldn't make any difference. You don't like me, okay, that's all right. I promise you won't have to see me after today unless you *want* to see me. I'm asking your help in a business matter, and that's all it is. Strictly." And she dipped her head to start writing something in her checkbook.

Mice were nibbling the ropes holding me to the mast. "Don't—don't write anything there," I said. "I'm not interested." (But I wouldn't have to see her. Bart and Art could have a final falling-out. Art could marry *and* disappear, and still get his two thousand every month.) (No no no no no. Remember your vow. Don't let greed get the upper hand.) (Remember the Main Chance.) (But you wanted to get *out* of this.)

She'd finished writing, *Rrrip* came a check out of the checkbook, and she leaned forward to float it like an aircraft carrier onto my desk. "That's extra," she said. "In addition to everything in the contract, just an extra little wedding present. To make up for the inconvenience."

Have you ever tried not to look at a check someone has just tossed on your desk? This one had a straight slash at the beginning of the number and then an awful lot of circles. It had a 1, and a 0, and a comma, and another 0, and another 0, and another 0, and a period, and still another 0, and then one final 0, and that was it.

Ten thousand dollars.

The mice ate through the ropes. The nibbled lengths fell to the deck, and oh, the sirens sang so sweetly.

Liz knew she had me. She didn't wait for me to say anything, she simply put the checkbook and pen away and got to her feet. "It's ten-thirty," she said. "I'll have a car out front for you in an hour." She started toward the door.

My hand rested gently, palm down, on the check. I could feel those zeroes against my flesh. "Wait," I said.

She stopped in the doorway and looked back at me, ready for anything. "Yes?"

"Make it an Alfa Romeo," I said.

36   36

CONVERSATIONS:

"Kairnair rezeedonce."

"Hello, Nikki, this is Bart Dodge. Could I speak with Betty, please?"

"One moment, pleeze."

nnnnnnnnnnnnnnnnnnnnnnnnnnnnnnnnnnnnnnnnnnnnn

"Hello, Bart?"

"Betty?"

"Bart, is this important? I was just rushing out to lunch, I'm meeting Dede at Bonwit's, she's in town for the day and—"

"It's important, Betty."

"Bart? Is something wrong?"

"I have to ask you a couple questions, Betty."

"Bart, you sound so serious. What is it, darling, what's the trouble?"

"I've just had a long talk with Art. He told me some things. I just don't know what to make of it."

"Have you two boys been fighting again? Has he been saying things to try to hurt you, sweetheart? Don't listen to things people say in anger, darling."

"He told me some things about you, Betty."

"About me? I have no idea what your brother could possibly find to say about me, in fact I don't even want to hear it, but surely you can see that things a person says in the heat of anger don't—"

"I have to ask you about them, Betty. You can see that, can't you, I do have to know."

"Well, I'll simply deny everything categorically, even before I hear it. What on earth could your brother know about me, we've hardly ever even seen one another, if he wasn't your identical twin I doubt I'd even recognize him on the street. I think it's very cruel of you to listen to malicious gossip against me. We've only been married eight days, and already you're doubting me, you're—"

"About the taxes, Betty."

"You're—the what?"

"Taxes."

"Taxes?"

"Art says you married me because you have to be married by the end of the year for tax reasons."

"This is about *taxes*? You wanted to talk about *taxes*?"

"Is it true, Betty?"

"Oh, ha ha ha ha ha. Oh *ho*, ha ha ha ha ha hau ha."

"Betty, this is serious. I have to know."

"Oh, ha ha, I know you do, ha ha, my darling. Oh, you sweet man, I could hug you and kiss you and eat you all up."

"Is it true? About the taxes, is it true?"

"That I'll save money if I'm a married lady? Yes, it is, sweetheart, absolutely true."

(Hurt silence.)

"Bart, dear?"

"I see."

"But sweetheart, that isn't *why* I married you. I married you because I *love* you, darling. You swept me off my feet, it was a whirlwind romance, I've never been happier in my life than I am right now, and the money doesn't have a thing to do with it."

"Then why didn't you ever tell me about it?"

"I was afraid to, dear."

"Afraid to? Why?"

"I didn't want you to think—ha ha—you know, that I was marrying you for my money."

"Are you sure, Betty?"

"Oh, sweetheart, don't you remember this morning?"

"Sure I remem—"

"And last night?"

"Yeah, I re—"

"And yesterday morning?"

"I remember it *all*, Betty."

"Then how can you doubt me? Sweetheart, we'll talk about it at dinner, but right now I really must rush, Dede's waiting for me at—"

"But what about the lawsuit?"

"What about the what, dear?"

"You and your sister are suing each other for control of the Kerner businesses, and it's important in the lawsuit that you be married."

"Did Art say that, too?"

"Yes, he did."

"Just where does he get all this information?"

"From Liz, I suppose. And I guess it's true, isn't it?"

"Darling, husbands and wives all over the *country* are a financial help to one another: they file joint income tax returns, they put businesses in one another's name, they do all sorts of money things for one another, but that doesn't mean they don't *love* one another."

"The question is, why didn't you tell me about all this? The taxes, and the lawsuit. Don't you trust me?"

"Of course I do, my darling. I just didn't want you to worry, that's all. I didn't want you to get the suspicions in your mind that you have right now. This is what I've been trying to avoid."

"By lying to me."

"I didn't *lie* to you, sweetheart, I just didn't tell you every last single bit of the truth. And that's only because I'm so in love with you."

"Then why did you go to bed with Art?"

(Stunned silence. But *stunned*.)

"I'm sorry, Betty, I don't think I can go on like this."

"Buh-Bart—"

"It's too late to deny it. Art told me everything, he told me . . . details, he told me things he couldn't have known if it wasn't true."

"Um. Bart, dear."

"The taxes, and then the lawsuit, and then this."

"Darling. Bart, please listen to me for a minute."

"You have to meet Dede at Bonwit's."

"Bart, I've been wrong. Yes, that did happen, what you said, what Art said. But I swear it wouldn't have happened if he didn't look so much like you."

"Oh, Betty, for—"

"It's true, darling, dearest. But oh, when we got to bed, I regretted it. He isn't a bit like you, he doesn't know how to make a woman feel like a woman. Not the way you do."

"You mean I'm better, huh?"

"Darling, let's start over again, brand new. We can still make it, I know we can."

"I'm sorry, Betty."

"Bart, what are you going to do?"

"I have to be by myself for a while, I have to think things out."

"Oh, my darling, it kills me to have hurt you this way."

"I'll . . . I'll call you in a day or two."

"Yes, Bart. Bart?"

"Yes?"

"Always remember, dearest, I do love you."

(Pregnant silence.)

"Bart? Darling?"

"I'll call you in a day or two."

* * *

Buzz.

"Yes?"

"A Mrs. Ralph Minck on the line."

"Tell her I've joined the Trappist monks."

"Yes, sir."

* * *

"Lo?"

"Feeney?"

"Yeah?"

"This is your landlord speaking."

"Oh, hi, Art, how ya dune?"

"Next Monday is Labor Day, Feeney."

"Oh yeah. I'll be outa here by then, don't worry. I'm packin' already."

"You'll be returning to Cornell, Feeney?"

"Yeah, man."

"That's wonderful. Feeney, do you know a bar in Ithaca named O'Hanahee's?"

"That's a dive, man, that's no place to hang out."

"Good, you know the place. Feeney, two of the regular patrons of O'Hanahee's are old friends of mine from union-busting days. They're called Brock Lujenko and Big Horse Tumwatt. You ever meet those fellas, Feeney?"

"They don't sound like the crowd I hang out with, man."

"Feeney, I was in the apartment last week. You were out."

"Oh, yeah? I guess it was kinda messy."

"It looked as though Laurel and Hardy had just left."

"Hee hee."

"The point is, Feeney, you're going to clean it up."

"Oh, yeah, sure."

"Spotless. Immaculate. Exactly as delivered to you."

"Certainly, man."

"Because otherwise, sometime during the fall semester, you will meet my old friends Brock Lujenko and Big Horse Tumwatt."

"Oh. Yeah?"

"Yeah. I'll be moving in Tuesday."

"It'll be clean, man. Don't you worry about a thing."

"I'm not worried. Believe me, Feeney, in the ebb and

flow of life you are the least of my worries."

"Yeah?"

"Yeah."

* * *

Buzz.

"Hah?"

"Miss Linda Ann Margolies."

"In person?"

"On the phone."

"Ah. Tell her . . . No, never mind, I'll talk to her."

"Mm hm."

Click. "Miss Margolies?"

"How quickly they forget."

"Eh?"

"If you recall, I believe we were naked on your office floor at the time, I said, 'Call me Linda,' and you said—"

" 'Call me irresponsible.' It all comes back to me. How are you, Linda?"

"My shoulder blades are healing up just fine. And how are *you*, Irresponsible?"

"Exactly."

"Who's on first."

"That's right."

"Well, what I'm calling about—"

"Sorry, miss, I gave at the office."

"Yes, I remember. And *you* remember my thesis."

"Is that what that was? You remember my pickle, don't you?"

"It's a dilly."

"No, Linda. We don't descend to material like that."

"The hell we don't. I want to send you my thesis."

"I'm not sure it'll fit on a card."

"Listen, Eerie, things are—"

"Listen *what*?"

"Eerie. That's short for Irresponsible."

"I'd rather you called me Sibyl."

"Fine with me. Listen, Sibyl, what I want is—"

"I'm not sure I came out ahead on that one."

"What I *want*, Jack, is for you to read my thesis and tell me what you think of it."

"I think it's the cuddliest, furriest little thesis I ever—"

"Sibyl."

"Right. I'd love to read your thesis, I really would, but I can't promise when. I've got a lot, uh, going on right now."

"That's okay, I have a month before it's due."

"Then send it along."

"You may not like the title."

"Oh? What is it?"

"Comedy: The Coward's Response to Aggression."

"Well, it's hard to tell without the music."

"It's a tango."

"So send me two copies."

"Oh, God."

"He's a dilly."

"Yours was worse."

"No, it wasn't. What did the cannibal give his sweetheart for Valentine's Day?"

"A box of farmers' fannies."

"Did you hear about the guy who parted his hair from ear to ear?"

"He thought it was wonderful till somebody whispered in his nose."

"Linda, is there no rotten joke you don't know?"

"There are three of them, in fact."

"Whi— Oh, no, you don't. Good-bye, Linda."

"Almost gotcha. Almost gotcha."

* * *

"Gloria, I've—"

"Hold on a minute, till I finish typing."

"Letter to your mother?"

"Company business. Tax form for the state."

"Don't show it to me!"

"I wasn't going to show it to you."

"Just sign my name and send it to them."

"There's a check should go with it."

"So enclose a letter saying, 'Please find check.' "

"Do I enclose a check?"

"Don't waste time with silly questions. I have a car waiting. Type, type."

Clackety clackety clackety clackety—zzzzip

"Okay, now what?"

"First of all, here's your paycheck."

"How come? It's only Wednesday."

"You'll notice it's postdated. So is this bonus check, in honor of Labor Day."

"A hundred— You don't think I'd try to cash this, do you?"

"Faith and patience, that's what you need. Now, *this* is a check and deposit slip for the Wonderful Folks account, which I'd like you to deposit for me."

"TEN THOU—"

"Hush! Hush!"

"Ten thousand *dollars*?"

"Miss Kerner is investing in Those Wonderful Folks."

"She's off her tree."

"Be that as it may, that check is as good as the girl atop the unicorn. Now, we're gonna close up shop right now, you'll deposit this check on your way home, by Friday the account will be full and green and beautiful, and you can cash these other two checks.

"Wait a minute. I don't come back after lunch?"

"No. And we're not opening tomorrow or Friday either. We'll take a long Labor Day vacation. I'll see you Tuesday."

"Well, that's fine with me."

"Gloria."

"What's up? You're up to something."

"You don't want to know about it."

"Agreed."

"But you *do* want to know what to say if anybody asks

you where my twin brother Bart is."

"Are you *still* playing that game?"

"I'm getting out from under right now. If it should happen that you are asked, if anybody wants to know where Bart Dodge is, it is your understanding that the brothers quarreled, and that Bart Dodge has severed his connection with this office and is unlikely to return."

"Amen."

"There's light at the end of the tunnel, Gloria."

"Pray it isn't a flamethrower."

"What a kidder."

37

LESS THAN THREE MINUTES after Gloria left, while I was still battening down the office hatches for an extended separation, the hall door opened and two guys walked in, strangers to me. They were wearing identical short-sleeved white shirts open at the neck, and they seemed larger than most people. "Sorry, gents," I said, "I'm just closing up."

"That's okay," one of them said, coming in the rest of the way, and shut the hall door behind himself.

"Listen," I said, "I'm in something of a hurry. I'm going away and—"

"That's right," the other one agreed, and extended a white envelope toward me. "Here's your ticket."

"Ticket?" Frowning at them, trying to connect the idea of a ticket with Liz having told me earlier that she'd send a car for me, thinking confusedly that these people must be from Liz or how would they know I was going away, I now saw that they were really very large indeed, thick-necked and broad-shouldered and heavy-armed. They looked like football players arriving at the stadium.

I took the envelope. They watched me with their heavy faces, neither of them saying anything, so I opened the envelope and took out what was obviously an airline ticket. Opening that, I saw my own name, plus those ranks of letters and numbers by means of which airline employees manage to communicate with one another without being overheard by the customer. It took a few seconds to sort out: the "JFK" after "From" would be Kennedy airport, where Bart had soared off for California. And the destination? "To: St. Martin."

"St. Martin?"

"That's right," one of them said. "It's an island."

"In the Caribbean," the other one said. "You'll love it."

"Wait a minute, now," I said. "Miss Kerner sent you here with this?"

They both chuckled, which sounded like the bass fiddle section tuning up. "It don't matter where the ticket come from," one of them said. "What matters is that you use it."

"I don't get this." Maybe I was slow, but I actually didn't get it. Tell me a joke and I'll get it; lean on me and you'll just confuse me.

"You're gonna take a trip," one of them said. "You're gonna lie around on the sand and enjoy yourself."

"And every day," the other one said, "you'll go to the post office at Marigot, on the French side of the island, and you'll ask is there a letter for you."

"And some day," the first one said, "there will be a letter. And in it will be a ticket to come back again."

"And," the second one said, "you won't come back until you get that letter."

"Are you two crazy?"

"Not likely, friend."

"What—what—who's idea is this?" I was trying to

think: a joke? Some confusion with Liz? It made no sense to me.

"You don't need to know who it is," the first one said. "Just think of him as a benefactor."

"A secret admirer," the second one said, and they both nodded and smiled at me.

"Volpinex!" I said, and I suddenly saw the whole thing. Their smiles turned to frowns. The first one said, "Throwing names around, that's not a nice thing to do."

"He's not getting away with it." Angry, I tossed the ticket on Gloria's desk and said, "You can give him that, and tell him I'm staying here and getting married."

"You're a very dumb fella," the first one told me.

"He needs an explanation," the second one suggested.

"Maybe so." The first one frowned—his manner was a bit impatient, a bit pedantic, but mostly disappointed in my denseness—and he said, "See, what our job is, my friend here and me, we send people away. This fella doesn't want that fella around any more, so we send him away."

"That's right," the second one said.

"Now, we got two different ways," the first one said, holding up two meaty fingers, "to send people away. The first is we take a fella to the bus station or the airport or whatever, and put him on board, and wish him like a bon voyage."

"That's right," the second one said.

"Now, the second way," the first one said, "is we take people to the hospital after some bones have been broken. Like leg bones, or maybe a back, maybe a shoulder. All depends how long the fella's supposed to be away."

"That's right," the second one said.

I stared at them. They were talking like the heavies in a B movie, they were talking melodrama. Therefore I laughed at them, right? Wrong. I looked at them, and I saw that if they wanted to pretend I was a beachball and toss me back and forth, then that's what they would do, and no way would I stop them. And I noticed that I was alone in this office with these two guys, and I further noticed that they seemed to be very conscientious workmen, dedicated to their job. I backed a step away from them, wondering if I could make it into my inner office, lock the door, phone the police (no, they'd break the door down before I finished dialing), and I said, "Now, look."

"What our job is this time," the first one said, going on placidly with his explanation, "is to take you to your apartment and help you pack, and then take you to the airport and put you on the plane."

"Unless you argue with us," the second one said.

The first one nodded. "That's right."

"In that case," the second one said, "our job is to take you to the hospital."

Comedy: The Coward's Response to Aggression. Inside I was raging, a death-red glow of fury and hate. I said, "Well, I'll go away with you, but I just know you won't respect me in the morning."

38   38

WHEN I SAW THE ALFA, I knew I couldn't do it.

Coming interminably down in the freight elevator, my two new friends standing on either side of me like temple columns ("my name, dear, is Simpson, not Samson,"), I had given myself any number of reasons why what was happening to me was not really a defeat after all, but might even be considered in some ways a victory. Art Dodge, driven out of town by Ernest Volpinex, would disappear from the scene. Tomorrow, Bart Dodge would

sneak back from St. Martin, have a wonderful reconciliation with Betty, and live happily for the foreseeable future.
With any luck, I might even get to keep Liz's ten thousand
dollars; if it cleared before she put a stop payment on it.
I'd known all along I should stop playing this twin game,
should settle into one persona and begin to harvest my
crops, so now circumstances were forcing me to take the
road I had already acknowledged to be the path of wisdom. And if the taste in my mouth was partly bile, if the
lump in my throat was partly rage, if the fact of my exile
was mostly Volpinex's victory rather than mine, so what?
Bart could get even with him for me later.

That was what I'd talked myself into during the elevator
ride. But when we stepped out to the street and I saw that
white Alfa Romeo illegally parked by the fire hydrant in
front of the building, dealer plates wired on and green-
shirted driver from the dealership waiting there to hand
me the keys, I knew I couldn't do it. I couldn't lie to myself about victory and defeat, I couldn't con myself into
wisdom or acceptance, and I goddamn well couldn't take
any airplane to any island in any Caribbean.

The street was its usual workday derangement of activity. The garment district is New York's version of the
Baghdad marketplace, with trucks instead of camels,
wheeled garment racks instead of burros, and taxis taking
the place of the vizier's horsemen. A ferment of tongues
is heard, all of them degradations of one or another major
language: spic, yid and black predominate, but wop, wog,
and various variants of chink are also featured, plus other
rarer spices in this or that section of the stew. (What the
fellas in the turbans speak I don't know, but it sounds like
warm shit being stirred by wooden spoons.)

"This way," one of my teammates said. "We're parked
around the corner." So the three of us turned right and
moved away from the building and the lovely white Alfa
(I knew better than to look back at it, though I wanted to)
and walked off along the buckled sidewalk into the di-

shevelment of the garment district.

We walked three abreast, of course, which wasn't easy in that crowd, and several representatives of society's disadvantaged races gave us dirty looks as they stepped off the curb to go around us; three white men taking up the whole damn sidewalk.

Soon we found ourselves moving slowly behind a drove of slow-moving garment racks, propelled by a rabble of spics and spades. The former spoke Cockroach, their version of Spanish, and the latter spoke Harlem, a bastardization of English composed principally of the noun *muhfur* and the adjective *muhfun*.

We were almost to the corner, walking closely behind this shuffling shoal, when I suddenly raised my head and yelled, "You fuckin' niggers move your fuckin' black asses out of the way!"

The number of eyes that turned in my direction was gratifying. Linking my arms with my bewildered comrades, marching forward, I loudly announced, "We're comin' through, jigaboos, so move it!"

The first punch was thrown by a musclebound black whose T-shirt fit him like Saran Wrap, turning his ripply chest and shoulders into a snowbound anatomical study. The punch was thrown at me, but I was no longer there to catch it. The instant I saw that arm rear back I turned and ran.

There was yelling behind me, some of it in actual English. Racing at top speed, skipping sideways between garment racks, hopping over fire hydrants and cardboard cartons, lunging through clusters of dolly-wheeling trolls, sliding along the plate glass windows of the button factory, I didn't look back until I was parallel with the Alfa, and even then I didn't stop. I took it for granted I'd have to leave the neighborhood for a while, and running would be faster than the stop-and-go single lane of taxi-truck-tourist traffic oozing along the middle of the street.

Yes, I would have to depart. Here they came, running

along after me, bowling over the pedestrians I'd skirted, creating secondary fist fights and shouting matches in their wake, and even from here I could see the murder in their eyes.

Not my friends of the airline ticket; they were way back where I'd left them, barely discernible in a whirling frenzy of pummeling arms and legs. It was a flying squad of jiga-boos, led by my friend in the form-fitting T-shirt, that was pounding after me now, and I really doubted St. Martin was the destination for me they had in mind. Facing forward again, knocking down a pair of fat female Puerto Rican sewing machine operators starting out for an early lunch (spic-ettes? spic-esses?), I bounded over their bar-relly bodies and ran for daylight.

39

AFTER THE CEREMONY I kissed the bride and she got into the Lincoln with the best man and left for parts unknown. The other witness, or maid of honor, was the JP's ugly daughter, and so remained in her original setting: picket fence, sagging sofa, black-and-white television set the size of the mouth of the Holland Tunnel.

My escape from the race riot I'd started had been accomplished with the help of a taxi ride up Sixth Avenue. When I'd come back twenty minutes later, police cars were clustered at the end of the block where the fight had begun, and much shouting was taking place back there. The green-shirted auto dealer man, unaltered, continued to lean on the Alfa's fender, one fixed point in a disintegrating age, until I identified myself. With neither small talk nor surprise, he handed me the keys and the provisional registration and an envelope containing instructions on where to meet Liz for the taking-out-the-license ritual in Stamford, and then he faded away while I entered my Alfa.

Life. It *can* be sweet. This creature smelled not like an ordinary new car but like the world's most expensive new glove. Starting the engine (a snarling purr), waiting while a police car full of bloodied blacks went by, I joined the ebb of vehicles, edged my way cautiously through the miserable traffic of midtown to the West Side Highway, then opened it up and just had a wonderful time on the Henry Hudson Parkway, the Cross Bronx Expressway, and the Connecticut Turnpike to Stamford. I got there first and hung around outside in the sunlight until the familiar black Lincoln rolled to a stop by a fortuitous fire hydrant. Liz got out of the back, with somebody she described as "the best man."

I looked at him. "Are you sure?" This creature was alleged to be a rock musician from Toronto, but appeared to be almost entirely rock, with little left for musician. The only word he knew in English was, "Yuh." I didn't try him on any other languages, but I doubt he would have shown much proficiency no matter what the tongue.

"Let's go get it over with," Liz said, and I handed her my three new speeding tickets, saying, "I suppose you have people who can take care of these."

She glanced at them, put them away in her shoulder bag, and said, "Don't make me a widow before the lawsuit's over, okay?"

"Your concern," I told her, "inspires me to greater heights of self-protection."

"Mm," she said, and we went inside to get the legal papers. Thence to the JP for a scene out of a thirties comedy—except that the old farmer marrying us wasn't wearing a ratty bathrobe and didn't have his false teeth out

—and by three o'clock the deed had been done. "So much for that," Liz said.

"Just think," I said. "We're Mr. and Mrs. Arthur Drew Dodge."

"Sure," she said, got into the Lincoln with Yuh, and off they went. The JP, Missis JP, and Daughter JP stood on the porch by the glider and waved and waved, till they noticed the groom was still right here. "Well, so long folks," I said, hopped into the Alfa, and spurred away. Behind me, they formed a tableau, lined up along the porch rail, mouths open, hands up to wave but not quite waving. Not what you'd call waving.

40   40

ERNEST VOLPINEX, PLEASE."

"Who shall I say is calling?"

"Art Dodge," I said, "Tell him I'm not on the plane."

"One moment, please."

I was briefly again in my office before heading north to some tranquil hideaway. Lake Placid, maybe; the sound of it was exactly what I had in mind. A placid time out, a rest period between halves. Perhaps on Saturday or Sunday I'd call Betty and reluctantly permit Bart to be drawn into a reconciliation scene.

"Volpinex here."

"Ah, yes," I said. "And this is Art Dodge, *still* here."

"My secretary said you wanted to talk about an airplane," he said.

"Oh, really? You're going to be innocent?"

"I do dislike hearing your voice, Dodge," he said. "If

there's a point to this call, would you mind stating it?"

"I married Liz at three o'clock this afternoon."

There was a short electric silence. I waited through it, smiling at the phone, and finally Volpinex said, in a quiet thoughtful voice, "I see."

"So you can call off your goons," I told him, "and forget about airplane trips to St. Martin."

He said nothing.

This time I didn't wait him out. I paused long enough to give him a chance to speak if he had anything to say, and then I added, "You can forget everything in fact. It's too late."

"Perhaps," he said. Still quiet, still thoughtful.

A little chill touched the back of my neck; I did my best to ignore it. "Perhaps? I told you, Volpinex, I'm married. Signed, sealed, and delivered." And then, remembering Ralph's having told me Volpinex was a widower whose wife had died on vacation in Maine, I added, "And I'm not going to Maine."

The coldest voice I've ever heard said, "What do you mean by that?"

"I mean it's all over. You've had it."

Click.

"Volpinex?" I knew he'd hung up, but I jiggled the phone cradle anyway. "Volpinex?" But he was actually gone, so reluctantly I too hung up, and sat there a minute frowning at the telephone.

The conversation had not been as satisfactory as I'd anticipated. The chill still hovered at the back of my neck, and the sound of Volpinex's cold voice still whispered in my ear.

I found myself rethinking my plan to drive north and spend tonight alone. A friendly face, a warm body, might be a much better idea after all.

But whom? Not Betty. Linda Ann Margolies? I could phone her, take her out to dinner, see what happened next. We'd already had sex, right here on this floor, so if she wasn't busy tonight there wasn't any reason—

The phone rang.

"Hello?"

"So there you are."

"Candy?"

"You have too many women, Art, is that it? You can't recognize voices any more?"

"I only recognize your voice when you're sweet to me."

"When *I'm* sweet to *you*!" Her shock and outrage nearly melted the plastic of the phone.

"Sweetheart," I said, "I've been so busy lately, it's just—"

"I'll just bet you have."

"Some day I'll tell you all a—"

"Make it today."

It was now shortly after six, approaching dinnertime. I said, "Candy, even if I had time to come out to Fair Harbor, I'd never make the last—"

"I'm in New York."

Flashback: vision of Candy entering this selfsame building as I was exiting it with Betty after the mirror trick. "Ah," I said. "You're in New York."

"I left Ralph."

"Oh, Candy, think what you're saying."

"I wrote him a letter, Art, I told him everything."

"A letter? To Ralph?"

"Everything, Art."

"Candy, are you sure you—"

"I'll show you the carbon. Take me to dinner and I'll show you the carbon, and we can talk."

Good God. An hysterical or overemotional woman at this juncture would have been bad enough, but a woman who tells all to her husband in a letter and makes a carbon is neither hysterical nor overemotional. No. Such a woman is a woman with something in mind. I said, carefully, "Candy, if you want to talk over your problems with me for old time's sake, I'll be hap—"

"Old time's sake? We had a lot more than old times before you started running around with that rich bitch."

"Candy," I said, "I hate to bring this up, but the reason we haven't seen so much of one another lately is because you threw me out. Remember that?"

"We'll talk about that, too, Art."

"Um. What does Ralph say, Candy?"

"About what?"

"About the letter, what else?"

"He hasn't seen it yet. I'm going to mail it to him tonight."

"Oh," I said.

"After you and I have our talk," she said.

"I see."

"You always were pretty quick, Art."

Candy hardly counted as a friendly face, but God knew she was a warm body. So much for Linda Ann Margolies —too bad. I said, "Where are you now, dear?"

"At home." Meaning the apartment on West End Avenue in the eighties.

"I'll come by for you at seven?"

"Have the doorman buzz me," she said. "I'll come down."

"You don't want me to come in, Candy?"

"First," she said firmly, "we'll talk."

41   41

WE HAD DINNER IN THE Library, a Broadway restaurant near her apartment. I'd asked immediately to see the carbon of this famous letter, but she'd said, "Let's not spoil our appetites with a lot of argument," so we'd had to go through the entire meal, spoiling my digestion if not my appetite, and at last over coffee she took a well-folded document from her purse and handed it over to me.

Two sheets of paper, typed. Sighing, convinced I was not going to be happy with this letter, I began to read:

Dearest Ralph,
   Darling, I want you to know that no matter what happens from this point in time forward in time I have never lost respect and love for you and I never will lose that respect and that love.
   However, I have come to the distraught conclusion that it can no longer be possible for you Ralph and me Candice to continue to live together as husband and wife. The gulf that stretches between us cannot be bridged by our best intentions no matter how good those intentions of ours might be.
   We are drifting apart, my darling, and I no longer see any possible way or circumstance in which we could drift back together again. Our problems of sexual and emotional incompatibility are simply too deep for us to be able to climb over them and find one another in the valley of love on the other side.
   You know that I have asked you repeatedly to see Doctor Zeeberger about your premature ejaculations and your occasional impotence and your general inability to satisfy me in the conduct of our conjugal affairs in the bedroom. I want to be honest with you, Ralph, now more than ever, and I do know that you have been to see Doctor Zeeberger, but I do not believe you could possibly have explained the situation to him or he would not have said it was *me* he wanted to talk to. *I* do not have premature ejaculations. *I* do not have occasional impotence. In fact, Ralph, if you will recall and be honest with yourself and with me, you will know that I have given you every possible verbal assistance and reassurance on this subject, saying such things to you as, "I'm sure it'll be just fine this time," and, "Don't get tense, sweetheart," every single time we go to bed together.
   Ralph, I have a confession to make. I am a woman, with the needs and desires of a woman, and in my frus-

tration and anguish I have turned to another man. Yes, you know him, Ralph, he is your dearest friend and mine, Art Dodge. In his arms I have found the fulfillment that fled me within my marriage. Art and I have had intercourse on a regular basis for over a year now, in a variety of settings. I am enclosing photostats of four motel registers where we registered as Mr. and Mrs. Arthur Dodge.

Ralph, I hate to cheat and lie. Desperation drove me to Art, but love has kept me with him. We love one another, Ralph, and we want you to give us our freedom so that we may marry and be honest before the world.

It was this summer in Fair Harbor, when the children became aware of what was going on, that I knew I could be a dishonest woman no longer. Yes, they know, Ralph, in their childish way. That's why I sent Art away, hoping against hope that you and I could somehow make a go of it, though the odds against us were astronomical.

Well, it can't happen. You will find a better woman than me, Ralph, I am sure. All I want is the children and child support, you know I would never be greedy. And don't think too harshly of Art. Love hit him like a ton of bricks, just like it hit me.

> Hail and Farewell,
> *Candy*

I finished reading this remarkable carbon, nodded slowly, refolded the thing on its original creases, laid it on the table, sipped at my coffee, looked at Candy sitting across from me like a sharper who'd just switched decks, and I said, "Do you really have those photostats?"

"They're in the envelope with the original."

"And where is this envelope?"

"Oh, no," she said. "You aren't getting that. Besides, I can always write the letter again, and I can always get more photostats."

"Uh huh." I tapped the folded letter, thinking things over. "Why, Candy?"

She frowned, not understanding me. "What do you mean?"

"Why me? Ralph makes a better living than I do, he's

more reliable, he's more blind and therefore more safe, and he likes your kids. I hate them, you know, and I always will."

"You'll get used to them."

"Why *me*, Candy?"

The look she gave me was both vulnerable and defiant. "Maybe I love you," she said.

"Christ," I said, in honest depression, "I believe you do."

"And I can make something of you," she said.

I half-closed my eyes when I looked at her; I didn't like seeing her head on. "Make something of me?"

"You've never had any ambition," she said. "You've just been content to live on what you can con and cheat and steal. You're very smart and very imaginative, and if you really tried you could be a big success."

Four hours ago Liz had married me, and here was Candy trying to turn me into a husband.

"The only kind of big success I want to be," I said, "is without trying. Money that's earned by the sweat of my brow is tainted; I won't touch it."

She pointed a triumphant red-tipped finger at me. "I'm going to change all that," she said. "I'm going to make you a success in spite of yourself. You'll have money, respectability, accomplishment. You'll be proud of yourself, and I'll be proud of you."

"You'll reclaim me from Satan."

"You could say it that way," she said, without flinching.

"And if I say no," I suggested, "you'll send Ralph this letter."

"If you don't think I should send it," she told me, innocent and wide-eyed, "then I certainly won't. I mean, if we're friends and I think you're somebody whose opinion I should listen to."

"Yeah, right." I tapped the letter again. "But what if you do send it? How is that any skin off *my* nose?"

"Your *nose?* I didn't say anything about your nose, honeybunch." How sharp her little teeth looked. "Now, with a lot of husbands," she said, "you might have to worry about your nose, because a lot of husbands might just come over and punch you on the nose a good one. But *my* husband is a lawyer. He isn't going to punch anybody."

"Right."

"But do you know what I think Ralph might do?"

"What might he do, Candy?"

"Well, he might call a friend of his in one of the big law firms, and all of a sudden your distributor wouldn't want to handle your line of cards any more. Or he might talk to some other friend of his in the New York City tax department, and they might look at the corporate taxes you've been paying. Or he might—"

Shades of Volpinex (another lawyer) and the ghost of the IRS. "Okay," I said.

"That's what a *lawyer* might do," Candy said. "A husband might poke you in the nose, but a lawyer would do other things. And believe me, Art, when it comes to being either a husband or a lawyer, Ralph is much more likely to be a lawyer. You can take it from me."

"I'm sure I can."

She looked very hard at me, and I could see that one insult, one outright rejection at this point, would send her right out into the street and directly to the nearest mailbox. When the only reason for my being here was to take her directly to bed.

On the other hand, would an immediate capitulation be realistic? Unfortunately not. "Candy," I said, "I noticed this carbon wasn't dated. Is there a date on the original?"

"There doesn't have to be," she said. "He'll get it when he gets it."

I looked troubled. I sighed. I gazed away at the other diners.

Candy said, "What's up?"

"These are new thoughts to me," I said. I gave her my

honest look. "Settling down, taking on the responsibility of a family, trying to make something of myself. I'm not sure I'm cut out for it."

"You'll do just fine," she said.

"It's such a new idea, though." Her right hand was on the table, and my left hand had been tapping the folded letter; now I reached across, took her hand, and said, "Do I have to give you my answer right now?"

Her first convulsive reaction was to pull her hand away, but then she relaxed a bit, let the hand stay there, gave me a look in which suspicion mingled with hope, and said, "You wouldn't be trying to stall me, would you?"

"How much time do I have, Candy? Will you mail that letter tonight? Or will you give me a chance to get used to the idea?"

"Or maybe you'd like a chance to skip the country, disappear someplace, put that crummy little card business up for sale, and take off."

"Take me home with you," I said, and gave her hand a squeeze.

She frowned at me. "What?"

I gave her as meaningful a look as I knew how. "It's been a long time, Candy," I said. "Take me home with you, let me—let me sleep on it. Then we can talk again tomorrow."

She was weakening, I could see it, but before she made any answer at all the waiter came by: "Check, sir?"

"Yes, thank you." I looked at Candy again, my heart melting into my eyes. "Shall we go home?" I asked her. "Candy?"

She held back a second or two longer, then abruptly nodded. "All right," she said. But to retain her tough-guy image she added, "So I can keep an eye on you."

"Right," I said. While I was rooting in my wallet for my Master Charge card I grinned at her and said, "Almost like a wedding night, isn't it?"

Y OU'RE MARRIED???"

"Yesterday was my lucky day," I said. I'd waited till Candy had made us both breakfast and I'd finished eating mine before breaking the good news. She was still sitting at the kitchen table, a half-empty coffee cup in her hand, and I was standing over by the swing door to the hallway, in case she decided to throw anything.

"You son of a bitch," she said, and then she said, "I don't believe you."

"Stamford, Connecticut," I told her. "The blushing bride was one Elizabeth Kerner, whom I believe you met a few weeks ago."

I stepped through the swing door, pushed it closed, heard the coffee cup smash against it, and stepped back into the kitchen again. "I could have told you last night, I suppose," I said, "but you were having so much fun lording it over me. Besides, you gave me a wonderful wedding night, one I'll never forget."

This time I had to step outside long enough for an egg-smeared plate to disintegrate against the door. Leaning cautiously into the kitchen again, I said, "Candy, you're just too emotional. You should try to be more calm."

"I'll send the letter," she said. "I'll send it right away, right this morning."

"Go ahead," I told her. "Burn your bridges while you're standing on them."

"You don't think I'll do it?"

"I don't *care* if you do it, Candy, because I'll deny every word of it."

"And the photostats?"

"Mr. and Mrs. Arthur Dodge. I don't see *your* name there, Candy. I was in those motels with Liz Kerner, who is now my bride, and who will back up every word I say."

She glared at me, very nearly speechless. "You'd *lie*?"

"Surely, Candy," I said, "you've heard of people lying before. Listen, breakfast was super, but I'd really better be off now. And my advice to you is to give poor Ralph another chance."

"You bastard! You bastard!"

Remembering my last experience with an enraged Candy, I doubted she was now pawing in that kitchen drawer for an ice cream scoop. "Well, ta ta," I said, and departed. Some sort of banshee seemed to be moving through the apartment as I went out the front door.

43   43

IT WAS THE THOUGHT OF the sleeping bag on the floor of my office that drove me at last to a reconciliation with Betty. I'd originally intended to make her stew a couple of days longer, but what the hell. Why not be magnanimous? Besides, there was no answer when I tried calling Linda Ann Margolies.

Having spent last night with Candy rather than on the northbound road toward some placid lake, I now found myself in the unlikely position of trying to get away from New York for a few days on the Thursday before Labor

Day. I had no reservations anywhere, and the roads were already beginning to fill up with those maniacal death-wish families from the provinces: three adults, seven children, and a dog in a nine-year-old Plymouth doing forty on the New York State Thruway. It was really too late to go anywhere, so I might just as well stay in the city.

The hot city. The muggy city. The impossible city. It had been your typical New York City August, coming in like an armpit and going out like a mass grave. The Alfa was well air-conditioned and my office was poorly air-conditioned, but that was about the limit of my options. Unless I wanted to nap all day in a movie house somewhere, which I didn't.

So, at four o'clock that afternoon, I phoned Betty. "Hello," I said, when she came on the line, and I made myself sound properly depressed.

"Bart?"

An imp suggested to me that I be Art again, that I spend the next few days with Betty not as her husband but as her brother-in-law; but I briskly gave the imp the back of my hand—enough complexity is enough—and said, "Yes, it's Bart."

"Oh, sweetheart," she said. "I'm so glad you called."

"I've been," I said, "miserable."

"Oh, so have I, darling."

"I wish I could get you out of my system, Betty, but—"

"Oh, no, sweetheart, no! Darling, where are you?"

"In the office. Art's office." My voice trailed away a bit. "Everything is Art's, I guess."

"But I'm not!" she cried. "That was one mad—moment, one crazy—fling that didn't mean anything, sweetheart, it was loneliness and self-pity and—"

"And I know how persuasive Art can be," I said. It was time to start giving her an out.

She's no dummy. She said nothing; she let the statement stand on its own teeny feet.

"Betty," I said, "I want us to try again."

"Oh, so do I, Bart, more than anything. We'll have to-night together, and then tomorrow we'll go out to the Island, just the two of us, no one around—"

"Won't Liz be there?"

"She's gone off someplace," she said. "She was here last night, with some very very strange-looking man, and the two of them left this morning. She won't come out to the Island, she told me so herself."

"We could make a new start," I suggested, tremulously, as though the thought had just come to me.

"A *real* start, this time. Oh, Bart, I'm so glad you called, I've been so unhappy!"

"So have I, sweetheart."

"I'll pack right now," she said, rushing her words together. "I'll have Carlos bring the car around, I'll be down to pick you up in twenty minutes."

"Twenty minutes?" Time enough to find a garage to stow the Alfa in; I wasn't about to leave a beauty like that out on the street for the next five days. "I'll be waiting," I said.

"From now on," she promised me, "life is going to be wonderful."

"I believe you," I said.

44   44

WHEN VOLPINEX CAME out on the terrace, I was sitting in a chaise longue, smiling at the sunny park out there, and rerunning in my head last night's Bart-Betty reconciliation. Betty herself was out right now with Carlos and the Lincoln, shopping for a surprise present for me, but she would be back before noon, when we would have the light snack—shrimp, lobster, and king crab salad—being prepared for us at this very moment by Blondell. Following which, we would leave at once for our weekend together on Fire Island.

I was so content in my setting and my memories that at first I didn't notice the arrival of Volpinex, but all at once there he was, standing beside me, looking down with a slight smile on his lips that did nothing to alter the coldness of his eyes. "Iy!" I said, startled, and sat up so quickly I spilled some of my champagne and orange juice. "Who let *you* in?"

"No one," he said. His voice was so soft I could barely hear it over the shwush of traffic from far below. "I have my own key," he said.

"Your own key?" What absurdity was that?

"From Liz." His thin smile thickened briefly. "I doubt she remembers I have it."

"Well, I'll be sure to tell her," I said, and pushed my glasses up more firmly onto my nose. Bart's priggishness was uncomfortably easy to fall into.

"I don't think you will," he said. The smile became so thin it nearly disappeared, then lived once more as he added, "But I don't intend to use it again after this, in any event."

"I should think not. You can't just walk into other people's houses."

"Or other people's lives," he suggested. "Or other people's plans."

The morning sun was behind this building, casting its stunted shadow onto Fifth Avenue and a bit of the park, so there was no direct sunlight here on the terrace. Nevertheless, the sky was very bright and I couldn't help but squint when I stared upward at Volpinex, whose face was little more than a silhouette, practically nothing showing but his cold eyes and that flickering humorless cold smile.

I thought of standing, meeting him man to man, but became suddenly hyperaware of that railing very near me, and the masses of empty air just the other side. Seven stories down were the concrete sidewalk and the blacktop street. I seemed suddenly to have developed a fear of heights, to feel more secure with my entire body below the level of the railing.

"Why don't you sit down?" I said. "As long as you're here. I mean, if you won't go away."

"It's your going away that I'm here to discuss," he said. He remained standing. His hands, resting calmly at his sides—approximately my nose level—were very long and very thin, but with a look of strength about them. My earlier image of Volpinex as part vampire returned to me, more insistently.

"I *am* going away," I said. "Betty will be back any minute—" it seemed for some reason important to make that point, that I wouldn't be alone for long "—and then we'll be off for Point O' Woods."

"I mean a different kind of going away." His right hand lifted and made a slender graceful gesture toward the park, as though inviting me to admire it. Or perhaps to fly over it. "Something more permanent."

What had failed with brother number one he was apparently now going to try with brother number two. I said, "I'm not leaving. I'm staying with Betty."

An expression of cultured disgust rumpled the smiling lips. "I know you two are married."

"Then that's an end to it," I said.

"Perhaps." He leaned toward me, placing his hands in odd flattened positions in front of himself, reminding me that he was a self-proclaimed karate expert. "And perhaps not," he said. His eyes glinted, and a muscle inside his left cheek began jumping, like a moth under a sheet.

"Oh!"

A female voice. It startled us both, and I suddenly realized I'd been sitting there like a hypnotist's subject, staring up at Volpinex open-mouthed, saying nothing, thinking nothing, feeling only a steadily increasing nervousness. My mouth was dry, my shoulders stiff. My heart was pounding.

"Meestair Dahjj. I deed not know you had company."

It was Nikki, blessed Nikki, in the living room doorway with the telephone in her hand. "Come out, Nikki," I called, hoarse-voiced, and gestured extravagantly for her to approach. Meanwhile, Volpinex backed away a pace or two, his face as sternly angry as a Mayan stone god.

Nikki came out, tripping in much her usual fashion, but with apprehensive looks toward Volpinex. "Meez Kairnair on the phone for you," she told me, and put the phone on the table beside me. She was in an uncharacteristic hurry to be off.

I said, "Mr. Volpinex was just leaving, Nikki. Show him to the door, will you?"

Volpinex stood glaring at me from under hooded eyes. I could almost see the gears of his brain ratcheting away in there. Leaning toward him, I said softly, "She'll remember you were here." His eyes flickered at that, and I added, "And so will I."

He expelled air; apparently he'd been holding it for some time. "We'll . . . talk again," he said, nodded curtly at Nikki, and followed her away into the apartment.

I watched them go, then picked up the phone. My hand was shaking so much I could see two receivers. I put them both to my face, where they rattled against my skull, and said, "Betty?"

"I don't want you to guess," she said. "About what I'm getting. But I want to know your favorite color."

"My favorite color." I reached out for my champagne and orange juice. "Orange," I said, and drank it down.

LABOR DAY WEEKEND AT
Point O' Woods. Four of the most pleasant and comfortable days of my life. I know that Betty too was having a
good time and I'm glad of it, all in all, considering how
it ended.

After Blondell's seafood salad on Friday, we had driven
out here with me at the wheel of Betty's present to me; an
orange Thunderbird. Two cars in three days; this was becoming my week.

Except for Volpinex, whom I couldn't get out of my
mind. Had he really come there to kill me, on that terrace?
It didn't seem possible. Volpinex was dangerous, of course,
capable of trying to injure me in that squash court, capable
of hiring toughs to drive me out of town or beat me up,
but was he really capable of murder? It had all seemed
very real at the time, but people don't actually kill people,
and particularly lawyers don't kill people. As both Volpinex himself and Candy had recently pointed out, lawyers
have too many other strings to their bow.

The former wife, dead in Maine.

"Nonsense," I muttered, and looked over my shoulder.

But once at Point O' Woods it all faded away. Betty
and I were here in this Episcopalian ghetto, and nothing
from the real world—or the unreal world of Ernest Volpinex—could possibly get at us. The weather remained
perfect: the sun a great dollop of Béarnaise on a sky of
shimmering blue china, sand the color of raw silk, ocean

the colors of mermaids, air a soft warm beneficent presence sailing up across the world from Brazil. The mosquitoes had all been burned off by the heat of midsummer, nor had any other obnoxious insects taken their place. Beauty, peace, contentment and suntan oil were spread o'er all.

As for Betty, the combination of her expressions of guilt for having betrayed me plus her joy at our reunion combined to make her the finest servant-wife since the last war bride was brought home from Japan. Did I wish to go to bed? Was there a position, a variation, possibly a rumor of an alternative method, which I would like to try? Absolutely, absolutely. Was I hungry? Betty blossomed into a cook before whom Blondell would have shriveled away in shame. Great sunlit breakfasts on the back deck, wonderful cold lunches of dishes like *salade Niçoise*, dinners so lavish and extensive and delicious that afterward I could barely bring the snifter of Rémy Martin to my lips.

Joy. Joy undiminished. Will I ever find its like again? No, not ever.

Partly, of course, it was my own doing that it all came to an end. Peace and joy bore me after a while, and I found myself itching again to do something. Something. So partly I do have myself to blame for what happened next.

But only partly. The rest of the blame goes to Volpinex, a sneak and a bastard and a poor sport if there ever lived one.

But first my own contribution to the acceleration of events. It was ten o'clock Monday evening, and we were both in bed, Betty and I, having repaired there for after-dinner calisthenics and having both fallen promptly to sleep. I was the first to awaken, finding myself semi-imprisoned by a Betty-arm and a Betty-leg flung across me. We were on Father's bed, as usual, and one lamp glowed on the night table. I lay on my back, studying the bedroom ceiling, aware of the summer house around me, the summer community, the summer island, and increasingly aware of the end of summer. One way and another, it was all coming to an end.

I tried to see through that ceiling and into the future, but it remained hazy. Who would I be in September? Betty's husband, true-blue Bart, respectable businessman, manager of his wife's vast business empire? Or Art, with his freedom and his Alfa and his little card business and his little marriage business with Liz? It couldn't be both, not any more.

Never make a business out of your hobby, you'll take all the fun out of it. Insult cards had been my business and fornication my hobby, and I'd been reasonably content. Now the card business was on the verge of being scrapped, I was on the threshold of making millions out of fornication, and look at me: staring at the ceiling, worrying about my future.

"Oh, fuck it!" I suddenly said, and pushed Betty's limbs out of the way so I could get out of bed.

She half woke up. "Swee-hart? Goin'?"

"For a walk on the beach," I told her. I patted her cheek, and then her other cheek. "Have a nice nap, I'll be back in a little while."

She moaned and smiled and rolled over, and I put on slacks, sneakers and a T-shirt, and out I went.

I walked aimlessly for ten minutes or so, brooding, and then I passed the phone booth. And I stopped and looked at the phone booth, and a thought entered my mind.

Just how reliable *was* Betty? If I was going to be faithful Bart, what about her?

There was a dime in my pocket.

She must have fallen asleep again; it was six rings before she answered, and then her voice sounded blowsy with unconsciousness. I said, "Hi, there, honey. Guess who this is?"

"Hello?"

"*You* know who it is, Betty."

"Art? Is that you?"

My heart was pounding; it surprised me. "That's right," I said. "Long time no see."

"Where *are* you? What time is it?"

"Early. I'm in Ocean Beach, I'm staying with friends. I could be there in half an hour."

"Oh, no!" She sounded truly shocked.

"No? Why not, honey?"

"Well . . . Bart's here."

"I don't believe it. Put him on."

"He—he just went for a walk. On the beach."

"Come on, Betty, don't leave me hanging here like this."

"He'll be back pretty soon," she said, and suddenly she was pitching her voice lower, as though afraid she'd be overheard. "He really will."

"Then you come out."

"Oh, I couldn't."

"Why not?"

"Well, your brother . . . He's staying here with me."

"You can still go out for a while. *He's* taking a walk, isn't he?"

"Oh, Art, this isn't right."

I didn't have to go on with it. I've had this conversation often enough with other women, I know when the argument is won and there's nothing left but the extra verbiage to help the woman feel she was overpowered; but there was a certain satisfaction in running the ritual right through to the end. "Of course it's right," I told her. "Anything that feels good is right, you know that."

"Art, you're terrible, you really are."

"I'll meet you at the beach end of the fence."

"I might not be there, Art."

"I'll wait for you," I said, and hung up, and left the phone booth, and went for a walk on the beach.

46   46

I WAS LYING AGAIN ON FA-
ther's bed, hands behind my head as I brooded at the
ceiling, when I heard her come in. The door opened and
closed, she moved about down there, and then there was
silence. Sitting up, I called, "I'm up here," and heard her
start up the stairs.

I hadn't been surprised to find her gone when I'd come
back here, but I had been disappointed, and I'd spent the
last hour and a half in a state of general depression. But
why? Did I love her, for Christ's sake? Did I love either
of those wretched sisters? In perfect truth I did not, but
what I was learning—and this was quite a bit worse—was
that I needed someone, someone, anyone, to love *me*.

(I don't count Candy. The architect's plans for my re-
modeling were already completed in her head, that was
how much she loved *me*.)

But I still didn't know what to do about anything, and
now Betty was back. Sitting up on the bed as I heard her
footsteps approaching, I turned toward the door and saw
Volpinex just reaching the head of the stairs.

I scrambled off the bed, pointing at him. "You did it!"
I shouted. "You really did! And you were going to do it to
me!"

I meant the wife in Maine, that Volpinex *had* murdered
her, and that he really had intended to murder me on the
terrace last Friday, two insights that had exploded belatedly into my consciousness the instant I saw him in that

194

half-lit hall, rounding the turn at the head of the stairs and walking toward me. That was what I'd meant, but I doubt there was any way he could have understood me from what I'd said. When a man begins a conversation by shouting, "You did it you really did and you were going to do it to me," it is not unfair to say of that man that he is speaking gibberish.

Volpinex, in any event, treated my outburst the way a sensible man treats gibberish: he ignored it. He said, "I'm not interested in you, Dodge. I'm looking for Elisabeth."

"Which one? She's not here. I mean she's in the bathroom!" Meaning I didn't want him to think I was alone in the house.

He paused, glanced at the open bathroom door immediately to his left, and gave me a one-raised-eyebrow stare. "Is that something comical? Another joke?"

"You won't get away with it," I warned him, which was absurd. He was between me and the stairs, nobody knew he was here, he was an expert in karate: he would get away with it.

"Your sense of humor continues to elude me," he said. He had come forward to the bedroom doorway, just close enough to be sure I was alone in this room. "I fail to understand what you're saying," he said, and now I saw he was holding a large manila envelope in his left hand. What was in it? Some murder device? Visions of silken twine slithered through my head. Or a slender case of surgical knives, as in *Arsenic and Old Lace*.

I said, "They'll suspect you. I left a letter with my lawyer to be opened in case of my death."

His frown of incomprehension continued a few seconds longer, and then all at once he smiled, broadly and insultingly. For a humorless man he had quite a collection of smiles on tap, none of them pleasant. "So you think I'm here to kill you," he said.

"You wanted to Friday, on the terrace."

"Did I?" The smile curled around his face like smoke,

and I noticed he didn't bother with a denial.

"That's why I left a letter with my lawyer," I told him.

He shook his head, impatient with me. "You did not," he said. "Don't be tedious."

"You think so?" Raging to cover my fright, I shook my fist at him and yelled, "Just murder me and see what happens!"

He stood there and looked at me, and we both listened to what I'd just said. It hadn't come out exactly right, had it? Hurrying right along, I said, "You didn't come here to see Betty, that's just a story."

"Oh, but I did."

"Why? You're not her lawyer."

"And you're not your brother," he said.

"What?"

"You have no twin brother," he told me, and the glint in his eye was triumph.

Oh oh.

Brazen it through. You can't prove a negative, this is a bluff, brazen it through, don't slip for a second, don't show him a thing. "Of course I have a twin brother," I said. "You've met him yourself, his name is Arthur."

"No," he said. "*Your* name is Arthur. There never was a Robert or Bart Dodge, no twin brother at all." He jiggled that manila envelope toward me. "I have the hospital records here, showing that yours was a single birth. I have school records, tax records. I have you cold, Dodge. I told you not to get into a game that was too fast for you, but you wouldn't listen. And I believe your next step is going to be the state penitentiary."

"Wait a minute, now," I said. "Hold on. What do you mean—penitentiary?"

"Your two marriages," he said. "The first you entered under a false name and with falsified papers. The second was fraudulent because you lied on your application about your current marital status."

"The Kerner family wouldn't want a scandal like that."

He laughed; oh, he was enjoying himself. "They'd like nothing better," he said. "If the girls tried to hush it up, the rest of the family wouldn't let them. And they'll both, of course, use it in their civil suits against one another. Oh, you'll be famous, Dodge."

"That's not one of my goals," I said.

"The time for choice is over," he told me. Turning away, he said, "I'll wait for Betty downstairs."

"Wait. Wait a minute." This was even worse than being murdered. Something like true terror was crawling around on the floor of my stomach. With two quick steps forward, I grasped his arm, saying, "Wait, let's talk this over."

He looked at my hand on his arm. "Take your hand away," he said.

I didn't. I said, "Look, you're smart, you're better off in partnership with me, the two of—"

He moved. First something horrible happened to my left wrist, and then I went sailing backward to crash on the floor and slide along it until my shoulders and head crashed into the night table. The lamp fell over, but stayed lit, and the drawer popped open, dropping itself and a scatter of playing cards, hairpins, and assorted garbage over my face and chest. I batted my way upward through it to a sitting position on the floor, and looked up to see Volpinex leering down at me like something on a cathedral cornice. "I enjoyed that," he said. "I'd enjoy doing it again." He kicked me encouragingly on the ankle. "Get up, Dodge."

"No," I said. My left wrist stung abominably. I splayed my right hand out behind me, for support, and my fingers bumped into something hard and unyielding.

He kicked me in the same spot, more determinedly. "I said get up."

My fingers closed on Daddy's gun, on the floor now amid the wreckage of the night table drawer, and I swung it around at arm's length. "God *damn* you!" I shouted, and I shot that grinning gargoyle right in his drain spout.

47

T HEN, OF COURSE, I WAS
really terrified.

"No no no no no!" I shouted, but there weren't enough
no's in the world to overpower that simple yes. But I
hadn't meant it. I'd never meant to kill anybody. Not even
to hurt anybody.

Maybe he wasn't dead. The gun still in my hand, as
though glued there, I crawled over on hands and knees to
where he was lying crumpled against the wall next to the
door, and I peeked at his face to see if maybe his eyes were
open.

Oh, dear. I swallowed a sudden hint of dinner and
looked very quickly away again. You don't have a face
like that if you're alive. That wasn't something you could
take to a fix-it shop, oh, no, that was something broken
for good.

Broken for good.

I have known terror before in my life, such as when I'm
in the closet and the suspicious husband is tramping around
in the bedroom and the wife is making shrill suggestions
that they go out to a movie, and I know what such terror
feels like. It feels hot and electric and red, full of buzzing
and tiny explosions. That was the terror I'd felt most recently when I had my hand on Volpinex's arm and tried
to talk him into making some sort of deal, and until now
that was the only kind of terror I'd ever known.

But now I'd met the real thing, the terror below that

one, the terror that makes that one seem like a simple case of hypertension. And I'll tell you what real terror is like. It's a wet green swamp with no bottom, and the filthy water coming into your nostrils. It's a small and slimy toad inside your body, eating your bowels and your stomach, leaving a bile-smeared hollow inside you from your brittle ribs to your exposed genitals. It's not being able to reverse time for even one second, for one tiny miserable second, to undo the unthinkable. It's Volpinex with a face like a First World War atrocity case and no more life in him than a sausage.

I don't know how long I stayed there, sunk back on my haunches as I refused to look any more at Volpinex, continuing to hold the gun because it hadn't yet occurred to me to put it down, but I was finally getting shakily to my feet—with no idea at all what I would do next, how I would get out of this, what the moves were that followed this one—when all at once Betty was standing in the bedroom doorway, staring open-mouthed at me, at the gun, at Volpinex. And then shrieking.

"Betty," I said, "listen to me." But even I couldn't hear my voice in the midst of those shrieks of hers.

And for what happened next I blame the motion picture industry of America. I had ceased to function as a thinking, planning intelligence, I had become a character in a specific sequence.

Three characters: two male, one female. One of the males is dead, shot by the other. The female arrives, sees, screams, turns, runs away. We've all seen this sequence, in how many movies? And she runs toward the staircase, she always runs toward the staircase. And the man with the gun lifts it and fires. That's what he does, every time.

Every time.

W HEN I AWOKE, THEY
were still there.

It was not callousness that had permitted me to go into
a deep and dreamless sleep right after committing the first
two murders of my life. At first I'd been so terrified I
couldn't think at all, and if I'd stayed awake I really believe I would have gone off the deep end. But my brain,
more equal to the emergency than I was, simply called for
a crash dive, and out I went like a stage hypnotist's shill.

And when I awoke, they were still there: Volpinex by
the bedroom door, Betty out in the hall by the head of the
stairs. It was after two in the morning and my mind was
clear. I came to consciousness all at once, remembering
everything and knowing exactly what I should do in order
to get out from under.

I started small, with that damned manila envelope full
of un-twinning. It was the easiest to get rid of, and gave
me confidence for the tougher part to follow. I burned it
in the bathroom sink, watching the yellow flames flare up
from the photostats, watching it burn down to anonymous
ash. I ran water, smeared it around, dried my hands on a
towel. Now for the other two pieces of evidence.

It was hard getting them downstairs. Dead bodies don't
feel like living bodies, and the differences kept making my
stomach churn. Over and over I had to pause in my labors,
stagger to the nearest open window, and pant the fresh air
for a while. Then back to it, tugging and toting and drag-

ging those two awkward misshapen creatures down the stairs and back to the kitchen. And now I know why corpses are called stiffs.

Flammables, flammables—I opened cabinet after cabinet. Charcoal starter, floor cleaner, various burnable liquids. Good good good. On went the oven and the four gas burners. I sprinkled my flammables over the remains, and from them in a line through the house and up the stairs and here and there at the scenes of the crimes. Then I carefully put all the cans and bottles back where I'd found them, stored just so.

Now the gun. Bring it downstairs, wipe it off with this dish towel here, then force Volpinex's reluctant fingers around it, grasping it tight. Good. Now remove the gun from his grip, careful not to touch it with my bare hand, holding the barrel wrapped in the dish towel.

Lights out, throughout the house. The smell of escaping bottled gas was now rather strong in the kitchen, less so toward the front door. Out on the porch I went, carrying the gun in the dish towel. I trotted down the slate walk, paused, then pitched the gun underhand into a thick clump of bushes on the far side of the concrete public walk. Then back to the house I jogged, to toss the dish towel inside, light the trail of flammable liquid, and watch the flame skitter like a kitten across the wooden living room floor toward its unborn big brother in the kitchen.

I was at the beach, but had not yet reached the Point O' Woods border fence, when I heard the explosion.

Gloria buzzed me at ten-fifteen.

"Yes?"

"Liz Kerner calling."

"Right." Click. "Morning, sweetheart. Have a nice wedding night?"

"Haven't you heard?"

"Heard? What, are they announcing your orgasms on the six o'clock news?"

"Then you don't know anything about it," she said. "The police didn't call?"

"Police? What for?"

"Don't go away," she said. "I'll be there in twenty minutes." And she hung up.

Twenty minutes. Good. It had been very very hard this morning to pretend I was still the same old Art Dodge and that nothing had gone sour in my little merry-go-round world. Starting twenty minutes from now, I'd be able to relax into the shock that continued to be my primary true feeling.

Last night I'd traveled for an hour across Fire Island until, at the end of a rundown dock in Robbins Rest, I'd found a motorboat with an unconscious seminaked couple lying in the bottom of it, sleeping it off in fond embrace. The key was in the ignition, and it was simplicity itself to get behind the wheel, start the engine, and steer toward Bay Shore. About halfway across, the male started to wake up, but I clonked him with the fire extinguisher and that was that. The girl never moved.

I didn't tie up to the dock at Bay Shore, but gave the boat a push and permitted it to drift away. Then I walked through town till I found an all-night diner, where I called a cab to take me to an address in Babylon, the next town toward New York. (There was no way to claim Bart's new Thunderbird, which was a pity.) Behaving as though I were half-smashed, I told the driver to let me off at the corner so I could sneak into the house without waking up the li'l woman. He grinned at me and blew cigar smoke around and wished me luck, pal. I thanked him, feeling I needed it.

Another walk in Babylon to another all-night diner, where I called a cab from a different company and traveled this time to Mineola, playing the same sort of role. From Mineola, another company's cab took me to Queens, and in Queens I picked up a regular New York City cab to bring me to my office in Manhattan, which I staggered into at twenty after six this morning. Directly into the sleeping bag I went, where I dozed fitfully, full of bad dreams, until Gloria arrived at nine. Since which time I'd been taking a lot of coffee and Excedrin, and assuring Gloria my condition was the result of several nights on the floor in that sleeping bag.

But another and much better excuse for my condition was on the way. Twenty minutes she'd said, but she made it in fifteen, brushing past Gloria just like last time and saying to me, "We have to talk in private."

"We have to talk about your manners," I told her. "Okay, Gloria, it's all right."

"If you say so," she said, and closed the door gently behind her.

Liz dropped heavily into the second chair. She looked even worse than I felt: strain lines, fatigue, nervousness. "I've never known how to break news gently," she said.

"Don't tell me you want a divorce." Art Dodge was a

role I'd played successfully for years; I might have mud-
died the part recently with my loan-out interpretations of
twin brother Bart, but the original characterization was
still there, full-fleshed and ready to go. And never had I
needed it as much as I did right now.

"Lay off the jokes," she said. "You'll just want to bite
your tongue in a minute."

I frowned at her. "Come off it, Liz," I said. "Nothing's
that serious, not in your world. What's up?"

"Betty and Bart are dead," she said. Just like that.

"Ha ha," I said, and then I brought myself up short and
stared at her. We kept our eyes solemnly on one another
and neither of us said a single solitary word while I silently
counted, very slowly, to one hundred forty-three.

At which number, she looked away from me, shrugging,
and said irritably, "I shouldn't have to tell you this. The
police should notify you, right?"

"Police? What was it, an accident? A car?"

She looked at me again. "Somebody killed them," she
said. "On purpose."

Now I permitted myself a slightly doubtful scoff. "Are
you saying murder? Don't be silly."

"They were shot," she said. "I swear to God. You can
call the police at Brookhaven, if you don't believe me."

"Shot? Liz, you mean for real? With a *gun*?"

"Whoever did it," she said, "tried to make it look like
an accident. He burned the house down. But it was too
suspicious and they did an autopsy right away and found
the bullets."

"But—but who did it?"

"They don't know," she said.

I couldn't believe it. What the hell was the matter with
the Suffolk County police? They couldn't find a goddam
pistol within fifty feet of a major crime? Was all my clever-
ness to go for naught simply because the police were too
inept to do their job properly?

Find the gun! Goddam it, Suffolk County police, I know

you can't find stolen bicycles and stolen sailboats, but for Christ's sake even you people should be able to find a *gun!* It's right out in front of the house, covered with Volpinex's fingerprints!

Had a child found it? Had a child taken it away, for magpie reasons of its own?

Liz had been saying something more. I said, "What? I'm sorry, Liz. I guess the impact is just hitting me." And I jumped up impulsively from the desk, staring in agony toward my dusty window. "Bart!" I cried. "Bart dead!"

"Betty gets billing, too," Liz said.

I blinked at her. "You've had longer to get used to this," I said. "Longer to think about it."

"It never gets much funnier," she said.

"But Bart," I said, gesturing vaguely, hopelessly. "He'd come back from the coast, we'd had such—"

"Yeah, yeah," Liz said. "Save it for the graveside. You and Bart got along about as well as Betty and I did."

"I wasn't *suing* him!"

"You would have, if there'd been any money in it. You liked Bart all right, and I liked Betty all right, and I feel just as lousy as you do, but we're still alive, Art, and we've got things to do."

"Undertakers," I said vaguely, "arrangements . . ."

"That's not exactly what I had in mind," she said.

What now? I said, "What else, then?"

"I need an alibi, Art," she said.

I gazed at her, dumbstruck, I mean truly dumbstruck. Possibilities raced through my mind like cockroaches when the kitchen light turns on. I said, "Did *you*—?"

"Oh, don't be stupid," she said. "If I was going to get rid of Betty, I'd be smarter than *that.*"

I might have considered that an insult, but more important considerations had the floor. I said, "Then why do you need an alibi?"

"We had the lawsuit going," she said. "There was bad blood between us, and a lot of people knew it. I don't want this thing pinned on me, Art."

"Neither do I," I said. And I was telling the truth. I wanted it pinned on Volpinex, where it belonged; and where it would answer all the awkward questions.

Liz said, "We were married last Wednesday. We've been inseparable ever since, right up till this morning. We've been in your apartment, so we wouldn't even have my servants around us."

"My apartment?"

"You know I'd show you my appreciation," she said. "I'm a generous girl, you know that."

Pop. Another complete movement dropped into my head. "You sure are generous," I told her. "You have no idea how generous you are."

Mistrust spread over her irascible features. "What's that supposed to mean?"

"How badly do you need this alibi? I mean, why not produce Joe Rock? He's the guy you were really with, isn't he?"

"He can't help," she said.

"Why not?"

"He's evading a couple of Federal warrants. Drug sales, possession, things like that."

"So it's me or nobody."

"What's your offer, Art?"

"No offer," I told her. "We're at the level of take-it-or-leave-it."

"Maybe I wouldn't mind a women's prison," she said.

"Lesbianism would make you fat," I told her, and buzzed Gloria. "Bring your pad in, will you?"

Liz wasn't liking any of this. "Just tell it to me," she said. "Let me say yes or no."

"Let me have my fun," I said, and when Gloria came in I dictated to her a new agreement between Liz and me that eliminated the entire former agreement from beginning to end. "The greater understanding, confidence, and trust of one another created since our marriage" was given as the principal reason for the change. From now on, this agreement said, our marriage would be ruled exclusively by our wedding vows, the laws of Connecticut, and the customs and mores of the social groupings amid whom we would make our communal life. Insofar as property was concerned, the community property statutes of the state of California would apply.

Liz sat stony-faced through all this, and Gloria speed-wrote it all with her usual aplomb. At the finish I said, "Date it yesterday, prepare it for both our signatures, and do it in four copies."

"Yes, sir," she said, deadpan, and left the office.

Liz crossed her legs the other way. "And what," she said, "makes you think I'd sign anything like that?"

"A real marriage, sweetheart," I said. "Wouldn't you really like that, after all?"

"No."

"Then it just comes down to preferences," I said. "Which would you rather have for the rest of your life? The State Penitentiary for Women, or marriage to me?"

"That's not an easy decision."

"Take your time," I said. We could both hear the clickety-clack from the outer office. "Gloria only types about thirty words a minutes," I said.

50   50

BOY WAS SHE MAD WHEN they found the gun!

That happened about three in the afternoon. By then

we'd both been interviewed by rumple-suited Suffolk
County plainclothes detectives, who sat uncomfortably in
the living room of the Kerner apartment in Manhattan
and treated us with the awkward polysyllabic deference
natural to cops confronted by power and/or money. We
had also started the funeral arrangements, and I had
started the details of a cover-up beside which Watergate
was at the level of who-left-the-top-off-the-grape-jelly?

The funeral arrangements were themselves part of the
cover-up, since I insisted on the simplest possible form.
Liz felt the same way for arrogant reasons of her own—
she hated the hoi polloi gawping at the edges of her life—
and so what was decided on was cremation and urnment
in the Kerner mausoleum up near Tarrytown, all to be
done as soon as the coroner and other authorities were
done with the remains, and the entire operation to be unac-
companied by services, wakes, or even announcements of
any kind. No prayers, no get-togethers, nothing. The bare
minimum. Burn 'em up, brush the ashes into the urn, clap
on the cork, shove it onto the shelf, and the less said the
better.

The next step of the cover-up, for me, involved cooling
out an incredible number of people who knew different
potentially incriminating parts of what had been going on.
Gloria. Ralph. Candy. Joe Gold. My sister Doris. The
list went on and on, and not everybody could be given
exactly the same story. Doris, for instance, knew damn
well I didn't have a twin brother, but it was just possible I
could convince Ralph that the twin brother had existed.

Oh, boy.

I started my cover-up campaign with Gloria. When she
finished typing up the agreement I'd dictated, she brought
it in and waited while Liz read it. Then Liz stalled a bit
by asking directions to the ladies room, and while she was
gone I said, "Gloria, I think I'm in a lot of trouble."

"What makes this day," she said, "different from any
other day?"

"No, seriously," I said. "You know that twin brother thing I was pulling?"

"I know you were doing *something*," she said "God knows what."

"It was harmless," I assured her. "Just a sex game, you know how I am."

She allowed as how she knew how I was.

"I'll tell you something," I said. "That woman there, that bride of mine, she just came in to tell me her sister was murdered last night out on Fire Island."

Appropriate shock from Gloria, followed by appropriate doubt. "Is it for real?"

"Apparently so," I said. "The snapper is, a guy was found dead with her, and *Liz* says the guy was my twin brother."

"Your—?"

"I know," I said. "That isn't possible, is it?"

"Not any way I know of."

"Now," I said, "Liz wants me to give her an alibi. She wants me to swear she was with me last night, and the truth is she wasn't."

Lowering her voice, Gloria said, "Do you think she . . ."

"I have no idea," I said. "But that's why I had you type up that agreement. Normally, she wouldn't sign a paper like that for anything. If she signs it now, she's up to something. I just want you to know, Gloria, in case something bad comes out of this later on."

She gave me a troubled look; part of the reason she stuck with this weird job is that she actually did like me. "You're in over your head, Art," she said.

"Truer words were never spoken," I said, meaning it, "but I don't see any way to get out of it. I've got to follow through to the end and hope for the best."

"I suppose so."

"If anybody comes around and asks you anything," I said, "anything at all, you don't know a thing."

"Right."

"Not even whether I have a twin brother or not."

"I'm a complete dummy," she promised me.

"Maybe I can still beat Liz at her own game," I said bravely. Then we both heard the outer door close. "She's coming back," I whispered. "Let's see if she'll actually sign that agreement."

Joe Gold I dealt with later that afternoon, following the visit from the Long Island police. The gun still hadn't been found, but the cops showed no real inclination as yet to consider either Liz or me prime suspects. We'd alibied one another, we'd expressed shock and horror, we'd told what we could of our late siblings' recent activities and associates, and then we'd been left, with apologies, to our mourning.

Immediately upon the departure of the fuzz I said to Liz, "Give me some of your stuff. Undies, lipsticks, crap I can spread around my apartment."

"Good thinking," she said, and quickly assembled a paper bag of closet sweepings, with which I rushed to my own place, a residence which no longer resembled the site of a Turkish massacre, but was still not quite so clean as a truckstop diner on a Saturday night. Oh, well, Feeney had undoubtedly done his best. Spraying Liz's detritus hither and yon, I made my way to the phone, which seemed to have had honey poured on it, and phoned Joe out there in sunny L. A.

"Listen, Joe," I said.

"What—more? Can't you join a commune?"

"Joe, I got a serious problem."

"I've said that for years, Art."

"There's been a murder, Joe. No fooling, no gags, no kidding around, an honest-to-God murder."

"In the immortal words of Samuel Goldwyn's ad-lib writer," he said, "include me out."

"Absolutely," I said. "Include us both out. But here's the thing, Joe. What I've been pulling here this summer is a twin scam. You know?"

"I don't want to know."

"You must have had *some* idea, from that conversation."

"Art, in cases of homicide I make it a rule not to hear conversations."

"That's wonderful, Joe. Except I think I'm maybe being set up for something. Maybe to take the fall."

"Art? You wouldn't be trying to pull one on *me*, would you?"

Of course I would, but that isn't what I said. I said, "Joe, I'm too scared to pull anything on anybody. You've got to listen to me."

"Maybe. Start talking."

"I met twin sisters. So I became twin brothers, so I could screw them both. A simple innocent game, right?"

"It bears your signature like Andy Warhol's on a junkyard fence," he said.

"So *then*," I said, "it turns out these two are rich. But *rich*. And they're suing each other for millions and millions of dollars. And last night, Joe, while I was with one sister here in New York, the other sister was getting murdered out on Fire Island."

"On the level?"

"Absolutely. I swear on my mother's IUD. But here comes the cute part. Joe, there was a guy out there with her. Killed with her."

"Yeah?"

"My twin brother, Joe."

"What? What shit is this?"

"Exactly the question I ask myself, Joe."

"Somebody's up to something," he said.

"I had the same feeling myself. Am I being set up for something? I'm scared, Joe, and no fooling. If I get out of this, I may well be cured for life."

"Amen," he said.

"Joe," I said, "the only safe thing I can see for me is that *my scam did not exist*. If the cops want me to have a twin brother, fine. I neither confirm nor deny. But if the twin con comes to light, what happens to me?"

"Art," he said, "are you asking me to lie under oath in a murder case?"

"Absolutely not," I said. "I am asking you to stay out of it entirely. If some cop calls you long distance and asks you did Bart Dodge stay with you for a few days you can say yes, because later on you could say you thought he said *Art* Dodge, and maybe you got the dates wrong, and what's the problem anyway? You're out there, you're safe, you're out of it."

"You're damn right I'm out of it."

"All I'm asking, Joe," I said, "is that you don't volunteer. I've *got* to cover the twin con, I've just got to."

"I begin to think," he said, "that this may turn out to be a wonderful lesson for you."

"You bet. Joe, can I count on you?"

"Art," he said, "you and I have been pals for years. You've always been able to count on me, and you'll be able to go on counting on me right up to the point where it becomes inconvenient."

"But you won't blow the twin con."

"I won't volunteer."

"You're a sweetheart, Joe," I said, and went back to the Kerner apartment, where Liz met me with fire in her eyes, saying, "Give me that agreement. I won't go along with it, I want to tear it up."

"You what? Listen, I gave you that alibi, I helped—"

"You can just forget that alibi, buster," she said, "and the agreement, too."

"Forget it? Why?"

"Because," she said, "that asshole Ernie Volpinex did it, what do you think of that?" She stood in front of me, arms akimbo, fists against sides, jaw jutting out. "They found a gun where he tried to hide it, his fingerprints are all over it, it was a goddam crime of *passion*! Ernie's run away, nobody can find him, he's guilty as sin, I don't need any alibi, and *I won't stand for that goddam-goddam-goddam-agreement!*" She shook both fists in my face. "Stop that laughing, you goddam hyena! Stop it right now!"

51   51

I DIDN'T THINK YOU'D COME to work today," Gloria said when I walked in.

"Ah, well," I said. "Life must go on."

"People have called from the *Daily News*, from ABC, and from Channel 11. They want an interview about your brother."

"No interviews," I said. What a thought: me on television, discussing the murder of my twin brother. That would finish me, wouldn't it?

"I told them you wouldn't be in today. I suppose they'll try you at home."

Meaning the nest fouled by Feeney, to which I was unlikely to be returning for quite some time. "Good luck to them," I said. "And if anybody else calls, friend or foe, I'm still not in. Period of mourning, unlikely to return to the office before next week."

"Right." She gave me a conspiratorial look. "Anything else from the Kerner woman?"

"I still don't know what she's up to," I said. "The only thing to do is just wait and see."

"Maybe you ought to talk to a lawyer," she suggested.

"I intend to. Get me Ralph Minck, you have his office number there."

"Right. Oh, your sister called."

"Doris? Call her back, I'll talk to her before Ralph."

I went to the inner office and sat down at a desk that somehow seemed less mine. I had altered into someone different in the last two days, and the cons and concerns of yesteryear no longer vibrated as they once had. The murder cover-up was all that counted now; it exhausted all my energies just to tread water in this mighty ocean.

But once I'd pulled it off, if I did, would I then be able to come back to my innocent former self, full of silliness and smut? In some absurdist way it seemed that in killing Volpinex I was becoming Volpinex. Where was my comedy? Where was my caustic center?

"A Birthday," I muttered aloud, "a Birthday, a Birthday." If I could still do them, if I could still come up with a greeting on demand, then there was nothing to worry about.

Buzz. "Your sister."

"Right." Click. "Doris?"

"Art, what on *earth* is going on?"

"About what?"

"The newspaper said your twin brother Robert was *murdered*."

"My what?"

"Art, you don't *have* a twin brother."

"I know that. What— Oh! That thing out on Long Island!"

"Fire Island. It said— Wait, I'll get the paper."

"I know what it said, I noticed that coincidence myself."

"Coincidence?"

"Doris," I said, "how many brothers do you have?"

"Barely one," she said. "You promise and promise and *promise* to call Duane, and you never do it."

"I've been busy, Doris, getting ready for Thanksgiving."

"But that isn't the *point*. The *point* is, what is this— Here, I've got the paper. 'Twin brother Arthur Dodge, Manhattan greeting card publisher.' What are they *talking* about?"

"A different Arthur Dodge, obviously," I said. "We don't exactly have an obscure name, you know."

"But a greeting card publisher?"

"Doris, do you know how many little outfits like mine there are, just in New York? And maybe he doesn't have his own outfit at all, maybe he's an executive with Hallmark or Gibson or one of that crowd. I mean, I can see reporters getting mixed up and calling me instead of this other guy, and believe me they've been calling all day, but Doris *you* know I don't have any twin brother."

"It's just a coincidence?" She sounded no more than half-convinced.

"Listen, Doris," I said. "I'm looking in the Manhattan phone book right now, right here. Do you know how many A. Dodges there are, just the initial? And this is just Manhattan, this doesn't count people living in Queens and Brooklyn and—"

"It was just such a surprise," she said. "The same name and everything."

"There are eight million people in this city," I said. "Some of them have the same names."

"At first," she said, "I thought maybe it was *you* that was killed."

"What would I be doing in a rich people's place like that?" I said, and oddly enough that was the convincer. The fact was, although I had insisted on being upwardly mobile, she had remained steadfastly rooted in a social level where old tires are placed on the front lawn as planters. So she laughed over the idea of my hobnobbing with rich people, and so did I, and then we had a little chat about the subject of coincidence in general, with some drab examples from her own life and times, and finally she got off the phone and I buzzed Gloria to get me Ralph.

Waiting, trying to think of a new birthday message, I went through the accumulation of mail, trying to get back some of my former *joie de milieu* by repeating once-pleasant activities, but even wastebasketing final notices didn't give me a charge any more.

And what was this? A large thick manila envelope, very like the one Volpinex had carried, the one filled with death weapons aimed at Bart. This new envelope was on my desk face down, with no identification showing, and my hands hesitated over it while the hairs on the back of my neck did little clenching things, as though holding tiny ice cubes. It looked exactly like the Volpinex envelope, which I remembered burning in the sink in Point O' Woods, watching the yellow flames hula over the photostats.

So this was a different envelope, that's all; why was I hesitant? I have never been a believer in ghosts or the occult or any of that mumbo jumbo. I don't even believe Mary was a virgin. So this was a different envelope, and my reluctance to touch it was the result of nervous tension, nothing more.

Exactly. When I did turn it over, a bit more emphatically than necessary, the other side showed me my name and address typed in the middle, a gallery of canceled stamps (Eisenhower with beards and moustaches) on the upper right, and the information "L. Margolies, 37 E. 10, NY 10003" on the upper left.

Comedy: The Coward's Response to Aggression.

Ah. Knowing more these days about aggression and the coward's range of responses to it, I opened the envelope with the expectation of a good rousing argument to come, but was interrupted by Gloria buzzing to tell me that Ralph was home sick. "Drat," I said. "Call him at home, then. But if a woman answers, hang up."

"Right."

I reached into the envelope again, and a Birthday came to me. At once I wrote it down: "Your birthday stone—is hanging around my neck."

What? I frowned at what I had written, like a coughing romantic composer looking at blood in his handkerchief. What the hell was *this*? "Your birthday stone—is hanging around my neck." Not only wasn't it funny, it wasn't even sensible. It didn't *mean* anything. What did it mean?

I muttered aloud; "I've lost it, I've lost it, it's all gone." I stared at my former product on the walls, and none of it was funny. None of *it* was funny. Here and there shreds of meaning clung to the sentences, like meat to a well-gnawed bone, but they weren't *funny*.

"I'm becoming Volpinex." I'm afraid I also said that one aloud, and God knows what else I would have announced if Gloria hadn't buzzed me again at that moment. I depressed the switch. "Hah?"

"Got him."

"Who?"

"Ralph Minck. Remember?"

"Oh." I averted my eyes from the birthday non-greeting I'd just written. "Right," I said. Ralph: time to cool him out in re twins. Rolling myself into one, I pushed the button and said, "Hello, Ralph?"

"Hello," he said, in a voice so faint and tremulous I could barely hear him. He didn't sound sick, he sounded suicidal.

I said, "Ralph? What's happening?"

"I'm afraid I can't talk to anybody right now." Dignity tottered among garbage cans in his voice.

"Wait, wait! Don't hang up. It's me, Ralph, your best friend Art. What's the problem, boy?"

A long sigh. A silence. And then: "She's left me, Art."

Oh, wonderful. "I'll be right there, pal," I said. "Don't you go anywhere."

Slamming the phone down, I noticed again the birthday greeting, stone and neck, and this time I took it for no more than what it was: a bummer. I'd had losers before, and I'd never turned into a six-foot cockroach. Distraction had dried the fount of my humor, it was as simple as that, a temporary drought. Crumpling the useless Birthday, I tossed it into the wastebasket, then fondly patted the envelope that was not in fact anything like Volpinex's. "Get to you later, sweetheart," I said.

On the way out, I told Gloria, "If my sister calls, I'm just out for a while. If anybody else calls, I'm in mourning. If we never meet again, I want you to know you've been a brick."

"And I want you to know," she said, "you've been a real change from Met Life."

52   52

THE LAST TIME I'D BEEN in the Minck apartment was my wedding night. It looked much different now; somehow, Ralph had managed in two days to create a setting that looked as though he'd been abandoned for three months. Dirty dishes all over the living room, ashtrays piled high with horrible butts, a stink of mildew and dirt and decay in every room, and a bathroom I won't attempt to describe.

The children, it turned out, were temporarily with some handy cousin in Queens. Candy was somewhere out in the great wild world, having left no forwarding address, and Ralph was sitting around in the kind of undershirt men haven't worn since the draft started in 1940. "She's gone for good," he said.

"Did she say so? Did she, well, leave a note, a letter, anything like that?"

"Yes. She's gone for good."

"Yes what? She left a letter?"

"Yes."

Oh, God. Not the famous letter I'd read at dinner the other night. "Where is it, Ralph?"

"She's gone for good, Art."

"Yes, but where's the letter? Her letter, Ralph, the letter she left you."

"It's over . . ." He gestured toward the planet earth.

I finally found it on the kitchen table, formerly crumpled but later resmoothed, smeared with stains of butter, coffee, tomato juice, liquor of some sort, and what might have been tears. Reading it, I found that it was and yet it was not the same letter Candy had shown me the other night. That is, it was the same letter except for me; "your dearest friend and mine, Art Dodge," as I had been previously billed, was no longer a character in this version of the epic. The appropriate paragraphs had been rewritten, quite neatly, as follows:

> Ralph, I have a confession to make. I am a woman, with the needs and desires of a woman, and in my frustration and anguish I have turned to another man. You do not know him, Ralph, I would not humiliate you or myself either by a cheap adultery with some so-called "friend." He is a man of honesty and value, Ralph, and in his arms I have found the fulfillment that fled me within my marriage.
>
> Ralph, I hate to cheat and lie. Desperation drove me to another, but love has kept me with him. I do not know what the future holds for he and I, but I only know I cannot go on as before. I had hoped against hope that you and I could somehow make a go of it, but this summer at Fair Harbor has convinced me that it cannot happen.
>
> You will find a better woman than me, Ralph, I am sure. All I want is the children and child support, you know I would never be greedy. And try not to think too harshly of me. I have loved you, in my fashion.
>
> Hail and farewell,
Candy

I went back to the living room, carrying the letter. It was sticky, rather like my apartment *après*-Feeney. "Well, that doesn't sound so bad, Ralph," I said cheerily, and plopped into the cleanest chair I could find.

"She's gone for good," he said.

"I just don't believe it," I said. "Ralph, I look at this letter, and what I see is a cry from a woman's heart."

He gazed at me, blearily. "A what?"

"A cry for help, Ralph."

"She's gone for good, Art."

"She loves you, Ralph, she says so right here. And she wants you to understand her, care about her, love her in the romantic way you did when it was just the two of you. No kids, no legal papers being drafted on the dining room table, none of this extra stuff. Romance, that's what she wants, Ralph, and she wants it from you."

"From somebody else," he said, and growled a little. "If I could find the guy, Art—"

"He doesn't matter, Ralph. He probably doesn't even exist, she just put that in there to make you jealous. Like my twin brother."

"I'll find him some day, and—" He blinked, slowly, twice. "Like what?"

"My twin brother."

"What twin brother?"

Good. I had his attention. I probably wouldn't have it for long, so I plunged right ahead. "It's a con, Ralph," I said. "Somebody's setting me up for something, but I don't know what. I was hoping you'd be able to help me, but I can see you've got troubles of your own."

He was bewildered, naturally. "Well, what happened? What's the matter?"

"That girl I was engaged to," I said. "Elizabeth Kerner, you looked her up for me."

"The heiress," he said.

"I went ahead and married her, Ralph. Just a week ago today."

Joy for me commingled with pity for himself, and he began to cry. "Congratulations," he blubbered. "May you be as happy as I used to be."

"Listen, Ralph," I said. "A week ago I married her,

and the night before last somebody murdered her twin sister."

I had his attention again. The waterworks dried up and he said, "Murdered? Are you sure?" Sniffing, he wiped his eyes and nose on his sleeve.

"Bang bang," I said. "With a gun. Out at Point O' Woods. Then the killer burned the house down, trying to cover his tracks."

"Good God!" He'd forgotten Candy completely by now.

"But here's the crazy part," I said. "There was another body with her, and the general opinion is that it was my twin brother."

"What? You don't have a twin brother."

"There are documents," I said, "to prove that my bride's twin sister was married last month to somebody who called himself Robert Dodge and who claimed to be my twin brother. And now that guy is dead."

"But that doesn't make any sense," he said.

"It gets crazier," I promised him. "Because the killer turned out to be that lawyer, Volpinex. Fingerprints on the gun, and he's disappeared, and there just isn't any question."

He sat back, wiping snot from his cheek with his other sleeve. "None of it makes sense, Art," he said.

"I'm afraid of it," I told him. "I don't know what's going on, Ralph, but I figure I'm the patsy if I'm not damn careful. So I haven't said anything to anybody. I haven't even denied the twin brother."

He frowned at me. "Why not?"

"Because I don't know what it means. Listen, there's a lot of money in that Kerner family, and somebody's after it. You know me, Ralph, I've done some pretty cute conniving in my day, I'm not sure I could stand a really tough police investigation. I mean, things that were perfectly innocent at the time could be made to look pretty incriminating right now."

"The truth is usually best, Art," he said doubtfully.

"I know that, Ralph. But this is all so weird, I'm afraid to make any move at all. If I just sit tight, maybe I'll find out what's going on."

"Don't sign any false statements," he told me.

"Ralph, I wouldn't sign a birthday card right now." (Or write one either, apparently.)

He nodded, thinking it over. "That's probably best," he said. "You aren't a witness or anything, are you?"

"I was in Manhattan with my bride while it was going on. I'm just an in-law. Or a relative, if you want to believe the twin brother story."

"Then you're probably right," he said. "Sit tight, and wait to see what happens next."

"And if something does happen, Ralph, can I come to you?"

"You know that, Art. How can you even ask? Aren't we friends?"

"I was just thinking. . . . under the circumstances . . ." And he began to dissolve again. "Ralph," I said, leaning forward to pat his knee, to console him. "She'll be back, Ralph."

"She's gone for good, Art."

"Ralph, I'll look for her."

He gazed at me in bleary hope. "You will?"

"I'll talk to her, if I can. I'll do anything I can to help, Ralph."

"Art, if you could— Art, I just—"

"We'll help each other," I suggested. "I'll help you with Candy, and you'll help me with this crazy twin brother thing."

And we fell into one another's arms.

T HE NEXT FOUR DAYS WERE
lived on tiptoe, but by God not a single egg got broken.
The police seemed to have swallowed my Volpinex-as-
murderer playlet, and lacking a denial from Volpinex himself there was nothing to jar their sweet certainty. Bart's
death certificate was as legitimate as the coroner's office
could make it; he had been such stuff as dreams are made
on, and his little life was rounded with a sleep, as he rested,
an unidentifiable mound of ashes, in a brass urn in the
Kerner family vault, beside his bride.

The cat's cradle of stories I'd told here and there held
up very well, mostly because it was never really tested. No
cop ever talked to Gloria or Ralph or Doris or Joe Gold,
and why should they? My ex-wife Lydia was cooled out
with the same coincidence gambit that had worked with
Doris, and everybody else went on believing the various
fantasies and half-truths I'd already delivered. With no
arrests or other postmurder development, the news media
lost interest in the BIZARRE SLAYING within two days,
and that also helped.

Gloria continued to run Those Wonderful Folks, with no
assistance from me other than erratic phone calls; I did
not drop by my office, any more than I visited my former
apartment. Ralph, based on the evidence of my few calls
to him, continued to drink and mope and feel sorry for
himself, with not the slightest thought for the outside
world. As for Candy, the only loose end left to be tied, I

had a story to tell her, of course, but she was unavailable
to listen to it. She had dropped, as the saying goes, from
the face of the earth, and could stay dropped forever for
all of me.

Which left Liz. For a day or two she remained indignant
and enraged in re the altered contract, but by the weekend
she had calmed down considerably and seemed prepared to
accept the inevitable, saying to me, "What the hell, I kind
of like you anyway. I could have done worse."

"You have," I told her. "Frequently. But that's all over
now." And we went for another romp on her big bed.

54   54

O N SUNDAY NIGHT, SIX
days after the double murder, Liz said, "Let's get away
for a while."

"Sure," I said. The danger period was over, the official
investigation having moved on to other concerns and un-
official curiosity having been generally appeased, so a vacation away from the scene of my broken-field-running
exploit might be very restful indeed. Also, Liz had become
increasingly docile and pleasant the last day or two, with
none of that nastiness I had come to expect from her; re-
moving her to a new setting might help turn this happier
personality into a permanent improvement. "Where to?"
I asked.

"Saint Croix," she said. "We have a house there."

Good God. "We do?" And what *more* wonders lay
ahead, yet to be unwrapped?

"We'll phone them in the morning to open it," Liz said, "and we'll fly down tomorrow afternoon."

So I'd be going to the Caribbean after all; wherever he was, I hoped Volpinex was pleased. "Fine," I said.

55   55

W E HAD IDENTICAL *Air France* bags, many-pocketed and pale blue. Mine had been Betty's, but as Liz pointed out, "Why let it go to waste?"

Monday morning, while she phoned the servants in Saint Croix and the airline at Kennedy, I went back, possibly for the last time, to my little black office in the garment district, carrying my new blue bag. Gloria was typing away, and had the usual pile of outrageous mail and phone messages stacked up. "Forget all that," I told her. "Remember that rabble of ungrateful illustrators that wanted to steal the company from me, couple of years ago?"

Gloria nodded. "In lieu of payment," she said. "I always thought they were crazy, myself."

"They had a lawyer," I said. "Look him up in the file, prepare a letter for my signature, no date, saying, 'I don't ask to be insulted. Mine was a serious question.' I'll sign it."

She frowned at me. "You do carry a grudge, don't you?"

"Not exactly. This afternoon, call that lawyer and ask him if his company of turncoats is still interested in making a deal. If he says yes, ask him to forward the details of their proposition. When you get it, put a date on that re-

sponse of mine and send it to him with all copies of his
proposition. Any time he calls, I'm out of town but expected back shortly, and you don't know where I can be
reached."

Gloria said, "You wouldn't really quit, would you?"

"Life goes on."

"And I go back to Met Life? That isn't fair! I've given
you the worst years of my life!"

"Don't dramatize, Gloria," I said, and went on to the
inner office, where I collected my emergency cache of ten-
dollar bills from behind the "Kiss me again" plaque, then
turned my attention to the desk. Was there anything I
wanted with me for an indefinite stay in the Caribbean?

A bottom drawer revealed an extra glasses case; startled,
I stuffed it out of sight into the wastebasket. Bart's glasses
had been consumed with his body, and Art would never
wear glasses again.

There were, however, some useful items: my passport,
my birth certificate, my immunization record. And what
was this on the desk top, this large manila envelope with
its combination of pleasant and unpleasant associations?

Ah, yes: the thesis of Linda Ann Margolies. In all the
activity of the last week or so, I hadn't given the thing a
thought. Now at last I opened it, and withdrew a sheaf of
Xeroxed manuscript pages, plus a brief letter. The letter
said:

Chief,
   At last. I have the plans for the new naval torpedo,
and Admiral Von Heffelwitz has the clap. For the glory
of France!
                                                Cherie
   Enc: Stolen plans for naval torpedo.

Right. I slipped the stolen plans into the *Air France* bag,
for later reading 'neath a tropical sun.

Gloria wouldn't talk to me when I left.

Sozzled with champagne, Liz snoozed as we sailed above the Atlantic. Washington, D.C., was on the horizon to our right, if anybody cared; nobody cared, at least not up front here in first class. This half-empty 747 was taking us all to Puerto Rico, where Liz and I would switch to some smaller mud jumper for the hop over to St. Croix. For now, the majority of my fellow passengers, somnolent with lunchtime wine, were sagging in their seats and waiting for the movie.

I couldn't quite sag, not all the way. We had no baggage other than our two *Air France* bags, now tucked companionably together beneath the seats in front of us, exactly where I would have preferred to tuck my feet. "I can't stand waiting for luggage," Liz had announced. "What do we need there anyway? A toothbrush and a bathing suit." So I had to keep my legs bent.

The stewardess came by with a fresh rum and tonic, gave it to me, and glanced over at Liz, pillowing her head against the plastic window. "Is your friend comfortable?"

"Very seldom," I said. "What's the movie today?"

"*Guolpo, The Reluctant Chihuahua*, with Fred Murray."

"Ah."

The stew went on her way, dispensing bloody Marys and bullshots to the off-season spenders, and I prepared myself for departure to the upstairs lounge. I would take Linda Ann Margolies's thesis with me. Where better to read a

master's thesis on humor than the upstairs lounge of a
747?

The envelope jutted up near the top of the anonymous
mélange in the bag. I unzipped, reached in, pulled the
thing out, zipped again, restowed the bag, and left my
seat. And not a moment too soon: the movie screen was
being drawn out of the ceiling at the forward end of the
compartment. Turning my back, I climbed the steep spiral
staircase and found the lounge unoccupied except for another stew, who was setting out drinkables on a counter
and who shouted above the plane noise, "Hello!"

"Hello!"

"Want a drink?"

"Got one!" I shouted, and displayed the glass in my
right hand and the manila envelope in my left.

She smiled broadly, then shouted, "Did the movie start?"

"Just about to!"

"I'll be back! I just love the part with Bill Dana and
Cher on the roller coaster!" And off she went.

I chose a seat with a window and a handy table and lots
of legroom, sat down, put my drink to one side, and placed
the envelope on my lap.

It was Volpinex's envelope.

The hairs on my forearms recoiled from my shivering
skin. I didn't move, I didn't breathe, I didn't blink. The
droning rush of airplane filled my ears.

It was Volpinex's envelope. There on the upper left
corner was the printed name and address of his law firm:
Leek, Conchell & McPoo, 7 Broad Street, New York,
N.Y. 10001. I'd noticed that name and address when I was
burning this—

Burning it.

Betty's name and address were centered, as before.
Elisabeth Kerner and so on; it blurred before my eyes.

This is a nightmare. I, too, have fallen asleep, overfull of
drink, relaxing at last from the tensions of August, and my
worst fears have come to me in a nightmare. I am not

awake, this is not Volpinex's envelope—which I burned burned *burned*—and it does not contain the proofs of Bart's nonexistence. I am asleep, I am having a nightmare.

It contained the proofs. I opened the envelope, undoing the metal clip at the end, and found inside a second manila envelope, not quite so large, with a note attached. On Leek, Conchell & McPoo letterhead stationery, some Uriah Heep named Gordon Alworthy was writing to Liz—Liz, not Betty—to say the enclosed envelope had been in the confidential Kerner file in Ernest Volpinex's desk. The said Alworthy, having been for some time the said Volpinex's assistant on the Kerner and similar matters (and the said Alworthy undoubtedly now snuffing around to take the said Volpinex's place), the said Alworthy was pleased to forward the said envelope (unread, need it be said) to the said Miss Kerner, for disposal as she best saw fit.

And inside the said envelope? The familiar photostats, Xeroxes of the familiar documents, the whole grim familiar package.

Eyes. I looked up, and Liz was standing beside my chair, looking down at me. The blurry red mark on her forehead from sleeping against the window did not detract from the coldness of her eyes or the grimness of her expression. "Give it back," she said.

I simply stared at her. The plunge from euphoria to doom had been too rapid: I had the bends.

She held her hand out for the envelope. "Give it back," she said, "or I'll call the stewardess." She didn't raise her voice, and yet I could hear every word clearly through the plane noise.

I opened my mouth. At first nothing at all would come, and then I surprised myself by asking, "How long—how long have you had this?"

"Since Friday. Give it back."

I closed the envelope with clumsy fingers and handed it up to her. "What are you going to do with it?"

"That's up to you," she said, and sat down in the nearest chair, facing me slightly from the left.

I gestured at the envelope. "You're not going to give it, uh, to the police, in other words."

"Not as long as you do what you're told."

Here came the crunch. Watching her carefully, I said, "Liz, what am I going to be told?"

"You'll live in the house on Saint Croix," she told me. "By yourself, except for the staff. No women."

"No women? For God's sake, what diff—"

"Shut up, Art." She was all ice. "I've inherited from Betty," she said, "so I'm strong enough now to bounce those freeloading cousins and uncles right out on their asses, and I'm going to do it. Every once in a while you'll get something in the mail to sign, as my husband. You'll sign it."

"Look, Liz—"

"If you don't sign, or if you leave, the houseboy will call me in New York, and this evidence goes to the Suffolk County District Attorney."

Was it something I could live with? I said, "For how long, Liz?"

"Till the lawsuits are over."

"Six months? A year?"

Grinning, she said, "More like ten years. Maybe fifteen."

"Good *Christ!*"

Holding the envelope, she got to her feet and said, "You ought to come down and watch the movie. It's a comedy, take your mind off your troubles." And she started away.

"No!" I couldn't let it happen like this, I just couldn't let it happen. Jumping up from the chair, I lunged after her, to hold her, stop her, force her to listen until I found the right things to say. Angry, she pulled away from me and cried, "I'll call the stewardess if you try anything with me!" And turned toward the stairs.

Among the beverages on the counter to my left was an unopened quart bottle of Popov vodka. I picked it up and let her have it across the side of the head. And, as she tottered into the stairwell, I plucked the envelope out of her opening hand.

57   57

THE AIRLINE WAS VERY RElieved when I decided not to be difficult after all. At first I made distraught references to overly steep and narrow spiral staircases, obvious safety hazard, I'd have my attorney look into previous damage suits, etc., etc., and generally I made as much noise and trouble as I could without making any *real* noise or any *real* trouble.

But the airline executives who flocked to San Juan and to my side like sparrows to a suet ball didn't know any of the background. All they knew was that the 747 spiral staircase *had* been criticized by safety experts in the past, and that now they had a dead woman and distraught husband on their hands. A *rich* dead woman and a *rich* distraught husband. So they stroked my shoulders and they offered me sympathy and Jack Daniels and they spoke as emotionally as I did about this unfortunate and unforeseeable accident. (However, they did also mention from time to time that the autopsy would determine the alcohol level in Liz at the moment of her final flight; they did drop that fact in from time to time.)

In addition to compassion for my trouble and a mortician for my bride, the airline did at last also lay on a suite at the El San Juan, in which I was to rest and recover from my emotional ordeal. Once alone in a room dominated by sun plaques, I placed an immediate call to Leek, Conchell & McPoo, got through to Gordon Alworthy, the legal assistant who had sent out that package of trouble to begin with, and told him the situation in twenty-five words or less. "Elizabeth Kerner is dead," I said. "I am Arthur Dodge, her heir and now controller of the Kerner interests. I want you on your way to San Juan by the next available plane, at Kerner expense, to handle the legal problems at this end."

He grasped the situation at once, as I'd known he would, and made a penetrating and brilliant remark. "Yes, sir," he said.

58   58

GORDON ALWORTHY WAS five feet two inches tall and as thin as the ice I was skating on. He had blond hair and blond eyebrows and an open boyish smile and a soft amiable manner of speech and a mind like an Arab oil minister. The airline's attorneys tended to chuckle when they first met him, and to be frowning later when they left his presence. I trusted him as far as I could pay him.

We spent four days in San Juan together, with frequent conference calls to other legal minds back in the New York office of Leek, Conchell & McPoo, and at the end of it I knew I never would have been able to do it on my own. And yet how easy it had been, with Alworthy.

Which was another fact I'd never before entirely understood about money; it buys brains and expertise to supplement your own. I'd gone pretty far with nothing but my own native wit and talent for scrambling to sustain me, farther in fact than I'd ever dreamed of going, and now I was at a plateau where I didn't have to do much of anything any more. If a drink was required, I could push a button and a drink would be brought to me. If conniving was called for, I could hire a fella who'd been taught conniving at Harvard Law School.

How much Gordon Alworthy knew or suspected I didn't know, nor did I care. Even assuming the worst, that he had read those damaging documents before sending them to Liz, what did it matter? If he turned me in it would cost him his job. The Kerner estate would be thrown into a chaos of cousins and uncles, and Gordon Alworthy would be thrown back into the faceless mélange of young assistant attorneys at Leek, Conchell & McPoo. Would he turn me in? Would *you*?

Neither did Gordon Alworthy.

The airline paid off, of course. If I'd been a poor man, an insurance salesman grabbing a week in the sun with his bride, it would have cost the airline five or ten thousand, no more. If I'd been moderately well off, it might have cost them a hundred thousand. But I was rich now, I had so many lumber mills behind me I looked like an exercise in perspective, so what *I* cost the airline was a feeder route between two Canadian cities.

The Kerners already had a Canadian airline—Laurentian Interior Air Service—but prior to this it had been strictly a small cargo carrier, principally of goods manufactured by other Kerner holdings. I was happy that my first act as head of the Kerner business empire was to diversify into yet another area of commerce. The new passenger division of our airline I dubbed Laurentian Interior Zealandia; we did not actually service Zealandia, a a town of two hundred souls in Saskatchewan, but that way the company's initials could be LIZ. She had, after all, made it possible; it was the least I could do.

CARLOS WAS GRUMPY AT being fired, but there was no point keeping him on. I would drive the Alfa myself mostly, or at times I might take the wheel of the Thunderbird I'd inherited from my brother, but the Lincoln I would sell, replacing it with a limousine service on an annual contract for those rare occasions when a chauffeured vehicle was needed. The car would come only when called for, and the driver need not be housed or fed. It was more economical, and more sensible as well.

I took care of all that on Saturday, the fifteenth of September, the day after returning with Gordon from San Juan. Nikki I moved into Betty's bedroom, but I myself stayed in the room I'd shared with Liz; thus I had access without too much familiarity. Blondell stayed on exactly as before.

New York, by and large, had remained unaware of the latest tragedy in the Kerner family. When a major airline wants to avoid publicity, it avoids publicity. A small item had appeared in the city papers, saying that a local woman, Mrs. Arthur Dodge, had been involved in a freak fatal accident aboard a plane bound for Puerto Rico, but no connections had been drawn with the Elisabeth Kerner Dodge who had been gruesomely murdered with her husband Robert on Fire Island the week before. Given no coincidence to worry their heads about, people did not worry their heads. And to the few Kerner relations and friends whose recent phone calls had to be returned, I simply said that Liz had died "in an airplane accident," permitting them to place their own incorrect interpretation on the phrase. No one—not the airline, the San Juan police, the attorneys, no one—ever suggested for a second that Liz's death had been anything other than an accident.

As to the fugitive, Volpinex, Alworthy sent me a clipping from *Newsday*, the Long Island newspaper, saying that the death of the late Mrs. Volpinex in Maine a few years ago was under renewed investigation, and that the original judgment of accidental death was likely to be revised. "The circumstances were very suspicious," a Maine sheriff was quoted as saying. If any confirmation of Volpinex's guilt in the Fire Island murders were needed, that was it. (The item, so far as I know, didn't make the New York City papers at all.)

I only had one bad moment that weekend: on Sunday afternoon, when I belatedly unpacked the two *Air France* bags. Unzipping one of them, I found myself looking yet again at that envelope, that same envelope, would it never leave me alone? Would nothing ever—

It was the other envelope. Laughing at myself, albeit shakily, I took it from the bag and it was indeed from Linda Ann Margolies, containing her thesis on humor. What with one thing and another, I'd never had a chance to read it.

So I read it now. Or tried to, I should say. From the first paragraph, the whole piece seemed to me sophomoric in the extreme. I got through two pages before I tossed it in the wastebasket.

On Monday I met with three of the senior members of Leek, Conchell & McPoo. At first they urged me to transfer Gordon's duties to some older and more experienced member of the firm, but I expressed myself as perfectly satisfied with Gordon's performance in San Juan and totally confident in his abilities for the future, so they gave up on that point and called him in for the rest of the discussion, which centered on our handling of the dissident Kerner cousins. Among them they owned no more than eleven percent of the family holdings, but unfortunately their combined strength lay in a few key areas: a major lumber mill, the television station in Indiana, one or two others. It was decided to buy them off individually, refuse to deal with them en bloc, and drive wedges between them wherever and whenever possible. Our goal was full consolidation within thirty-six months. The attorneys were pleased with my decisiveness after nearly a year of bickering between the Kerner girls, and I was pleased with their grasp of the company problems and potentials. We shook hands all around—Gordon displayed his gratitude with a manlier-than-ever grip—and I left.

I still had some remnants of my former life to deal with, so off I went to that scruffy office in the garment district. Gloria was typing a letter to her mother when I walked in, and she looked up in surprise, saying, "By God, I remember you."

"Of course you do," I said. I didn't have time for nonsense. "Did we get a response on the sale offer?"

"My, we're in a hurry." In leisurely fashion she went to the filing cabinet and got me the folder. The attorney, some hole-in-the-wall grub named Mandel, had replied to Gloria's call with the expected unacceptable offer. My prepared response had gone out, and in today's mail another offer had arrived which came closer to making sense. "Good," I said. I gave Gloria the LC&McP number and said, "I'll want to speak to Gordon Alworthy." Then I carried the folder on into my office.

How had I ever stood this place? Squalor everywhere. Sitting at my desk, I took out my checkbook and went steadily through the accumulated mail. Some of these people, I thought with amusement, would be quite startled when they received payment in full.

Buzz.

"Yes?"

"Mr. Alworthy."

"Thank you." Click. "Gordon?"

"Yes, Art. What can I do for you?" (No secretary delay *this* time.)

I gave him a backgrounding on the Wonderful Folks negotiations, and he said he'd send a messenger up for the folder and would carry the deal from here. Then I buzzed Gloria, asked her to call my sister, and return to paying bills till the call came through.

"Doris?"

"My goodness, another phone call. Is this going to happen every month?"

"I'm afraid not, Doris. Basically I'm calling to say goodbye. I've—"

"You never even said hello! Fine brother you are. Did you call Duane? You did not. And you prom—"

"Doris, I will never call Duane. I think a Legal Aid attorney would be much more useful to you than I could possibly be."

"I don't see why you can't simply call him and—"

"I've sold my business, Doris," I said, "and I'm going to Europe."

"You *what*?"

"Possibly for a year, possibly longer. I've been feeling the need for a change for some time now."

"But—" A speechless Doris was a rare and beautiful thing. She stammered a bit more, then said, "Europe? Where in Europe?"

"I'm not sure yet. I'll send you a postcard."

"You never will," she said accurately.

"We'll see. Good-bye, Doris," I said, and hung up. Then I finished paying the bills and turned to the phone message memos. Wastebasket, wastebasket, wastebasket—

Candy.

I stared at it, her name on the phone memo, and the walls folded in on me. Everybody else had been dealt with, but what about Candy? What story did I have left for her?

Then I noticed the number she'd given, and it was her apartment, Ralph's apartment. What was all this?

I dialed the number myself, and Candy's sharp voice promptly answered. "It's Art," I said. "Don't tell me you and Ralph had a reconciliation."

"Marriage is something you have to work at," she said. "You wouldn't know about that, Art."

"Well, I'm very happy for you both."

"Ralph and I both agree," she said, "to just forget the past. You follow me, Art?"

"You mean that letter you gave me?"

"You might think it would be fun some time," she said, "to send that letter to Ralph. I know the way your mind works."

She didn't; I'd long since destroyed the copy she'd given me. But I said nothing, and heard her out.

"You've been up to something yourself, you know," she said.

I held the phone more tightly. "I have?"

"I don't know exactly what," she said, "but you've been running some kind of confidence racket or something. I think I could make a lot more trouble for you than you could for me."

No doubt. I said, "Candy, I wish you and Ralph nothing but eternal joy and success."

"And don't you forget it," she said, and broke the connection.

Well. Much relieved, I put down the phone, wrote out a severance check for Gloria, and brought it outside. "This is my last day here," I told her. "I'm definitely selling the company."

I was amazed to see her eyes well up with tears, but relieved that none actually fell. She said, "I knew this was coming."

"Of course you did," I said soothingly.

"You've changed a lot in the last few weeks, Art," she

said. "You may not like me saying this, but it's that Kerner woman's money."

Obviously she hadn't seen that tiny item about Mrs. Dodge's demise. "I appreciate your concern for me, Gloria," I said, "but I think I can take care—"

"Jesus, Art," she burst out, "what's the matter with you? You never talked like that before."

It was possible my intense association with attorneys over the last week had had some temporary influence on my speech patterns. "I've never sold a company before," I pointed out, "nor have I ever fired a good friend and a valued employee." And I stuck my hand out with the check in it. "Severance pay in lieu of notice."

She took the check, and stood for quite some time looking at it. The tears had receded from her eyes. "Two thousand dollars," she said softly, and looked up with what might have been an ironic smile. "Well, at least you feel guilty about it."

"Not at all," I said. "You have been invaluable here, and I think you know that yourself, and this is really a very small token of my appreciation."

Squinting as though looking at me through drifting smoke, she said, "Art, won't you need a secretary wherever you're going?"

"This company isn't folding," I told her. "Why not call that lawyer Mandel, meet with the illustrators? Who knows the business better than you do?"

"You do," she said.

I smiled at the compliment. "Not any more," I said.

She hesitated, then turned away, holding the check and shaking her head. "I'll just finish up this letter here."

"Take your time."

"Oh. This came for you." She turned back with a legal-size white envelope. "I didn't put it with the business things."

It was marked *Personal*, and Linda Ann Margolies' name and address were in the upper left-hand corner.

"Thank you," I said, and carried the thing back to my office with me.

I very nearly tossed it out at once—something about my brief encounter with that girl bothered me, I couldn't say what—but curiosity got the upper hand. Opening it, I found a greeting card inside of the kind I used to publish, though not one from my company. The front showed a man in the front half of a horse suit, with a theater's stage in the background. Inside, it said, "I just can't go on without you."

Was that supposed to be funny? I threw it away.